Niq Mhlongo

Way Back Home

Kwela Books

Kwela Books,
an imprint of NB Publishers,
40 Heerengracht, Cape Town, South Africa
PO Box 6525, Roggebaai, 8012, South Africa
www.kwela.com

Copyright © 2013 N Mhlongo

All rights reserved
No part of this book may be reproduced or transmitted in any form or by any electronic or mechanical means, including photocopying and recording, or by any other information storage or retrieval system, without written permission from the publisher

Cover design by publicide
Typography by Nazli Jacobs
Set in Utopia
Printed and bound by Interpak Books,
Pietermaritzburg, South Africa

First edition, first impression 2013

ISBN: 978-0-7957-0478-9
ISBN: 978-0-7957-0479-6 (epub)
ISBN: 978-0-7957-0599-1 (mobi)

"I hate purity. I hate goodness. I don't want any virtue to exist anywhere. I want everyone to be corrupt to the bones..."

– George Orwell, *Nineteen Eighty-Four*

"Why write this book? No one has asked me for it, especially those to whom it is directed. Well, well, I reply quite calmly that there are too many idiots in this world. And having said it, I have the burden of proving it..."

– Frantz Fanon, *Black Skin, White Masks*

I, *Kimathi Fezile Tito*, do solemnly declare that I am a soldier of the South African revolution. I am a volunteer fighter, committed to the struggle for justice. I place myself in the service of the people, The Movement and its allies. I take up arms in response to the wishes of the masses. I promise to serve with discipline and dedication at all times, maintaining the integrity and solidarity of the people's army. Should I violate any of these, I accept that I should be punished by all means, not excluding death. A tooth for a tooth; an eye for an eye; a life for a life.

13 August 1986, Angola

Chapter 1

Amilcar Cabral camp, Kwanza Norte province, Angola, 1988

"Are you ready to talk, or what?" asked Comrade Pilate as he paced about the interrogation room. The cross-examination had been going on for four hours, and he was beginning to get frustrated.

Comrade Bambata chewed nervously on his fingernails. On the desk next to Comrade Idi were a piece of paper and a pen. All he had to do was tell them what they wanted to know, but he had nothing to disclose.

Suddenly Pilate lunged at Bambata like a hungry lion, hauling him out of his chair and slamming him against the wall. The back of Bambata's head hit the cement and, disoriented, he fell to his knees. Pilate kicked him in the face with his boot.

"Which one of you betrayed The Movement?" shouted Pilate as Bambata coughed up some blood.

"I swear . . . I-I don't know, anything."

"Today you'll regret the day I ever heard your name," Pilate said as he jerked Bambata up and punched him in the face.

Bambata staggered backwards, blood coming from his nose, but Idi was behind him, and as he turned to get away from Pilate, Idi hit him in the face again. Bambata fell backwards, his head banging hard against the floor.

"We are not done with you yet," said Pilate to the unconscious Bambata as he and Idi left the room. "I'm sure you'll be ready to talk when we come back."

* * *

Comrade Bambata regained consciousness about an hour later. His mouth was full of blood and his left eye was so swollen that he could hardly see out of it. He rolled on his side and spat onto the floor.

"Stand up, you traitor!" ordered Comrade Pilate. "And take all your clothes off."

"What?" Confused, Bambata looked up at Pilate. He was standing over him, holding an acacia stick that had some white thorns on it.

"Faster," shouted Pilate as Bambata struggled to his feet and reluctantly took off his clothes. "Put them down over there and come to the desk."

"But why are you doing this to me, comrades?" asked Bambata, starting to sob violently, his eyes filled with fear and surprise.

"Stop asking stupid questions," barked Pilate as Comrade Idi took hold of Bambata and dragged him towards the desk.

With Bambata pinned firmly against the desk by Idi, Pilate raised the stick and aimed for his penis. Bambata hunched his shoulders, trying to break free, but Idi was too strong.

There was a loud scream as Pilate brought the acacia stick down. It was one of those blows that a man remembers to the grave.

Pilate gave Bambata a furious glance. "If you don't talk I will hit this thing of yours until it comes off," he said sadistically, pointing at Bambata's manhood.

"No, please!" Bambata cried as Pilate raised the stick again. "It . . . It was her . . . She did it."

"Who is this 'her'?" asked Idi. "Does she have a name?"

"Lady Comrade . . . Lady Comrade Mkabayi," Bambata said slowly, nodding his head.

"What did she do?"

"She . . . she gave information to the Boers and U-UNITA."

"What else did she do?"

"She . . . she . . . she agitated us to turn against The Move-Movement."

"I want you to write that down," said Pilate, pointing at the pen and paper, which had fallen to the floor. "Write an affidavit and say exactly what she said to you, word for word."

Bambata could only nod; the pain and the idea of betraying his innocent comrade were too much to bear.

"We'll be back within an hour to collect the affidavit," said Idi as he let Bambata slump to the floor, clutching his groin.

"You must remember one thing," said Pilate as he opened the door of the interrogation room. "This Lady Comrade Mkabayi of yours is the darkness to your light. She is very dangerous. You believed in her lies without thinking." He paused, watching as Bambata crawled towards the pen and the piece of paper. "But, if you correct your mind now, the rest will fall into place. It's never too late to do that. Change doesn't just happen; it is created by dedicated people like us, people who love The Movement."

Chapter 2

"Shut up! Shut up!"

Kimathi woke up from the nightmare screaming. It was already eleven, on a Sunday morning. He found himself sprawled on the bedroom floor of his Bassonia mansion. After rubbing his eyes several times, he became conscious of the fact that he was still fully clothed in his suit, shoes and tie. An empty whisky glass lay on the floor next to him, where he had obviously dropped it the night before.

This was the third time in a row that he'd had the same dream. Its terrifying detail had made him afraid to go to bed alone. *Shit! No matter how strong you are, the memory of something frightening always comes back to you in a bad dream*, he thought as he sat up. Not much of it made sense to him now. It had all happened more than two decades ago, while he was still in exile, and he could not even recall most of the faces, or what had happened to them.

Kimathi stood up and removed his tie, jacket and shoes. He staggered, aware that he was still drunk from the previous night's binge at the Hyatt Regency Hotel in Rosebank. He couldn't even remember what time he had arrived home. *Around two or three in the morning*, he thought as a burning tide of bile rose in his throat. With his hand on his mouth, he walked to the bathroom, feeling the cold tiles underfoot. At the sink, he closed his eyes and started retching and heaving repeatedly, but only a bitter, yellowish liquid came out. His head was heavy and felt ready to split open. Even when he drank water directly from the tap, the pounding in his head went on. He held on to the sink for support, and then remembered that he hadn't taken his medication. The prescription said two tablets in the morning and three in the evening.

Lurching back to the bedroom, Kimathi opened the bottom drawer and took out two pills. After popping them in his mouth, he went back to the bathroom to wash them down. The headache did not stop, so he dragged his body to the bar, where he poured a double tot of Rémy Martin, hoping it would chase away the hangover. He swallowed the cognac in one go, studied the empty glass for a moment and then poured a second one. With the glass in his hand, he opened the front door and went outside.

His chest heaving with the freshness of morning life, Kimathi sat down on a white lounger next to the swimming pool. From a distance, he looked like a bull seal basking on the rocks of Duiker Island. He took a sip from his glass, put it down, and then rubbed his hands together. As he reclined in the chair and crossed his legs, he started to calculate mentally. What occupied his mind at that moment was no longer the nightmare. He was thinking about the afternoon meeting he would have the following day with Ludwe, the director-general of the Department of Public Works, and his business partners. *Money is on its way*, he thought. He smiled to himself and stroked his forearm.

The sound of a car in the driveway interrupted Kimathi's thoughts. He craned his neck and saw his ex-wife's silver Golf V pulling up. Anele was with their seven-year-old daughter, Zanu. He had not seen them in two months, and he smelled trouble. He and Anele had been separated for two years, and Anele now lived in Killarney, where she owned an apartment.

Kimathi picked up his glass, but by the time he had raised it to his lips Anele was standing in front of him. Looking at her, he felt she had put on weight. She was dressed in a black dress with white polka dots, embellished cat's-eye sunglasses, black straw-wedge shoes and a gold starfish bangle. It was obvious to Kimathi that she had just come from church, as she carried a Bible in her left hand. He made no effort to rise and hug her, or even to shake hands.

"You have been avoiding my calls for the past two months," Anele said, getting down to business immediately, a tone of urgency in her voice. "So I thought I should come personally to discuss Zanu's maintenance with you."

Kimathi nodded wordlessly as he took in her red tassel earrings and the creamy black eyeliner close to her lash line. Her nail colour was the same shade as her lips – orange-red. *She looks amazing*, he thought.

Sensing that he was making his desire for her too obvious, Kimathi turned to look at Zanu. He then looked at the colourful birds chirping loudly on the red-tiled roof of his neighbour's house. Some of the birds were circling a nest in the tree next to the house.

"Oh, maintenance?" he said as if the topic did not interest him. "I'll try to put some money in your account at the end of this month. At the moment I'm broke."

"She is already four months in arrears at her school and here you are living large by drinking your expensive whisky," Anele retorted, her voice laced with anger as she looked at the glass of cognac in Kimathi's hand. "When are you going to pay for your child's education? I know for sure that you can afford it. Why don't you sell those expensive whiskies and raise the money, huh?"

"Honestly, I'm hung over right now," Kimathi said, taking a sip from his glass. "Can't this wait until I'm sober enough to fight with you properly?"

Anele looked at him as if he had just ordered her to drink a cup of his spit. Kimathi saw the annoyance on her face, but he ignored it. They were silent for several seconds, both of them lost in bitter memories.

"Why are you doing this, huh?" Anele finally asked with revulsion. "Why? Tell me."

"In order for me to answer your question, you must allow me to ask you one first," said Kimathi, fixing his bloodshot eyes on her. "Who insisted on putting her into that expensive school? You, of course, because you know it all." He raised a finger at Anele. "I told you that we must enrol her at a cheaper school, not that Sandton place. I warned you that we couldn't afford ninety-five thousand a year. Look now!"

"Stop right there!" Anele's tone was hostile. "For the last time, Zanu's fees are five thousand and fifty per month, or sixty thousand six hundred per year. Unless you have another child that I don't know of, and you are paying ninety-five thousand rand a year for that child, you must stop mentioning that figure to me."

"What's the difference anyway?" Kimathi replied. "Whether it's ninety-five thousand or sixty thousand, you took her away from me. Why should I give you the money to go and have a nice time with your boyfriends? How will I know that the money is spent on my daughter?" he concluded, but felt stupid the moment the words left his lips.

Anele clicked her tongue in disgust. "Sies! You know what, Kimathi Fezile Tito? You might have learnt everything in exile, except how to be a human being," she said, her eyes brimming with tears. "You are a nauseating excuse for a human being."

Zanu began to cry – bitter, frustrated sobs that set her small body shaking. Kimathi squatted in front of her, so that the two were eye to eye. Looking confused, Zanu simply stared at him with eyes that were damp.

"I'm sorry, my baby. Just wait until Daddy gets his foot on the ladder, my sweety pie. Everything will be great," he said, breathing cognac all over her. "At the moment the bureaucratic wheels are still turning slowly for Daddy, but soon it will be okay."

Anele stared down at him, clenching and unclenching her fists with annoyance as Kimathi nuzzled his daughter's cheek. Zanu's face came alive with glee as Kimathi reached out and took her little fingers in his.

"You keep saying that to her every time. Do you think she understands what you're saying?" interjected Anele, obviously fighting back her tears. "Do you have any idea of the stress and pain you're causing us?"

"Daddy, it was my birthday yesterday," said Zanu, showing her sad face again. "Why didn't you say happy birthday and buy me a cake?"

"Sorry, my angel, Daddy was too busy this week." Kimathi drew her closer to him. "Daddy loves you every day, and twice on your birthday," he said. "I'm going to make a huge birthday for you at the end of the month, and we will hire a jumping castle for you and your friends."

Pulling away from him, Zanu's small eyes searched his face as if prospecting for lies. Anele shook her head and her eyes narrowed. In response, Kimathi tried to restore his dignity by searching his trouser pockets. His right hand came out with a two-hundred rand note that he gave to his daughter. "Here, go buy yourself a big birthday cake," he said, offering her the money.

"Stop patronising us and insulting my daughter's intelligence," Anele growled, her eyes narrowing with a look of exaggerated scorn. "We are not that cheap."

Fighting back her rage, Anele took Zanu by her hand and pulled her towards the car.

Kimathi grinned. "All you need to stop that anger is Vitamin P," he shouted in a condescending tone. "Your body has an over-secretion of salt. You must get laid."

Anele clicked her tongue in disgust and cursed under her breath. Opening the car, she asked Zanu to wait for her. Then, as soon as their daughter was safely inside, she walked slowly back to Kimathi and stood in front of him.

"Thanks, doctor! But I don't appreciate you talking like that in front of my daughter. Never do that again! Never, Kimathi!" She paused and looked hard at him. "You'll be surprised to learn that divorced women are not necessarily loners, like you think they are. Maybe they are just tired of hearing stupid men like you refer to their tiny deformed stump of a male organ as Vitamin P."

"Go to hell!"

"No!" Anele shook her head. "Not to hell. To court!"

"Is that a threat?"

"Yes," she said with finality that told him it was indeed over between them.

Kimathi tried to speak, but his throat produced no sound. Instead, he slumped in his chair, limp and defeated. He felt weak, lonely and helpless. Swallowing a mouthful of cognac, he closed his eyes and exhaled. As he opened them again, he realised that his headache had returned. He balled his left hand angrily into a fist as he watched Anele walk away.

* * *

Kimathi had first met Anele at the Union Buildings in Pretoria during the inauguration of President Thabo Mbeki in June 1999, eight years earlier. She was only twenty years old then, beautiful, and had matriculated from Benoni High School the previous year. He was working in the President's Office as an economic advisor, and she was with the Mzukwana Catering Company, which was providing food for the president-elect's guests. He could not keep his eyes off her as she made her way around the dining hall, putting different dishes on the table. She had smouldering eyes, perfect cheekbones and a heart-shaped face that was wide at the forehead and tapered to a narrow chin. She wore black wide-leg pants, a caramel blouse, black sequined shoes, a snakeskin-print blazer, a coral necklace and gold bangles. Kimathi found Anele extremely attractive. Somehow she reminded him of his mother, Akila. He had wanted to kiss Anele's beautiful lips in front of everyone, to feel the orange-red lipstick on them. Instead, he had only managed to give her his business card. She confessed later, when they had been together for a while, that she had lost the card the same day.

Kimathi had spent the next few days tracing the Mzukwana Catering Company. When he finally had Anele's contact number, he had tried to ask her out on a date. She was not comfortable with it at first, and refused, giving him silly excuses. In fact, she only agreed to go out with him after he had done something extraordinary.

It was Friday, 25 June 1999, a day that Anele had often – when they were still together – claimed to be the most romantic day of her life. After asking some of his female colleagues for romance tips, Kimathi had called Nkele's Florist, at the corner of Church and Beatrix in Pretoria, and organised for twenty-four bouquets to be delivered to Anele at her workplace in Proes Street. As soon as this was arranged, he'd called Anele's manager, Mrs Smith, to let her know of the deliveries, which would arrive throughout the day – four per hour. He remembered Anele telling him that all the girls had envied her on that day. Every one of her colleagues had wanted to meet Kimathi, the romantic guy. At least that is what she had told him when they were still together.

Kimathi had delivered the twenty-fifth bundle himself at four-thirty sharp. It was Anele's knock-off time and she was completely overwhelmed by his romantic gesture. He had met her at reception as she was about to go home, and when he had asked her to meet him for dinner at eight o'clock sharp, she hadn't even tried to resist. During their candlelit dinner at the Baobab Restaurant in Menlyn Park Mall, she had told him that Sisa, her boyfriend, was a thug and a car thief. She was not happy with him, she'd said, because Sisa had lots of women all over the Barcelona section of Daveyton township, on the East Rand. After two more dinners, she decided to leave Sisa, and she and Kimathi started dating seriously.

Their wedding took place on 14 February 2000. They had sat for hours with Mapaseka, their wedding planner, explaining their elegant wedding dream. And it had been worth it, as every supplier suggested by Mapaseka had surpassed their wildest expectations. The wedding itself took place at Makiti Weddings and Functions in Kromdraai Valley, an exclusive venue in the Cradle of Humankind. The guests had come from as far away as Tanzania, Angola, Zambia, Australia, England and the USA. They were four hundred and fifty in total. Kimathi had chosen Ludwe and Sechaba as his best men, while Anele's bridesmaids, Aya and Yolanda, came from Daveyton. The day was filled with love, laughter and joy. He had even serenaded her – "Always You" by James Ingram – under the big old trees beside the river that meandered through the garden. It had been their favourite song. Immediately after the song, she had said to him, "You stole my heart, Kimathi Fezile Tito, so today I'm planning to revenge myself. I'm going to take your last name."

* * *

A black ant biting him on his left hand brought Kimathi painfully back to reality. He squashed the ant with his finger. *It is over*, he thought. Even the expensive diamond ring that he had given her had been traded at the pawnshop. When he had asked about it, she'd told him that she had sold it to raise money for Zanu's school fees.

Kimathi looked down into his cognac glass; some ants had drowned inside. He threw the remaining cognac into the garden and, craving a refill, stood up and went back inside the house. But instead of going to the bar, he instinctively opened his bedroom door. As he walked into the room he had once shared with Anele, he tried to force some pleasant images of her into his mind. Opening a drawer, he picked out a red bustier and matching G-string. These had belonged to Anele, but he had hidden them from her when she'd moved out. Souvenirs, he called them, to remind him of her. From the dressing table he retrieved Anele's favourite fragrance – Lancôme Trésor Midnight Rose – and sprayed it on both the bustier and G-string. Sucking in his breath, Kimathi sat down on the bed holding the lingerie. He stared at the wall, in deep thought. *Forget it. Nostalgia is always self-delusion. She is no longer yours. You have lost her forever. You have to move on, brother. She has.*

Chapter 3

Kimathi was a real son of exile. He was conceived in an act of unromantic lust in the village of Mazimbu Darajani, also known as Dark City, near Morogoro in Tanzania. His father, Lunga Tito, was a Xhosa man from Dimbaza, a township some twenty kilometres outside of King William's Town. His mother, Akila, was a Swahili from Kwa-Ngiriki. Kimathi spoke both Xhosa and Swahili fluently. His parents had met in Kwa-Ngiriki in January 1969, when Lunga was in exile in Tanzania. Kimathi was born the same year, on 31 October, which meant he shared a birthday with his father's struggle hero, Mau Mau leader Dedan Kimathi Waciuri.

Kimathi's father died in 1985, after suffering from depression and being suspended as camp commissar at Morogoro. Reports claimed that Comrade Lunga had become frustrated and shot dead six of his colleagues in their sleep before turning the gun on himself. As a commissar he held a critical position in the camp when it came to the education of new recruits. The Movement had suspended him because of allegations that he had lured new female recruits into his bed by providing them with supplies he stole from the logistics section, including clothes, toothpaste, meat and alcohol. On the night before he killed himself, Comrade Lunga asked a young comrade, Ludwe Khakhaza, his most trusted student, to look after his son. He pleaded with Ludwe to take Kimathi to Dimbaza with him once the struggle was over.

After he killed himself, The Movement decided that Comrade Lunga's actions were despicable and amounted to desertion; therefore he was not given the respect other struggle heroes were afforded. Kimathi's mother died eight months later.

Ludwe fulfilled his promise to Lunga when he assisted Kimathi with his application for indemnity and a South African identity document in 1991. Obtaining the indemnity was important for exiled freedom fighters like Kimathi, as it was the only way to enter South Africa legally. Otherwise, he would have risked prosecution for crimes committed as a member of The Movement. He entered South Africa on 27 July 1991.

With the compensation that he received from The Movement, which was less than three thousand rand, Kimathi had rented a flat in Hillbrow. He knew little about Johannesburg and South Africa. Before he came to the country, he had imagined cities built on gold. At least, that was what his father had told him during one of their many walks on the banks of the Ngerengere River, near Morogoro. This particular walk had taken place after one of his playmates at Likobe Primary School had derogatorily called him "wakimbizi wa Africa kusini", Swahili for "a refugee from South Africa".

"I want you to fight for your country, South Africa," his father had said to him when Kimathi came home from school crying. "Tell those morons in Dark City that you're not a wakimbizi, but a social reformer. Tell them you're from a country where the cities are built on top of gold and diamonds. You are a revolutionary."

It was on that day that Lunga decided that he needed to send his son to military school.

Kimathi began his life in The Movement as a student at Solomon Mahlangu Freedom College, or SOMAFCO for short. He became active in 1984, when a rumour circulated that the school might be targeted by the Boers. He was then tasked, together with other youths in exile, with digging trenches all over the campus. It was during this time that he met Comrade Ludwe properly for the first time – he was supervising the trench digging – and learnt of his connection with his father.

Chapter 4

Kimathi hummed aloud to Jonas Gwangwa's "Flowers of the Nation" as he drove along the M1 North freeway. With one hand firmly on the steering wheel of his X5, he relit his cigar as he passed Gold Reef City casino. Puffing on his cigar, he watched the smoke billow towards the windscreen. He was happy that his gambling habit wasn't as out of control as it had been in the past. The last time he had been at the casino was about six months earlier, when he lost twenty-five thousand rand in one night.

It was about quarter past eleven when Kimathi arrived at the "super sex market" of Oxford Road in Rosebank. After drinking countless tots of cognac alone at his home that day, the need for passion was bothering him, demanding his utmost attention. He needed a sexual encounter as a matter of urgency and he knew a few girls along Oxford who, for a small fee, specialised in making lonely men like him happy.

Kimathi parked his car on a dark, tree-lined street near the Nelson Mandela Children's Foundation. His aim was to avoid the prying eyes of anybody who might recognise his car. The street was completely deserted except for a car parked in the shadows a few metres ahead. *Maybe somebody like me is also searching for the kind of passion that comes without the exchange of tender words?* He remembered Ludwe confiding in him, during one of their sexual escapades in Mafukuzela Camp, that sex is one of the most basic needs of life because society has to reproduce.

Careful not to attract attention, Kimathi switched off the X5's lights, picked up the half-smoked cigar he had placed in the cup holder next to the gear lever and lit it again. His mood brightened at the sight of three prostitutes in bikinis. They were standing across the road under a streetlight, which made their heavily made-up faces glow. While Kimathi's lips sucked at his cigar, his eyes scanned the three prostitutes as he checked for the assets he desired. Large breasts, a big behind and dark pigmentation were his obsessions.

While Kimathi was studying the three women, two tall black transvestite prostitutes with long false nails, large earrings and wigs appeared from his blind spot and knocked on the window – their eyes talking to him in a suggestive language. Kimathi removed the cigar from his mouth and grinned at them, before pressing the button to roll down the window slightly. It was evident that he was not interested in them, as he covered his face with his hand briefly before giving a loud sigh.

"Not tonight, thank you," he said with exaggerated politeness.

A white armed-response vehicle passed by, and the two male prostitutes banged the roof of his car in disappointment. They walked away. Across the road Kimathi spotted a lady with shining thighs. She was wearing a very tight miniskirt, and her smallish head was crowned with a blonde, Brazilian-weave hairpiece. He recognised the hairpiece because another prostitute had told him about it on one of his previous visits.

Kimathi emitted a low whistle to attract her attention, and she walked seductively towards his car. Her skirt was split halfway up the left thigh, and she shook her body like a samba dancer as she walked towards him. Kimathi wondered if that was just the way she walked or whether she was doing it to arouse him. As she neared the car, most of her left leg showed, awakening his lust. In his mind, she became a pure, pink, twenty-seven carat diamond from the Big Hole of Kimberley. His cognac-addled brain convinced him that she was of a rare quality that he didn't expect to see along Oxford Road.

With a wave of his hand, Kimathi invited the lady inside his BMW. As she opened the car door, he noticed that she had huge eyelashes and thick make-up. She was the perfect shape for his desire. Her breasts were like the halves of watermelons, and she smelled of musk. *That's it, she's mine tonight*, he thought.

"How are you, sweetie?" Kimathi asked, his mouth curling into a smile as the lady put her small brown handbag on the dashboard.

"Hot and horny as hell, and how about you, my darling?" she replied, rubbing him between his legs. As she did so, she made sure that her miniskirt rode up.

Kimathi was already in a state of excitement. "How much will your company cost me tonight?" he asked, breathing quickly, his eyes glued between the lady's thighs.

"It depends on how much fun you want, darling," she responded with a false smile. "Five hundred for a suck and fuck."

Kimathi smiled and licked his lips. He didn't mind the scar below the lady's bellybutton, which was an obvious indication that she had produced a child.

"Shit! Inflation is a bitch in this country, isn't it?" he said, not meaning it.

"Like the Americans say, 'In God we trust, but in business we pay'," she replied jokingly.

"There is something familiar about you," Kimathi concluded after scrutinising her face again.

"Oh, really?" She shrugged while playing with her long red fingernails.

"Yes. Your voice sounds like someone I know." He gave her a conspiratorial look.

"Is she also in this business?" the lady asked as she looked in the rear-view mirror before glossing her lips with lipstick retrieved from her handbag.

Kimathi looked at her face and her breasts, and then between her thighs, but he said nothing. It was as if he was trying to discover the source of her attraction.

"Well, I think you forget easily, my dear. I'm Lakeisha from Tanzania, your favourite one. Remember me?" She winked at him and smiled. "I gave you Greek last week."

Kimathi briefly covered his face with his hands, but he couldn't remember her. All he knew was that he did not like the idea of taking prostitutes to his house. Instead, he preferred an exclusive spot in Saxonwold, a big guarded estate belonging to some white businessman. It cost only a hundred rand to park there for three hours, and once you found your spot, you could do a quickie behind the steamy windows. It was cheaper than booking a room in a hotel, which was why Kimathi fondly called it the "budget hotel".

"Oh yes, Lakeisha," Kimathi finally said, dropping his hands from his face. "Now I remember."

Kimathi kept quiet for a moment as if he needed time to digest what he had just said, then, on a sudden impulse, he put his left hand on her right thigh. Lakeisha smiled and showed him her slightly protruding teeth, which nearly spoiled her beauty. Her right hand reached out and he felt it touch his left thigh. With her eyes closed and mouth open, she fell back on the seat and spread her legs. Her hand moved between her legs, her middle finger moving as if she was stimulating herself. He was no longer sure if she was faking it.

"How much is fun with you today?" Kimathi asked again as he sucked in his breath.

Lakeisha did not answer him immediately, but continued playing with herself, shutting her eyes and moaning. The heat between Kimathi's legs was hammering harder as he watched what she was doing. He did not resist as she curled her fingers around his erect penis and massaged it.

"The usual price," Lakeisha whispered in his ear. "A thousand at your place."

"Give me a good price, Lakeisha." As he spoke, Kimathi moved his hand up Lakeisha's thigh. "You know I'm your best customer, don't you?"

"I know that," she said, digging her fingers deep into his scrotum. "But business is business, darling."

Kimathi felt a glorious energy spreading through his veins. He wanted to be on top of Lakeisha, to devour her. He could not endure it any longer, and moved his hand between her thighs. As he did so, Lakeisha reached for his wallet, which he had placed between the seats. Kimathi didn't complain as she removed a wad of notes, lust was running through him and he didn't care how much money she took.

Kimathi was still enjoying the delight that prostitutes afforded lonely men like him when he heard a window breaking nearby. This was followed by the sound of a car alarm going off and as Kimathi watched two guys ran past his car and disappeared behind some big trees. Seconds later two Chubb security vehicles raced past him and stopped by the parked car. Kimathi thought of driving away, but decided against it. He didn't want to attract unnecessary attention from the security people.

As he was about to chase the prostitute out of his car, there was a tapping on his window. A torch flashed on to reveal the scene between him and Lakeisha inside the car. Lakeisha opened her eyes wide; two police officers were standing outside, looking at the wad of notes lying between them. Upon seeing the two officers, Kimathi permitted himself to get angry and began selecting the precise wording of his official protest.

"What do you want?" he asked them as he opened the window slightly.

"Step out of the car, please," demanded the shorter of the two policemen. His breath smelled of raw onions.

"Why? Are you arresting me now for asking for directions?"

"Yeah, right, asking for directions with your finger on her shaved pussy," jeered the officer with the onion breath.

"That's an assumption," Kimathi responded, trying to contain his temper.

"You'll tell that to the magistrate," the taller officer said. "But now we are going to the police station with you."

"You can't do that," Kimathi protested. "I'm calling my lawyer." He took his cellphone from the dashboard and held it in his right hand. "I will sue your asses for defamation."

Before he could dial, the taller officer opened the car door. "Have you been drinking, sir?" he probed, looking at both Kimathi and Lakeisha accusingly.

"No," Kimathi replied, his face tensing with anger. "Do I look like I have been drinking?"

"You have to come with us to the police station so we can breathalyse you," said the taller officer with malicious delight.

"Why?" enquired Kimathi, rearranging his facial muscles into a frown. "I think you are now violating my rights, gentlemen, and that is against the constitution of this country."

"You are coming with us in the van," said the officer with the onion breath. "I will drive your car while you sit in the back of the van."

"No way," Kimathi said, his anger nearly choking him. "You are not arresting my car, are you? I will drive it myself."

"Not when you have been drinking," said the taller officer. "You can't drive the car."

"I told you, I'm not drunk," Kimathi insisted.

"Well, we now have three charges against you," responded the officer with the onion breath, shaking a warning finger at Kimathi. "One, resisting arrest; two, interfering with police duties; three, buying sex from a prostitute. How about that?"

"Do you know who I am?" asked Kimathi. "I know people in high places. I will call the Commissioner of Police, and you'll both lose your jobs."

"We don't care who you are," said the taller officer. "This is not Holland. Prostitution is still illegal in South Africa."

"Who said I was buying sex?" Kimathi responded, sounding offended. "I was just asking for directions."

"Yes, we know, with your zip open," the officer with the onion breath responded sarcastically.

"Fuck off! You imbeciles! You will all pay for this!" Kimathi threatened as the two officers dragged him out of his car and began to force him into the back of the police van.

The two officers didn't answer him. Instead the officer with the onion breath dismissed him with a wave of his hand and the taller officer gave him a look that said: don't fuck with us. He then got into Kimathi's BMW with Lakeisha.

As they drove in the direction of Hillbrow police station, Kimathi's eyes bulged with terror as the reality of the situation started to dawn on him. His libido was diverted, there was a more pressing matter at hand – the possibility of sleeping in a police cell. He was already imagining the embarrassing headlines in the newspapers, and the damage they would do to his chances of winning the tender he was about to apply for. The last time his reputation had been at stake was when he had been working in the Presidency and a female colleague had accused him of sexual harassment. Although the case had been dismissed, due to a lack of evidence, it had done a lot of damage to his relationship with Anele.

Chapter 5

It was Ludwe who reunited Kimathi with his family in Dimbaza in February 1992, six months after he had arrived from Angola. This was the happiest day in Kimathi's life. His father had told him a lot about his aunt, Yoli, and seeing her for the first time was a great thing.

Kimathi had carried with him two old photos of his father, taken at SOMAFCO when he was still a commissar for The Movement. In both photos, Lunga wore two-tone Florsheim shoes, khaki bell-bottom trousers and a floral shirt that hung open to expose his hairy chest. He also sported a huge Afro.

Yoli was unable to conceal her joy. "Oh, God is alive. He left here in August 1968. In fact, he just disappeared." His aunt smiled as she looked at the pictures. "He only wrote to us once, saying that he was in exile, but did not specify where." She paused and expelled her breath through stiffened lips. "I assume he is no longer alive."

Yoli looked at Kimathi for a reply, but instead it was Ludwe who spoke. They had agreed that he would do all the talking, especially in relation to Lunga's death.

"He died in Tanzania from gunshot wounds in 1985," Ludwe said with exaggerated grief. "He was my father figure in Tanzania. I left to go into exile in 1977, at the age of twenty. Comrade Lunga was already known as mgwenya, a veteran, when I arrived in Tanzania. He made sure I was well fed and clothed. He was my teacher."

"Was he shot by the Boers?"

"Yes," answered Ludwe, wiping an imaginary tear from his left eye. "He asked me to bring his son back before he died. He talked so much about you."

"Is your mother still alive?" Yoli asked, addressing Kimathi directly.

"No, she passed away in 1986," Kimathi answered.

Yoli spat on the ground to express her sympathy. "Shame, what was her name?"

"Akila."

"Were they married?"

"No, they were never married," Kimathi said, smiling sourly.

Yoli wiped her nose and then pinched it. Her eyes closed tightly, then opened and focused on Kimathi. "Don't worry, this is your home. I'm your mother and your aunt now."

"Thank you," said Kimathi, licking his lips.

"When were you born?"

"October 1969."

"How come you know Xhosa so well?"

"My father used to teach me, and there were lots of South Africans in Tanzania."

"Do you have a Xhosa name?"

"I'm Fezile."

Yoli hid her surprise with a satisfied smile. "That was your grandfather's name," she said, nodding energetically. "I'll take you to your grandmother's grave tomorrow."

"Thank you," said Kimathi. "And Grandfather, is he still alive?"

"Unfortunately we did not bury your grandfather. But tomorrow we will slaughter a goat, and I'll introduce you to your stepbrother as well."

Kimathi looked confused.

"Oh, didn't my brother tell you that he had a son while still in high school?" Yoli asked. "When he left in 1968, in August, his high school girlfriend, Bulelwa, who was also my friend, was six months pregnant. The two families were planning to meet and negotiate the damages when my brother disappeared. Nakho was born in November of that year."

"Where does he live?" Kimathi asked.

"He is in Dikeni." Yoli paused. "That's where his mother was originally from. In fact, my daughter Unathi stayed at their place when she was studying at Fort Hare. I'll call him later."

"I can't wait to meet him."

"He is a very sweet boy." She paused. "We are originally from Middelburg. I was thirteen years old, going on fourteen, when we were forcibly removed to this place. Your father was two and half years older than me. We came here by truck in 1967. The Boers simply asked my father, Fezile, where he originally came from. The next thing, they gave us a day to pack our things. The following day they locked our house and told us to wait for the truck that would take us to our new home."

"That was very cruel," said Kimathi.

Yoli lapsed into silence for a while, her eyes filled with tears.

Ludwe palmed his shaven head, then sat back in his chair, flipping one leg over the other.

"I remember it was raining on that day. Your father was about to finish school; he was very brilliant in maths. The Boers didn't even let him finish his final year of school, or write his exams, which were coming in three months' time. He had wanted to go to Fort Hare to do medicine or law. My father was arrested because he had initially refused to move here to Dimbaza." She stopped to wipe away a tear.

"Was Grandfather also a politician?" asked Kimathi.

"No." Yoli shook her head. "He had big land where we planted maize, beans and potatoes. He also had many goats, pigs, and sheep. When he was taken to jail, we were brought here to Dimbaza, to this house, which was initially a wooden shack with a zinc roof. My father only joined us here six months later, but when he came, he decided to go and check his farm in Middelburg. There he found out that it was now owned by some Boer called Viljoen, who had also inherited our livestock. That's when my father joined The Movement."

She paused and then continued, "One day, during the night, he went back to Middelburg and killed Viljoen. After that incident, our family was constantly harassed by the Boers, and that's when your father left for exile. My father was caught in 1972 and hanged. We were never given his body to bury."

They shared a second of eye contact and Kimathi saw a spasm of hatred pass across Yoli's face – she was obviously not the forgiving type.

"This house was improved by my mother, Nomakhaya," Yoli continued. "When we came here in 1967, it was just a leaking structure, but as you see now, it is a beautiful four-bedroom house. She used to work in King William's Town, making dresses in a factory until she passed away of cancer three years ago."

"That's not long ago," said Kimathi.

"Amabhunu ayizinja, mntanami. They are dogs," Yoli concluded. "When we were forcibly removed, our six-year-old brother passed away in the back of the truck because of the cold. Now they want to reconcile? Reconciliation se voet! I'm glad my brother Lunga taught you politics. You and me must go back to Middelburg and claim our ancestral land from the Viljoens. Our great-grandparents' graves are there. Now we cannot go and perform our traditional rituals because of those white bastards."

Yoli paused for breath, and then continued, "I went to the council to reclaim that land and they say I must come with title deeds. Where do they think I'll get that paper, huh, mntanami? When I told them that our farm stretched from the two tall fig trees to the stream, they didn't believe me because those trees are gone now. The Boers have chopped them down to hide the evidence. Those trees separated our farm from the Bacelas, who were also evicted."

She stopped and looked at her fingernails as if to examine the dirt beneath them. "Those council people looked at me as if I was a mad woman when I told them that those trees were our title deeds before the Viljoens occupied our farm. I'm no longer voting for any political party because they are failing to solve our problem of land."

At that point, a lady with an oval face entered the house. She was wearing a beige floral-print dress, a multi-strand necklace and brown showstopper heels. Ludwe's eyes settled on her for a very long moment. Her face was flawless.

"This is my daughter Unathi," said Aunt Yoli.

That night, before they slept, Ludwe spent some time talking to Unathi. She was interested in knowing more about her Uncle Lunga, and he seemed to be the right man to talk to. They exchanged contacts and Ludwe promised to use his network to try and get her a job in Joburg.

The following day, the family prepared a great feast for Kimathi and Ludwe. A goat was slaughtered to welcome Kimathi home. After the party, they went with Nakho, Kimathi's stepbrother, to the cemetery where their grandmother was buried. Nakho looked exactly like their father. However, despite everything, Kimathi felt no connection with his father's home. Unathi and Ludwe, however, continued to talk, and on that day he was even able to put his arms around her. She agreed to visit Kimathi in Johannesburg, and she and Ludwe were married a year later.

Chapter 6

Kimathi sat silently in the back of the police van with a faraway look on his face. He bit his lip; he was filled with nervous expectation, and he remained silent for a while as if hunting for options in his mind. He could not bear the thought of sleeping in a police cell.

When they reached Hillbrow police station, Kimathi was taken to an office where there were four female police officers.

"It seems you have netted a big one today, officers," said one of the female officers, who was sitting at a table writing something in a book. She had a smallish oval face.

"Yes," the officer with the onion breath responded, "a rich BEE."

"Where did you get him?" she asked.

"From between a prostitute's legs," said the taller officer.

There was laughter, and Kimathi looked embarrassed.

"Did you take the picture of his thing?" asked the flat-chested female officer who was sitting in the corner. "I want to see how big he is."

"It's all in my cellphone, but you'll have to pay to see the bioscope," teased the taller officer. "And he is a celebrity. He knows the Police Commissioner."

"I'm sure he'll be pleased to see his friend's porn movie."

There was another ripple of laughter.

"What's your name, sir?" asked the officer standing next to a small machine that looked like a till.

"You can't charge me with anything," protested Kimathi, staring at the breathalyser. "I'm not under the influence of alcohol."

"Yhooo!" said the fourth officer sarcastically. "This one seems to know a lot."

"But I'm not drunk," Kimathi insisted. "Why should I tell you my name?"

"Whether you want to tell us or not is irrelevant, mister," said the lady behind the desk. "One way or another you'll have to tell the magistrate."

Standing up, she opened a drawer and took out a tube that she connected to the breathalyser. She then demonstrated to Kimathi how he should blow into the device.

"Just so that you know, sir," started the female police officer before handing Kimathi the tube. "It is illegal to drive with an alcohol concentration of more than the limit of 0,24 milligrams."

She handed the device to Kimathi, but instead of doing as the officer had demonstrated, Kimathi started sucking air into his mouth and breathing it out so that the device could not read his level. This angered all the officers in the room.

"You have three chances to blow into this breathalyser properly, mister," said the female police officer with the oval face. "You must not waste our time."

"I told you, I didn't drink any alcohol," said Kimathi with obvious irritation in his voice. "And your German device concurs with me."

After failing to blow into the device correctly for the third time, the officer with the onion breath ordered Kimathi to stop.

"Well, sir," said the taller officer with a look of utmost hostility, "we'll have to go to the clinic to take your blood."

"What does that mean?" asked Kimathi with a frightened look on his face.

"Hawu, I thought you knew it all, mister," answered the taller officer in a sarcastic tone. "But, for your information, we are going to check the alcohol concentration in your bloodstream; it will prove that you are drunk."

"Let's go!" said the officer with the onion breath.

"Don't forget to show us his thing before the video hits the cinemas," said the flat-chested female officer as they exited the office.

"This one belongs to Hollywood," said the taller officer. "The South African movie houses won't be able to afford it."

"Don't forget us when you make those millions," she replied.

A few minutes later Kimathi and the two police officers arrived back in the parking lot where they had parked Kimathi's car and their van. When they opened the back of the van, Kimathi saw that Lakeisha was sitting inside. Looking at her, he knew he was in deep trouble. He was shaken. On the spur of the moment an apology came from his mouth.

"Okay, guys, I admit I'm in the wrong," he started in a softened tone. "Can we solve this matter peacefully?"

"What do you mean?" enquired the taller officer.

"How much will my freedom cost me?"

"A lot," responded the officer with the onion breath. "Especially now that we have already gone to all the trouble of breathalysing you."

"How about a thousand rand, and we forget this ever happened?"

"Bribery is a serious offence, do you know that?" said the officer with the onion breath. "It is called defeating the ends of justice, and you can go to jail for it."

"Please, guys. I'm begging you. My career is at stake here."

The two police officers remained quiet for a moment, as if they hadn't heard Kimathi speak. They then looked at each other and nodded in agreement. After a few seconds, they turned their heads in unison and looked hard at Kimathi. The taller officer took out his gun and played with it as if it was a toy. "If you fuck with us, you'll die," he said. "Do you understand me?"

"I will never, sir," Kimathi replied, his heart gripped with fear. "Please forgive me. And yes, I'd had a few glasses to drink when you met me. I'm guilty as charged. I swear it will never happen again."

"You bet it will never happen again. Do you have the cash with you?" asked the officer with the onion breath.

"Yes, I do."

"Okay, then. You give us the cash and disappear. But you'll have to add another five hundred for wasting our time."

"That's fine," Kimathi said, taking out his wallet. "I'm prepared to do that for my freedom."

The taller officer narrowed his eyes. "The girl remains with us," he commanded as Kimathi handed the cash to him. "We'll take very good care of her," he continued, splaying the bills out between his fingers. "She's in good hands."

Kimathi looked at Lakeisha and then nodded at the police officers. He didn't care if they took her away. She was a liability to him. Lakeisha started to cry like a child, as if pleading with Kimathi to rescue her. Kimathi watched the tears trickling down her cheeks.

"No," she protested feebly.

"She's all yours, officers," Kimathi affirmed in a tone that let them know he didn't care.

"Of course she is," said the officer with the onion breath, tossing Kimathi his car keys. "By the way, I saw a pack of cigars in your car. Can I have one?"

"With pleasure," said Kimathi, opening the car.

"Please don't leave me here," pleaded Lakeisha. "Take me with you. I beg you. Please."

Kimathi ignored her and handed the wooden Cohiba Behike cigar box to the tall officer. "Here, take the whole box," he said, climbing into his car – there were only three cigars left in the box and he had four boxes left at home.

Lakeisha started to sob. Kimathi looked at her briefly as he started his car. The tear he saw on her left cheek lingered in his mind as he drove away, but any feeling of guilt lasted just a few minutes.

Chapter 7

8:45 am, Mafukuzela camp, Kwanza Sul province, Angola, 20 August 1987

"Take cover, comrades!" Comrade Pilate shouted, looking upwards in an attempt to locate the origin of the roaring sound that filled the air around him. "The Boers are attacking us! Take cover!"

People came sprinting from all corners of the camp, dust rising up as five South African Air Force Puma helicopters, each with a white letter painted on its belly, descended on the camp.

Pilate screwed his eyes shut, opened them again and then blinked several times as if he couldn't believe what he was seeing. "It's a raid!" he shouted over the sound of the engines. "Run to the trenches!"

Rat-tat-tat-tat-tat!

The sound of gunfire came from the helicopters as they came in to land. Three people behind Pilate fell to the ground. One of them had been shot in the neck, and he began to kick both his legs as the blood spurted from his wound.

Ducking close to the ground, Pilate ran towards the escape trench. Two metres deep, it was surrounded by tall trees and thick bushes and ended in a dry riverbed that lay on the other side of the large maize field behind the camp. It had been dug for a moment exactly like this.

Boom!

A grenade exploded a few metres away, showering Pilate with dirt and throwing him to the ground. Climbing to his feet, he looked around in confusion. People were frantically running for cover, but very few of them were carrying their AKs, even though their lives were at stake. As Pilate watched, a woman clad in fatigues fell to the ground just outside Soshangane block. Another woman tried to help her to get up, but she was tripped by two men who were trying to get away.

It was already too late for the comrades in Ndlela ka Sompisi block. The building was on fire, smoke billowing from the shattered windows. High-pitched screams filled the air as burning debris began to fall on those inside.

Pilate tasted blood. Looking down, he saw two bodies at his feet. He touched his face. Blood from his two fallen comrades was congealing around his nose and mouth. "Shit," he whispered, his teeth clattering against each other as if it was a cold day. "We're dead people."

Chapter 8

It was almost a done deal; there was every reason for Kimathi and his business partners to celebrate their achievement with Johnnie Walker Blue Label King George V Scotch whisky at six hundred and fifty rand a tot. Money was not the issue here, not with the multi-million rand government tender that they were about to land for their company, Mandulo Construction.

Since five o'clock that afternoon, Kimathi and his three business partners, Sechaba, George and Ganyani had been drinking with Ludwe Khakhaza, the director-general of the Department of Public Works, in the bar of the Park Hyatt hotel in Rosebank.

"So, what's my role in this whole thing?" asked Ganyani of his long-time exile friend Kimathi. Ganyani's dark, round face and his big stomach gave him an aged look although he was only forty-seven.

"Relax, comrade, you don't have to do much here, but I promise you that we'll all make good currency." Kimathi smiled, forking at his plate of grilled tenderloin strips served over greens and dressed with crumbled Gorgonzola and tomatoes.

"Com, you can't call me all the way from Limpopo and book me into this expensive hotel for doing *nothing much*, as you say. Remember, I was also once a politician." Ganyani paused and looked across the table at Kimathi and Ludwe. "I know when somebody is promising a bridge where there is no river. What inspired this kindness? That's what I'm interested in."

"But isn't it great, chief, to be remembered when you are far away in sleepy Elim?" asked Kimathi after a short, mocking laugh. "All we ask of you is to bring your very sharp knife, not a sickle. The fat cow has finally fallen and we don't want you to complain later when you only see its horns and skin. We are the ones who know the secret jungle where this fat cow is, but we require your expertise in skinning beasts. That's all."

They all laughed, except Ganyani, who looked up and cupped his chin in his hands. He gave his face a vigorous rub, as if he hoped it would help to clear the fog in his brain.

Ganyani Novela had been a member of The Movement's military wing, although he had never held any prominent position. Like Kimathi, he was a comrade who'd got involved in business. He was not interested in running a company, but he had gained financially from doing so. Because of their strong political connections, both Ganyani and Kimathi had become successful businessmen upon their return to South Africa. In fact, when the ruling party promised to build one million new homes for the poor during its first term in office, Ganyani's construction company, GAZA, had benefited by closing a thirty million rand deal to construct houses in the Elim area of Limpopo province. Ganyani had long forgotten his past as a primary school teacher in Elim; his huge stomach dominated the corner of the Hyatt hotel bar.

Kimathi put all three of his cellphones on the table, including the one he had just taken from his cream Dunhill jacket. Ganyani sipped his whisky without talking. Kimathi winked at him joyously, and held up his glass. "Relax and enjoy your whisky, com," he said, studying the amber-coloured liquid before sipping it. "You Shanganese like to complain a lot, just like you did in exile."

There was mild laughter from the others, including George, who was the only qualified engineer among them. George worked for TTZ, one of the country's "big five" construction companies, which had in the past benefited from government tenders of more than one billion rand. Ludwe, Ganyani, Sechaba and Kimathi had known each other since exile days, but George's link to this group of comrades was his company's need for a recognised BEE partner in order to be considered for tender applications. This was the only reason TTZ was interested in Mandulo, which belonged to Kimathi and Sechaba.

"Point of correction, comrade," interjected Ganyani after the laughter had subsided. "It's actually Shangaan, not Shanganese. You mean to tell me that since you came back from Angola you haven't learned anything about our country? You don't even know how to pronounce the word 'Shangaan'? You are pathetic, comrade."

"You can't blame me for being born in exile, com," Kimathi said defensively. "It was not my choice, but the revolution's. Anyway, there is only one language in this world, and that is what brought us together here. Currency, comrade! Money!"

There were nods of approval around the table at the mention of the word "currency". Kimathi sipped from his glass again, popped an olive in his mouth, removed the pit and put it on the plate in front of him.

"All right, this is what your role is, Mr Novela," said George to Ganyani.

George was the only white man in the group. A Greek-American, originally from Ames, Iowa, had grown up on the banks of the Skunk River, and had studied engineering at Iowa State University. He wore a cheap blue shirt, a beltless pair of old blue jeans and his beard needed trimming.

George retrieved a file from the table and opened it. He paged through to a map. "There are about thirty farms in this area of Soutpansberg Coal Reef in the Vhembe Region," he said, running his finger along the map and pointing at an area around Louis Trichardt. "Your job will be to inspect them for us," he paused, "and since we assume they know you there, you can talk to the chiefs and farmers about the possibility of buying them out. That is, if it's necessary."

"Is that all you want me to do?" Ganyani's asked.

"Exactly that," said George.

"Like we said, it's nothing much," emphasised Kimathi, after George looked at him for approval.

"And what's my cut on this *nothing much* job?" asked Ganyani sarcastically.

"Comrade, this is not a big job, as you can see," said Sechaba. "We are prepared to give you seven per cent."

"Seven what?" asked Ganyani, feigning surprise. "No ways, comrades! Why are you guys asking me to bring just a knife if you're bringing machetes for the so-called fallen fat cow? I didn't join the struggle and go into exile to be a poor man when liberation came. I cannot betray the spirit of our noble revolution by taking such a small percentage while you guys walk away with the lion's share. I also have kids to feed, comrade."

"We know, chief." Sechaba's tone was conciliatory. "Of course, the spilled blood of our 1976 student revolution has oiled the wheels of economic change. But we promise you that your kids will be well taken care of for the rest of their lives. Just imagine how much seven per cent is of nine hundred million? It's a lot for doing nothing really. From today on, consider yourself a multi-millionaire, comrade.

You can buy the whole Elim village and all of the surrounding villages with that kind of currency."

They all studied Ganyani, but his dark face gave nothing away. Only a gold pen glimmered from the pocket of his navy Valentino jacket.

Kimathi picked the olive pit off his plate and rolled it between his fingers. "Comrade, perhaps let me tell you how we came to the seven per cent," he reasoned, realising that Ganyani was not going to respond as quickly as they had anticipated. "First of all, you know that your construction company doesn't have a level nine rating. So we –"

"What are you talking about, comrade?" interrupted Ganyani, his brows creasing. "I won a thirty million rand tender with my company nine years ago, and I had just formed it then. So, I don't think there is an issue with my rating."

"That's true. But I guess that's also the reason you abandoned the project, comrade," answered Kimathi, using both his hands to emphasise the point he was making. "It's clear that you didn't have the capacity; what you had were the contacts. And now you're in the bad books of the government in Limpopo."

"He's right," affirmed George as if it was obligatory for him to speak.

Although TTZ was registered as a South African company, it was actually owned by PMB, its sister company in France. One of the first major tenders TTZ had scored from the government was for the resurfacing of the N3 between Johannesburg and Durban. Their formula for securing the job, then as now, had been to partner with small black-owned construction companies. To win the Soutpansberg tender, they desperately needed both Ganyani's company and his contacts in government.

Ganyani began to think about what Kimathi and George had just said, but at that moment he saw a waitress appear at the far end of the bar and waved at her. As she approached the table, he emptied his glass in two swallows and ordered another drink. Kimathi, Sechaba and Ludwe also ordered more drinks as the waitress wiped their table and removed the empty dishes and the menu. The waitress left the table. Kimathi took out a toothpick from the small glass next to him and put it between his teeth.

"Maybe let me remind you of something, chief," said Sechaba, adjusting his silk tie on his pink Fabiani shirt. "According to the Construction Industry Development Board you are at the lower rating level."

"So what if I have a lower rating? Am I going to be discriminated against because of it?" Ganyani asked. There was arrogance in his tone.

"Obviously, comrade. You know for sure that out of the one hundred and eighteen contractors with the highest rating, only two are black-owned. You are not one of them, of course."

"Bad, but what does all of this have to do with me, then?" asked Ganyani. "If I don't have the right rating?"

"We will help you to get a higher rating from the board if you work with us," Sechaba offered. "We have friends on the board."

The waitress arrived with their drinks. There was a moment of silence as she put the glasses on the table. Kimathi smiled mirthlessly as she left.

"This is different, comrade," said Kimathi, removing the toothpick from between his teeth. "We are talking here of a nine hundred million rand tender. Nine hundred million, comrade," he repeated, lifting his whisky glass.

"I know, but –"

Kimathi would not let Ganyani finish his sentence. "You definitely need us and our level nine rating to win it, and of course we also need you." He took a swig from his glass. "You can't go it alone. Even if we gave you all the time in the world, I don't think you'd ever reach the requirement. Not because we'd undermine you, but because there is a serious lack of engineers and other professionals in this country." He pointed at George and Sechaba. "We have been around for a long time now, and we have all the necessary skills."

"We'll see about that when the tender is announced," said Ganyani, unconvinced.

"May I remind you again, chief, that you need a minimum of seventy million yearly turnover, eighteen million employable capital and at least two qualified persons," said Kimathi. "You need an engineer or architect, and a quantity surveyor or project manager on your payroll. Where are you going to get that kind of money and the necessary skillls if you don't join us in this venture?" He opened his eyes wide. "We have already secured the personnel from PMB in France; that's why we're in partnership with them."

Ganyani remained quiet for a while, obviously trying to make some sense of Kimathi's speech. It seemed the words had passed through his ears without being digested properly, and had brought his mind into disorder. A faint sweat forced itself out on his forehead.

"So, what are you saying, chief?" probed Sechaba.

"I'll have to think about it." The words had fallen from Ganyani's mouth before he was even conscious he had said them.

"All we are saying is that you must never bite the hand that is trying to feed you, com," said Kimathi, with exaggerated concern. "If you join us, we will supply all the skills necessary to do the job. Comrade Ludwe here has strongly recommended that we make a joint venture with a company from the Soutpansberg area to make our bid even stronger." He cleared his throat, smiled and glanced at Ludwe. "As you are aware, he is the director-general of Public Works and has the final say in the matter. That is the reason we chose your company. We are fully aware that you are also interested in the tender, but you have to make a choice now. Otherwise, you will lose the bid to us. We want to empower your area through you, you know? We just want you on board, comrade."

Ganyani looked at Ludwe and smiled, exposing his gums. He folded his arms as if he was letting the words sink in. He was fully aware that Ludwe had an interest in the whole tender, but was not yet sure how. He had only seen the name of Ludwe's niece, Sindi Yeni, on Kimathi's company profile. She had been given an executive chairmanship, although Ganyani knew that she was only twenty years old and hadn't even passed matric.

Ganyani was not aware that Ludwe was to receive a ten per cent cut from the project. Sindi, meanwhile, would earn five hundred thousand a year, although with no medical aid, car or cellphone allowance. She would not receive any dividends from her shares, though she owned twenty per cent of the company according to the company papers registered with the Department of Trade and Industry.

For the first time, Ludwe addressed Ganyani directly. "Our people need electricity as soon as possible," he began in a concerned tone of voice, his eyes pleading with Ganyani. "You have built houses in Elim, so you know what our people's burden is without electricity. Our power at Sasol is very bad, comrade."

Ganyani cast his eyes down briefly as a sign of respect to Ludwe. "I'm with you, comrade. We just had a black Christmas with no electricity at Elim," he said.

"Exactly my point," Ludwe said. "This 2007 is already showing that our country is facing a power crunch, with the demand for electricity having begun to outstrip the supply."

"I fully agree." Ganyani nodded, his Adam's apple rising and falling.

"There is a major shortage of electricity," Ludwe said, with a look of deep contentment on his face. "That is why our government is ready to increase the supply of this cheaper electricity from coal." He paused. "So far, as you know, only Eskom, which is government-owned, supplies this cheaper electricity. Billions of rand are set aside to construct new power stations to meet soaring demand." He looked around the table.

"I hear you, comrade." Ganyani nodded again.

"A proposal that sets out deliverable targets by teaming up leading companies like George's TTZ, which has a great history and valuable connections in France, with local companies that can create jobs for our people will convince the department that you are the right people for the job. I can guarantee it. As for the department, we'll not only give you the coal tender but also resources for infrastructure development, upgrading of railway lines and dams," concluded Ludwe, searching everyone's face for signs of mutual understanding.

Ludwe looked at Ganyani's amused expression and smiled. It was not because he felt there was anything worth smiling about; it was simply a tactic he always used to buy the confidence of people he wanted on his side.

"Well, it seems I don't have any option, do I?" said Ganyani, smiling as if it was obligatory to do so. "I guess the seven per cent that you are offering is final."

"We are afraid so, chief," confirmed Kimathi. "Sometimes in life you have to surrender before you win."

Kimathi pulled at his jacket sleeve to look at the Rolex Yacht-Master II on his left wrist. It was twenty-five minutes before midnight, South African time. The Breitling on his right wrist showed New York time. According to him, it was necessary to wear both watches at all times so that he knew when to call his American business partners. He was definitely not showing off.

"I have to go, comrades," Kimathi said, yawning. "I haven't slept properly since I came back from my New York trip a month ago."

"I'm playing golf in Kyalami tomorrow," said Ludwe as he stood up. "So I should also get some rest."

"Oh, before I forget, here is your parcel," said Kimathi, handing a large brown A4 envelope to Ludwe. "It's exactly a hundred grand."

"Thank you very much," said Ludwe, smiling as he took the envelope. "I'll make sure that everything is in order."

Kimathi grabbed the keys to his X5 and wove his way out of the Park Hyatt bar. He ran his tongue around the inside of his cheek several times to remove pieces of food stuck there. Realising that the action was unsuccessful, he looked around before inserting his forefinger into the corner of his mouth. Having removed the food, he licked his finger and swallowed. In the lobby, he stopped and exchanged a few words with the receptionist, who was wearing large silver earrings. Pulling a wad of rolled-up banknotes out of his jacket pocket, he gave her a generous tip before he exited. The receptionist smiled broadly at the unexpected gift.

"With that smile, baby, I'm sure you won't sweat finding a rich man like me," Kimathi said in a self-satisfied tone as he staggered towards the door like an overfed penguin.

It had started to rain while he had been in the hotel, and the air outside smelt of wet soil, probably from the construction site for the Gautrain. Kimathi inhaled deeply, enjoying the moment, but as he did so, the streetlights went out and the whole neighbourhood was enveloped in darkness. He had completely forgotten the announcement he had heard on the radio earlier that day about the power being cut off from sometime around midnight for about four hours.

Kimathi still limped towards the parking lot. Although it was drizzling, he decided not to run to the car. His left leg had been weaker than the right ever since he had been injured while fighting UNITA rebels near the Kwanza River in Angola.

As he pressed the "open" button on his car key, Kimathi heard an owl hoot from the top of a nearby tree. The sound scared the breath out of him. Since childhood, Kimathi had hated owls, as they were regarded as an omen of witchcraft in his culture.

As he started the car, his headlamps picked up the bird as it flew away. In his whisky-addled brain, he was sure that the owl's eyes looked straight through him as he drove away.

Chapter 9

Driving south along Oxford Road, Kimathi put on his favourite CD by the Branford Marsalis Trio, *The Beautyful Ones Are Not Yet Born*. He had bought it to console himself after his divorce from Anele. Since their split, which had happened about two years earlier, Kimathi had started to get treatment for bipolar disorder. It was this condition that had led to their separation in the first place. During several manic episodes, he had spent huge amounts on his credit cards on gambling and prostitutes, which had made his wife suspicious. When he became delusional and started having sleeping problems, Anele asked him to consult a doctor. However, before he'd had a chance to get properly diagnosed Anele had found him naked in their bedroom with their domestic worker, Moliehi. This was the main reason for their divorce. Although Kimathi pretended to have forgotten Anele, the screen in his mind was filled with her image each time he was drunk and craved sex.

It started to pelt with rain as Kimathi came to a stop at the Bolton Road traffic lights by the Engen garage and McDonald's. The asphalt ahead of him shone, the headlights reflecting off the water on the road. The area exuded wealth and exclusivity during the day, but became something different at night because of the prostitutes. Kimathi watched with keen interest as his headlights picked up some women running towards the 14th Avenue bus shelter. He hungrily ogled one lady wearing a tiny dress as she tried to flag down a car coming from the opposite direction, savouring the shaking of her enormous behind.

Oxford Road was the only street in the country where Kimathi got an erection every time he drove along it. Just reading the graffiti got him horny. *Good Lord, she looks younger than the Glenfiddich single malt Scotch in my bar*, he thought as the sight of the lady's huge ass brought on an erection. He put his left hand inside his trousers and twiddled the short hairs around his pubic space.

He was still admiring the lady's assets when a car behind him hooted. Only then did Kimathi realise that the Bolton Road traffic lights were not working. As he drove slowly across the intersection, he saw what looked like an owl flying in front of him. It was as if the bird was guiding him home.

On the side of the road just before Cotswold Street, some prostitutes waved at Kimathi. They were standing at the bus stop next to the Nelson Mandela Children's Foundation building. Although he was a regular customer, Kimathi had told himself that he would fight the temptation to buy an hour of passion with one of them. The previous night's encounter with the two policemen and Lakeisha was still fresh in his mind. However, from his many emergency visits to Oxford Road, he knew that there were women there to suit every taste. He'd had unforgettable hours of passion with Zimbabweans, Swazis and Tanzanian goddesses. Tonight, he chose to look only at the familiar graffiti on the white wall of a law firm near 3rd Avenue. He read the words to himself as if they were new to him:

THE STREET OF 1000 WHORES

and below it:

WELCOME TO HORNYWOOD

and:

DRESSED TO FCUK.

As Kimathi crossed Riviera Road, there was a roar of thunder, and blinding lightning interrupted his fantasies. However, that did not stop him from synchronising his lips to Branford Marsalis's saxophone.

Immediately after joining the M1 South freeway, Kimathi heard a thump on the bonnet of the car. Thinking he had run something over, he reduced speed and was surprised and terrified to see a dead owl on the bonnet. Instinctively, he swerved the car over the yellow line, came to a stop and put on the hazard lights. His heart was pounding in his chest. Moments later the car's headlamps brought a faceless, blurry figure into view. He could see the raindrops hitting the figure's body and Kimathi watched as the figure looked up as if wondering why the rain was falling.

As the figure approached the car, Kimathi thought it was an old woman because of what looked like a walking stick in its hand.

Threads of lightning flashed across the sky as the figure knocked on the misted passenger window. Kimathi sat frozen inside the car, his lower lip quivering. Suddenly there was complete darkness. Kimathi blinked for several seconds then tried to open his eyes as wide as possible to accustom them to the lack of light. As he did so, he heard the passenger door open and someone sat down on the seat beside him. The lights came on, and, to Kimathi's utter astonishment, the owl flew off as if the lights had just resuscitated it. Slowly, the figure took off the white cloth that covered its head and part of its face. As it did this Kimathi noticed two owl feathers in its plaited hair and fear engulfed him. When he looked at the figure again he saw that it didn't have a left eye. He fainted for a few seconds.

When Kimathi opened his eyes, there was a beautiful young woman sitting next to him. She wore a tight pink T-shirt and blue jeans that were completely dry, as if she hadn't been out in the rain. Although his hands were shaking, her beauty immediately dispelled Kimathi's fear. He smiled. *Maybe I'm just drunk*, he thought to himself as he read the inscription on her T-shirt: *MR CHICKEN: GORGEOUS THIGHS & THICK JUICY BREASTS*. The air in the car was suddenly laced with an expensive perfume. He was familiar with the smell – *Anele's favourite, Lancôme Trésor Midnight Rose*, he thought.

"Why are you . . .?" He didn't finish his sentence. "Sorry, never mind. Maybe I've had too much to drink and was imagining things."

The woman smiled, but let the moment pass without responding to him. It was as if she had looked into his heart and read what was written on it – *fear*. Kimathi rubbed his eyes to drive out the intoxication running riot in his brain. He suddenly remembered that he hadn't taken his medication. While the woman watched him, he opened the cooler in the armrest and took out a Red Bull. Then he took three pills from a side pocket in the door and popped them into his mouth. He washed them down with the Red Bull and belched loudly.

"Eish! You gave me a hell of a fright," he said, speaking like a man who had just bounced back from the brink of a nervous breakdown. "I thought I was witnessing a true vision of the apocalypse, the real Armageddon."

"Sorry," the woman said in a smooth voice.

"Where is a beautiful lady like you going in this rain and thunder? Or are you Indira the goddess of thunder and rain herself?"

"I'm on my way back home."

"Way back home?" There was surprise in Kimathi's voice. "Where are you coming from, beautiful lady?"

"Work."

"Work?" he repeated, sounding irritated. "Show me that insensitive white bastard who is exploiting our black people at this time of our freedom by turning our hard-fought democracy into prison."

Without a word, the woman pointed at the small print on her pink T-shirt. It read *Malusi Nyoka Business Initiative*.

"Oh, I see. Is Mr Nyoka your boss?"

The woman nodded.

"Mr Nyoka is a great man, isn't he? I know him from exile," Kimathi said in a more upbeat tone. "But why are you here on the freeway?"

"My transport didn't fetch me and I was hoping to get a lift home."

"Why are you not wet? I mean, you've been standing in the rain."

When she didn't reply, Kimathi glanced uncomfortably at the dashboard clock. It was already seventeen minutes past midnight. He started the engine.

"By the way, I'm Kimathi," he said, giving her his hand to shake before withdrawing it quickly.

"I'm Senami."

"So, were you planning to walk in the weather at this time of the night until you got a lift?" He paused and cleared his throat. "It's not safe, you know that. Criminals will take advantage of you."

"Well, I was just trying my luck."

"Trying your luck?" he repeated. "Are you sure you're not from Oxford Road?" Kimathi laughed at his own joke, but Senami didn't join in. Embarrassed, Kimathi turned up the music to give himself time to recover from what he had just said.

"Where do you live, Senami?" Kimathi said eventually, having recovered from his embarrassment.

"Soweto. Protea North," she answered without looking at him.

"Do you like jazz?"

"I don't hate it."

"The guy that is playing here is called Branford Marsalis and the album is called *The Beautyful Ones Are Not Yet Born*." He paused, trying to choose his next words carefully. "You know, Senami, ever since my wife and I divorced I have told myself that there are no more beautiful ladies around. But today I'm thinking differently."

"What are you thinking?"

"That if some women were not as beautiful as you are, then the world would not go round."

Kimathi opened the glove compartment and took out a box of Cohiba Behike cigars. He asked Senami to open it for him, and took out two cigars. He offered one to Senami, but she declined by shaking her head.

"It's not a local one, you know. It's a pure Cuban gem. Try it," he insisted.

Her eyes warned him off and she shook her head vehemently.

Kimathi shrugged his shoulders and concentrated on the road. "Obviously you don't smoke, I see."

Silence fell as Kimathi thought of what to say next. Before he lit his cigar, he drew it to his nose and smelled it deeply. He was reluctant to light it, but felt obliged to do something – the silence in the car was unbearable. Taking the lighter from next to the cup holder between the seats, Kimathi lit the cigar. He reached for the window button and rolled it down a bit before puffing out the smoke with satisfaction. It seemed he had regained his air of superiority. Senami did not complain about the strong smell. They exchanged glances.

"It's the first time I'm seeing a lady this beautiful in years," Kimathi declared. "May I have the civilised enjoyment of accompanying you home? Otherwise I'll never have peace with myself."

"Thank you."

"I'm telling the truth, Senami. With every fibre in my revolutionary bones, I swear I'm not lying," Kimathi said, trying to impress her. "I think that I have already fallen in love with your smile, and I'm willing to go to hell with you."

"Big mistake," she answered.

"Why?"

"Because it's bad to love someone you can't have." Her words sounded like a stern warning. "Besides, I don't like politicians."

"Listen, I don't know what ideological horrors lurk in your mind right now, but may I ask why you don't like politicians?" Kimathi asked, contentedly puffing on his cigar.

"They are greedy, and they broke my spirit," Senami said sincerely, looking directly at Kimathi's Adam's apple. It was as if she was referring to it.

Kimathi laughed and stole a glance at a scar on Senami's left cheek. It suggested to him the reason for her dislike of men and perhaps male politicians in particular.

"True. Your political associate today can be your jailer tomorrow, I know. But that's the nature of politics. But let me tell you that it's not only politicians who break people's spirits. My ex-wife fractured my soul, and she didn't even know what *The Communist Manifesto* looked like," Kimathi said, searching Senami's face for a hint of a smile. There was none.

"Maybe I hate politicians because a conversation with them means talking about their wealth. Our democracy has only taught them to speak in huge figures and about the property they own," Senami said with some bitterness.

Kimathi hesitated before replying. "Oh, now I see. It is because of the guy you used to date that you think badly of politicians, isn't it? I guess it's true that one crazy bastard can make all beautiful women hate all the innocent guys," he said, plumes of smoke issuing from his nostrils.

"Not really. It is because most politicians are corrupt, I guess." Senami turned her face away from Kimathi as if trying to get away from the cigar smoke. "They learnt only one thing while on Robbers' Island." She paused and looked at Kimathi briefly. "How to steal. I think God created terribly flawed human beings when he created politicians, don't you think? He must be blaming himself up there," she concluded, and pointed at the roof of the car as if God was residing there.

Kimathi smiled to break the tension, but he felt a pang at the truth in Senami's words. He was surprised at how challenging she was; it felt like he was being granted a free assessment of politics in South Africa.

By then they were nearing Southgate Mall.

"I'm really enjoying your views on politicians. You sound very wise for your age, I must say . . ." Kimathi paused and glanced at Senami, his small eyes shining with pleasure. "But you must understand that we are living in one of the most challenging moments in the history of this country. It is therefore important to learn to accept what you cannot change. As the true sons of this nation, we must be in charge. We must not be apologetic about it."

Senami became silent again, as if digesting Kimathi's pretentious and condescending words. She had not yet smiled or given him any other kind of encouragement.

"I know it may appear to you as if I've sold out my country because I drive this car and smoke only Cuban cigars. But the nature of the world today is such that we have to survive and make money. Even the staunchest communist would agree with me on this one: a hungry man is a hungry man. Our problems cannot be solved by reading *Das Kapital*. I have sweated to be in this position, and yet I'm still sweating."

There was a frown of contempt on Senami's face and distrust in her eyes. She twitched her nostrils and looked at Kimathi as if he had just farted. Kimathi changed the subject immediately.

"But why are you wasting your time and talent working for a fried chicken outlet? Is it because of the politician?" he teased.

"No," she answered flatly.

"Why, then?" he insisted.

"I guess it's because I live in another world."

"What do you mean?" Kimathi looked at her briefly and drew in some cigar smoke.

"You and I might seem to live under the same sky, but I don't think we share the same horizon," Senami said with honesty.

"I still don't get it," Kimathi said. "Is it because you think I'm a politician and you're a worker?"

"What if I told you that what you see in front of you today is just an illusion?" Senami didn't wait for him to answer. "You know, my mother always used to tell me that there is another reality beyond what we choose to see with our eyes."

"I'm really lost," Kimathi acknowledged. "Can you put that in plain English?"

"Okay." Senami closed her eyes and exhaled. "I am saying that you must ask yourself whether we are living in this world or in an illusion."

It was about a quarter to one in the morning when they reached Protea North. Kimathi parked his car next to the house Senami had pointed out as her home. It was not far from the police station. Before she left the car, she gave him a friendly and light-hearted kiss as if she was acknowledging his courtesy. It took him by surprise.

"Thank you for bringing me home."

"Senami," he hesitated, "if you have nothing important to do . . ." He paused and tried to rephrase, "I mean, if the idea of spending a day with a lonely politician is not frightening to you, I should be glad to come and pick you up here at one in the afternoon tomorrow for lunch."

He looked at Senami's serious eyes. The scar below her left eye looked like a teardrop. Inwardly Kimathi was cursing himself for awkwardly advertising his loneliness to a virtual stranger. He was convinced that she would not accept his offer as she had unequivocally shown her abhorrence of men like him.

"Not a good idea." She shook her head.

"Oh please, beautiful. Just one lunch! I just want to be with a beautiful person like you. I promise I won't bore you with political talk."

"Sometimes beauty can deceive you, allow you to ignore something about someone." Senami smiled briefly. "Our eyes always choose to see what our hearts wish were true."

"I'm a good man, and I'll take care of you. I promise," Kimathi pleaded, forcing a smile onto his face. "I'm also divorced, if that is important for you to know."

"It is always the deeds that have goodness or badness in them, not the politician. But sometimes our eyes are liars because everything that seems real is merely part of the illusion."

Kimathi looked at Senami, wondering how a young woman like her came upon such words.

"You are really profound, you know that. But please, I beg you, just one lunch."

Senami looked at Kimathi and then gave him the answer he was dying to hear. "If you insist."

"Is that a yes?"

The smile on Senami's face burned Kimathi's eyes with its beauty while his heart raced with excitement.

"But definitely not tomorrow," she added.

"When is the right date?"

"Let me see." Senami paused as if mentally calculating something. "Today is already Saturday and we are having a traditional unveiling. Monday will work for me."

"What time is good for you on Monday?"

"Half past twelve," she said with a smile.

Kimathi felt drawn to Senami's beauty and intelligence and was convinced that if he could make a girl like her smile, then he was halfway up her legs. He did not remember ever having been so totally satisfied with a woman's company. He opened the glove compartment and gave her his business card:

> *Mr Kimathi Fezile Tito*
> *Master's in Fine Arts, Underground People's University of Siberia*
> *Chairman, Mandulo Construction*

There were cellphone and landline numbers on the back of the card. Senami looked at it briefly before opening the car door, then, like someone who didn't want to make too much fuss, she quickly waved goodbye to Kimathi.

"It will be great to hear your voice again," Kimathi said, smiling at her.

"Why? Were you auditioning me?" she asked jokingly as she stepped out of the car.

"I definitely was," Kimathi winked and smiled, "and I am a hundred per cent sure that you have made it to the next round of *Idols*."

"You better prepare your eyes for reality the next time we meet."

From the curl of her smile, and the happiness in her voice, Kimathi inferred that indeed she was also looking forward to seeing him again.

"A looter continua, Mr Politician!" she shouted sarcastically, raising her fist.

As she walked up the small paved driveway towards the house, Kimathi watched the movement of her hips and legs. She swayed suggestively as she walked.

"Yeah, *a luta continua*, comrade!" he exclaimed involuntarily, and raised his fist.

Kimathi watched Senami open the door to the house, and disappear inside. He felt like he had been deserted by someone he loved. At the same time he felt blessed and remade at the thought that they were going to see each other again soon. With sweet thoughts of Senami still in his mind, he drove home convinced that his ancestors were smiling down on him.

Chapter 10

Mafukuzela camp, Kwanza Sul province, Angola

Comrade Pilate wiped away the tears. He, Comrade Idi and the others who had made it to the escape trench had positioned themselves where they could look back through the maize field at what was happening in the camp. Most of the structures were now on fire and the flames were spreading quickly to the trees as the two dozen or so SADF paratroopers began to make their way through the camp. Pilate watched as people came out of the buildings coughing, some raising their hands in surrender.

"Skiet hulle almal!" one of the paratroopers shouted. "We're taking no prisoners on this one. They're all terrorists!"

Rat-tat-tat-rat-tat-tat!

The sound of gunfire and screams filled the air as the comrades fell to the ground.

Having swept the camp, the paratroopers began to advance into the maize field, making their way towards the trench. Pilate smelled confrontation and, using sign language, signalled for Idi and the other comrades to spread out along the trench and ready themselves for battle.

The paratroopers stopped, and then moved forward again. Pilate's breathing grew heavy as they advanced carefully through the maize towards the trench. He saw a flicker of impatience in the eyes of his comrades as they waited for the order to shoot, but he knew that they would only have one chance to spring their trap.

"Fire!" Pilate ordered.

Before the most advanced paratroopers could react, Lady Comrade Mkabayi jumped up and fired her AK-47. She hit one of them in the head and he dropped dead. Comrade Makana shot another paratrooper in the back as he turned to run.

Startled by the unexpected attack, the paratroopers began to retreat, firing randomly into the maize field as they went.

Ten minutes later, all five helicopters took off again.

Chapter 11

A dog ran in front of Kimathi's X5 near Police View, Protea South, in Soweto. He was sure he had hit it, but did not stop to check if there was any damage to his car – he was busy talking on the phone with his long-time comrade, Aluta Pooe, who now owned Perro Restaurant in 7th Avenue, Parkhurst. He wanted to impress Senami and had therefore asked Mrs Pooe to reserve a table for two and ordered a six hundred rand bottle of Moët & Chandon. The restaurant had also confirmed that his grilled ostrich and pineapple salad would be ready when he arrived at one that afternoon.

Perro was an obvious choice for Kimathi because of its exclusive nature. It was the only restaurant in Gauteng with a "wall of fame" covered with photos of the famous people who had dined there – the likes of Bill Clinton, Bono and Denzel Washington. A big guestbook at reception had the signatures of all the celebrated individuals who had dined there as well as their comments on the restaurant's great service and internationally renowned food.

Kimathi's intention in dining at Perro was to make Senami see the kind of people he associated with. He wanted her to catch a glimpse of the photo of him with Nelson Mandela and Will Smith, taken at one of the 46664 AIDS charity concerts in March 2005. The picture showed Kimathi standing between the two great men with his hands on their shoulders.

At about ten past twelve, Kimathi was already parked outside Senami's house in Protea North. A thrill of expectation shot through him. He looked at the Rolex on his left wrist as if he didn't trust the clock on the dashboard, he then looked at himself in the rear-view mirror to make sure he was presentable. His clothes spoke of money – he was wearing his favourite orange Valentino jacket, blue Hugo Boss jeans and purple Valentino shoes. Satisfied with his look, he glanced at Senami's house again to see if there was any sign of her, but the door to her house remained firmly closed. With nothing else to do, Kimathi opened the glove compartment and took out a bottle of Acqua Di Giò Homme, his favourite fragrance from Giorgio Armani, which he always kept in his car to make an impression on special occasions. As he rubbed the fragrance around his neck and on the back of his hands, a swarm of bees buzzed past and settled in what looked like a beehive in front of Senami's house. Distracted by the bees, it took Kimathi a few seconds to realise that Senami had opened the door and was beckoning to him.

Kimathi's eyes shone with excitement as he got out of the car. A few metres away, a group of young men were idling about. As he closed the car door, he studied the young men, checking out the way they were dressed. They were all wearing their pants below their cracks.

Kimathi opened the gate, warily scanning the yard for signs of the bees, but he saw nothing. He stood in front of the door for a while as if gathering his thoughts, then he raised his hand to knock. Moments later a neatly dressed middle-aged man opened the door and ushered him inside. A strong smell of boiled cabbage attacked Kimathi's nose, confirming for him the lower economic status of the household. The man's wife was sitting on a black leather sofa when Kimathi entered. She was in her late forties or early fifties and wore a black dress. Her head was covered with a black cloth and the whites of her eyes were bloodshot, giving the impression that she was mourning the death of someone special to her. Kimathi saw a framed picture of Senami on the wall. She was standing with an elderly woman.

After Kimathi had mumbled his greetings, the man in the house introduced himself as Napo Tladi, Senami's father. He introduced the woman sitting on the sofa as his wife Lola, Senami's mother.

"Are you sure it's her you're looking for?" asked Napo after Kimathi had introduced himself.

"Yes, sir. But I can see that I probably came at the wrong time," Kimathi replied, looking at the crying woman.

"When was the last time you saw her?" asked Napo, ignoring what Kimathi had said.

"Well, I met her on Friday night and I brought her home because it was raining." Kimathi offered them a brief smile. "She said I could come today. In fact, we are having a date."

"What?" Lola's face was clouded with disbelief and she blinked a few times as further tears formed in her eyes. Her fingers were trembling, and Napo sat down next to her and put an arm around her as she sank into the sofa and shut her eyes.

"Did I say something wrong?" Kimathi asked apologetically. "Maybe I should come back another time."

"No, you can stay," insisted Napo. "You actually came at the right time."

Napo stared intensely into Kimathi's eyes before standing up and going into another room. Lola was busy wiping her tears and blowing her nose with a handkerchief as Napo returned carrying a family photo album.

"Do you think you can identify her in this album?" Napo asked as he handed it to Kimathi.

A bolt of fear struck Kimathi as he flipped through the album, but he didn't know why he should be afraid, he had done nothing wrong. His eyes settled on a picture of Senami standing between two school buildings – she looked like she was sixteen or seventeen. When he showed the picture to Napo, Lola sobbed deeply as if Kimathi had caused her great anguish.

"Senami is presumed to have died in exile in 1991," said Napo, obviously trying to keep calm. He paused and looked at Kimathi. "She didn't return home when everyone else was coming back to the country."

"No, it can't be true." Kimathi paused and stared at Napo for a long moment. "But . . . but I just saw her standing outside now and waving at me to come in."

Napo narrowed his eyes, and Kimathi's heart thundered as he wondered what was happening to him.

"Very strange," said Napo finally.

"But she called me in here just minutes ago." Kimathi was adamant.

Lola winced as if she was in pain. She shut her eyes and cried out. As if to try and resolve the confusion in his mind, Kimathi's eyes roamed around the room. He thought he was imagining things, having delusions.

"This is not the only strange thing to happen. On Thursday we went to the cemetery to do some traditional rituals, " Napo said, handing Kimathi a copy of the *Sowetan*. "But when we got there, we found the bodies of two policemen between the graves of Senami and her grandmother. Their uniforms were hanging on her tombstone. They were stark naked and had cigarette burns all over their bodies."

Kimathi shot an uneasy glance at the picture on the front of the newspaper and blinked in both disbelief and horror. The gruesome image showed the two dead policemen lying between two tombstones marked *SENAMI DESIREE TLADI – BORN 22 FEBRUARY 1929, DIED 27 JULY 2005* and *SENAMI TLADI – BORN 1 JUNE 1970*. It did not mention when she died.

"Senami was named after her grandmother, who died two years ago," stated Napo, the tension in his voice immediately apparent. "She disappeared at the age of seventeen, a year after the declaration of the state of emergency in 1987. We only found out in 1988 that she had gone into exile. We heard from someone who was her classmate at Pace Commercial High School in Jabulani that she had left with her friend Lwazi Sibisi. He also did not return."

Fear coursed through Kimathi as he looked again at the picture on the front page of the newspaper. He suddenly recognised the men. How could he forget them? They were the ones who had arrested him and Lakeisha in Oxford Road. He had given them fifteen hundred rand and some cigars to buy his freedom.

"We tried the Truth and Reconciliation Commission, but they told us that they were sorry but they could not locate her."

Napo paused and looked at Lola as if hoping she would say something. She was sitting quietly, looking at the wall and yet seeing nothing in particular.

"We then went to the ANC head office in Shell House in Johannesburg to talk to someone who was then dealing with such things." Napo continued. "His name was Ludwe Khakhaza – he is now the director-general of Public Works." He paused and shook his head as if it would delete the incident from his memory.

"And what did Ludwe say?" asked Kimathi.

"That man was very rude," said Napo, sounding angry. "He told us that in every struggle there are bound to be casualties."

"Is that so?"

"Yes. Hold on," Napo said thoughtfully, standing up and walking to one of the bedrooms.

There was silence for a while. Kimathi looked at Lola, who was still staring silently at the blank, whitewashed wall.

Napo came back carrying a letter, which he handed to Kimathi. Kimathi's heart began to pound as he recognised Ludwe's signature. The letter's tone was dismissive:

> Every member that went into exile joined the struggle voluntarily. The Movement cannot be held responsible or accountable for every single individual who disappeared or chose not to make their way back home when the situation normalised in the country. The bones of our comrades lie in the mountains, hills and plains of southern Africa. The Movement deeply regrets that there are those comrades whose fate we may not know, but their death is not in vain.

Kimathi looked confused and nervous at the same time. He felt a terrible dryness in his mouth and all the way down his throat.

"We waited for years for her return from exile. Eventually, just over a year ago, a traditional healer advised us to have a symbolic burial and a funeral for her in Avalon Cemetery. He said that if we did this her spirit would rest in peace and not haunt us." Napo paused and glanced at Lola. "That was after my wife complained that she was seeing her ghost every day."

A sudden wave of panic rose in Kimathi. He began to sweat through the pores of his nose and his palms.

"This past Friday, which is the day you say you brought her here, was actually the day the sangoma completed the rituals," Napo continued. "It was exactly a year after Senami's symbolic burial. We had to cleanse ourselves so that nothing disturbed the process for a period of a year. We were not allowed to eat pork, fish, nuts or dairy, or sleep together as husband and wife." Napo paused and looked at Kimathi, who nodded nervously. "This Friday we slaughtered a white goat and two white chickens to end the process. The sangoma bathed us in cold water mixed with herbs and gave us beads to put around our ankles. We buried the goat bones in Senami's symbolic grave at around one in the morning on Saturday. He then told us to wait."

"So, all this happened this Saturday," said Kimathi absent-mindedly.

"Yes," affirmed Napo. "You see, my wife and I are Christians, but we agreed that we would do anything we could to bring our daughter back. When she started having frequent disturbing dreams and going into trances, that's when we decided to consult a sangoma." He paused and looked at Lola, who was still staring at the wall.

"I'm sorry to hear that," Kimathi said.

"I can only hope for the best," said Napo, shifting his eyes around the room. "I have exhausted all the places in search of her. I don't remember how many times my wife and I have visited the NPA offices in Silverton in the hope that the Missing Persons Task Team might have discovered something new. We have gone through all the photographs of political activists compiled by the apartheid police, but she is not there. We even began to hope that she could have been one of the activists that were kidnapped, tortured and murdered by the apartheid police between 1960 and 1990 . . ."

"When did you say she left for exile, by the way?" asked Kimathi as if he was trying to link something in his head.

"Well, I knew when she joined COSAS in April of 1986 that she was going to put herself into trouble," Napo replied indirectly. "She was doing Standard Seven at Pace Commercial High School then, and mixing with the wrong crowd, people that called themselves 'comrades'. She was obsessed with the struggle. They would meet here every time and all they talked about was freedom, socialism, Marx and the Boers. We wanted her to be a doctor, and she was good at mathematics." He paused and looked at Lola, who was wiping the tears off her cheeks. "Sometimes my wife and I still hear them talking at night."

The way Napo spoke of Senami, it seemed as if he was doing a kind of psychological autopsy on her.

"I can only imagine. It must be hard for you," said Kimathi as he stared at Napo for an instant before swinging his eyes towards Lola.

"Yes. We last saw her on the morning of 12 June 1987, when she went to school. She left after sixteen of her schoolmates, who were activists, were detained during a march. She used to be a very nervous kid. She was quiet at first until she took up politics. I guess she was afraid she was going to be jailed too."

Lola burst into loud sobs. Seized with terror, Kimathi staggered towards the door. He could not believe that he had shared such a brilliant moment with a charming dead person. Within seconds, he found he could hardly see. His head began to ache and his feet were swelling. Napo and Lola watched as he hobbled back and collapsed in confusion on the sofa.

Napo went to the kitchen and returned with a glass of cold water for Kimathi. But Kimathi was so overcome with terror that the glass slipped from his hands and shattered on the tiled floor. He cast fearful glances at Senami's picture on the wall while silently pointing at it. He saw her image in all four corners of the room. She was smiling at him.

"No," Kimathi cried, while wiping his damp forehead with the back of his wrist. "Leave me alone!"

The perimeters of Kimathi's visual field gradually turned grey, then black, blotting out the light.

Convinced that he had passed out, Napo and Lola helped Kimathi into Senami's room, where they put him on the bed. The room was stuffy and dark. The windows had not been opened since Senami's symbolic burial as the sangoma had performed some rituals in the room to try and stop Senami's ghost from haunting the family. Lola had often heard her voice – she would talk and laugh the whole night, especially when it was raining or there was a thunderstorm. Napo and Lola were sure it was Senami's voice. Sometimes they would find the room in a complete mess, with clothes scattered on the floor.

In order to chase the ghost away, the healer had painted the room red and smeared the inside of the windows with ash. There were five white candle stubs, each stuck into the mouth of a one-litre Coke bottle filled with water from the ocean. There was a bottle in each of the four corners, and the fifth stood on the dusty windowsill. A white sheet that had also gathered some dust had been used to cover the dressing table mirror next to the window.

Standing to one side of each Coke bottle was a carved wooden spirit figure. The first was in a squatting position. It had a heavily bent back and huge feet and hands. The next one had a large stylised head and cowrie shells for eyes. The third one had a concave heart-shaped face, and its notched arms held up its legless body. The fourth carving was a doll-like female figurine with slender dangling arms. It had a small rope fixed around its neck. A fifth figure had been placed in the middle of the room. It was a standing figurine with stump arms and bowed legs. It was blackened, except for a white face.

On the white wall next to the door was an old picture of Patrice Lumumba that had obviously been cut from a newspaper. Below the picture were the words:

> History will one day have its say, but it will not be the history taught in the United Nations, Washington, Paris or Brussels, however, but the history taught in countries that have rid themselves of colonialism and its puppets. It will be a history full of glory and dignity.

On the wall by the window, there was a picture of Nelson Mandela's head. The words below it read *FREE MANDELA*. Next to it was a picture of Robert Sobukwe with *IZWE LETHU, MAYIBUYE I-AFRIKA* written beneath it. Below that was a picture of Bantu Steven Biko with the words *VIVA BLACK CONSCIOUSNESS, VIVA* scrawled across it.

Lola took Kimathi's shoes and socks off while Napo unbuttoned his shirt. Napo then sprinkled some water on Kimathi's face, hoping he would regain consciousness, but it had no effect. Seeing this, Napo went away to call Makhanda, the sangoma.

Chapter 12

Kimathi was still out cold when Makhanda arrived about one and a half hours later. Makhanda was dressed in khaki trousers and a blue short-sleeved shirt that was dotted with what looked like gravy. His open brown sandals revealed blackened and dusty feet. He had a large head, with a beard that concealed a long face.

Makhanda had brought crushed umzilanyoni berries, which he asked Lola to boil in milk. When the milk was boiling he added bark from the umgudo tree into it, which immediately turned it a dark colour. They waited in the dining room for about thirty minutes for the concoction to cool down.

"I wonder what this is?" said Napo, pointing at the bedroom where Kimathi was still out cold. "A man comes to my house, starts talking about my disappeared daughter, and then he faints. What kind of coincidence could this be?"

Before Makhanda could answer, Lola came in with a plastic cup to be used for the ritual. After Makhanda motioned her to go into the bedroom, she gave the door a push and walked in. Makhanda and Napo followed her. Inside, Kimathi was lying on the bed with his mouth open. Sweat was pouring from his forehead in cold rivulets.

"I guess this is the moment I have been telling you about," Makhanda said as he tilted the cup and poured the medicine into Kimathi's mouth. "Remember what I told you when we were doing her symbolic burial? Your daughter may be dead, but her spirit wants to come home."

Napo nearly cried aloud at Makhanda's words, but restrained himself, as Sotho culture does not permit men to openly display grief in front of their wives.

"We miss her so much," Napo said eventually. "But I don't understand why she chose a complete stranger to return in her place."

"I think I know why," replied Makhanda as he shifted his attention back to Kimathi. "This is the man who is going to give us a clue as to your daughter's whereabouts. She has sent him to us," he continued as he wiped Kimathi's mouth with the back of his hand. "He is her messenger, and we must listen to him carefully."

"The only thing that made life bearable for me and my wife was the hope that one day Senami would find her way back home alive. It has been difficult for us to accept that we will never see her again. And now this . . ."

"Kuzolunga. It will be fine," said Makhanda, trying to soothe Napo. "You need to grieve in order to heal. If you don't, the sadness will just reside inside your heart and worsen your mind every day." He paused and looked at Napo for confirmation, and when he saw him nodding, he continued, "This is why it is so important that we do all the rituals properly, so that you are able to grieve. After this I want you to feel calm, confident, optimistic and relaxed."

Napo gave a faint smile and nodded again. At the same time, the unconscious Kimathi was licking his lips. Makhanda stepped closer to the bed and put his fingers on Kimathi's neck as if he was checking his pulse. Kimathi made a clicking sound deep in his throat. As if satisfied with the power of his medicine, Makhanda looked at Napo and smiled. Then he took a deep breath and patted Kimathi on the chest.

"Until when should we let him sleep in my daughter's bed?" asked Lola.

"Relax, mama. Let babuMakhanda do his work. Hopefully time will heal our family," Napo said, with a shrug of his shoulders.

Makhanda nodded in agreement. A single ray of sunlight filtered through the dusty window as he drew the curtains slightly. He smiled, exposing the black smudges around the edges of his neglected lower teeth. Then he lit each of the five candles in the room and muttered something in what sounded like a foreign language while clapping his hands at each wooden sculpture. He greeted each one with a slight bow, saying "Thokoza, Gogo".

While the candles were burning, Makhanda instructed Lola to boil some more milk to be mixed with iqwaningi roots. When this mixture was ready and cooled, half a cup was forced into Kimathi's mouth. Makhanda took out a new razor blade and made small cuts on Kimathi's ankles and wrists. As the blood oozed out of the wounds, he mixed black medicine that looked like snuff with some Vaseline. He then rubbed this muti into the cuts while intoning healing incantations in isiZulu. The bleeding stopped after a few seconds and the three of them stood beside the bed watching Kimathi, as if waiting for a poison to take effect.

The concoction seemed to transport Kimathi to another world. He yawned twice and mumbled something inaudible as if unable to move his tongue. Then there was silence and froth began to collect at the corners of his mouth. With an air of great satisfaction, Makhanda instructed Napo and Lola to wash their feet with the cold water that had been placed behind the door after Senami's symbolic burial a year earlier. The water was reddish, as it had been mixed with pulverised umnqandane wezimpisi roots, and smelled foul. After they had finished washing, Makhanda ordered Napo and Lola out of the room, before he too left Kimathi alone, closing the door behind him.

Chapter 13

Mafukuzela camp, Kwanza Sul province,
Angola

The smell of burning flesh filled Comrade Pilate's nostrils as they re-entered the camp. He looked at Comrade Idi, then at Lady Comrade Mkabayi, then at Comrade Makana as the moans of the dying echoed in his ears. His eyes were full of anger.

"Why are these Boers so cruel? Why?" Pilate asked nobody in particular as a tear rolled down his left cheek. He wiped it away with the back of his hand.

Slowly, the surviving comrades emerged from their hiding places and gathered in the centre of the camp. The whole raid had lasted for only about half an hour, but it quickly became clear that over fifty comrades were missing or dead.

"Somebody please explain to me how the Boers knew our camp was here?" Pilate said to Idi as he removed a bottle of water from the pack of a dead paratrooper.

Tension filled the space between them as a sudden fear brightened Pilate's eyes. He kicked the dead man's head as if trying to revive him.

"How?" he asked as he kicked the paratrooper again and again. "How did you know? How? Answer me, settler!"

With his eyes also filled with tears, Idi held Pilate back. They stood there for a few minutes, with their arms around each other, crying. Finally, Pilate pulled away, opened the bottle of water and drank.

"That's a very good question," Idi said as he watched Pilate use some of the water to wash the tears from his face. "The raid is very suspicious indeed. But we have to ask the relevant people, not the dead Boer."

"You're right, comrade. Do you think there are spies amongst us?" Pilate asked as he dried his face with his uniform, unable to believe the thought that had leaped into his mind. "If someone is betraying The Movement, we must find out who they are before it's too late."

"I indeed smell a rat here," said Idi. "They caught us off guard, and it was not a coincidence."

At that moment Lady Comrade Mkabayi and Comrade Bambata appeared, carrying the body of a dead woman. The fallen comrade's camouflage uniform was bloodied and torn, and she had a big wound on her left thigh.

"Let's first report to the leadership and suggest that we move the camp to another location," said Pilate in a defeated tone, as he watched the two comrades lay the body down next to their other dead. "After that we will deal with whoever betrayed us."

Chapter 14

Kimathi slowly regained consciousness. It was about nine in the evening and he was sweating profusely. Having been unconscious for eight hours, he was disoriented, but he quickly worked out that he must still be in Napo and Lola's house. He yawned and looked around. There was no one in the room, but the wardrobe was open and all the clothes had been thrown onto the floor. He thought they must be Senami's clothes, but he was not sure. His head was pounding, and the stuffiness of the room and the uncomfortable bed weren't helping.

Kimathi sat up on the bed and began to put on his socks and shoes. He looked around the room again in confusion. The carved figurines scared him. At the same time, he tried to figure out what might have happened. He searched his pockets – all three cellphones were still there. There were about seventy missed calls in total. Kimathi stood up and grabbed his jacket, searching for his car keys. Walking to the door, he checked his wrists and was pleased to see both the Breitling and the Rolex. His face softened, but he cringed when he saw a gecko staring at him from the doorframe.

"Leave me alone!" he shouted at the gecko as he stormed out of the room.

Walking across the dining room and into the kitchen, Kimathi realised that there was no one in the house. Both Napo and Lola had obviously gone out somewhere, though strangely the doors were unlocked. Kimathi left the house cautiously, as if his legs could not keep pace with his soul. His car was still parked on the side of the street.

The realisation of what had happened to him struck Kimathi as he drove home on the N12 freeway.

"Why me? Why?" he asked himself loudly as he slammed his fist on the dashboard.

He was chewing the end of an unlit cigar, but then remembered he hadn't taken his medication. He took two tablets before listening to some of the messages on one of his cellphones. Most of them were from George and Sechaba, reminding him of the meeting they were supposed to have had that afternoon at the Hyatt. Obviously he had missed it. Kimathi threw the cellphone onto the passenger seat without reviewing the rest of the messages.

When he reached his mansion in Johannes Meyer Drive in Bassonia, Kimathi opened the gate with the remote control. Deciding to leave the car in the long driveway rather than in the garage, in case he went out later to buy food from the Spur in The Glen Mall, he collected three bundles of daily newspapers from the overgrown lawn, shaking off the drops of water on each bundle. When he looked at his car again he realised that it had a nasty dent in the right fender. He inspected it and mumbled in displeasure, but he failed to remember where he might have picked up the dent.

As Kimathi approached his front door, he saw a brown envelope on the doorstep. He picked it up, unlocked the door and went inside, turning on the lights and tossing the newspapers on a table to his left. With the envelope in his hand, he wiped his feet on the large Persian carpet in the middle of the room and walked to the bathroom.

In the bathroom, Kimathi turned on the water for a bath, sat down on the edge of the bathtub and opened the envelope. It was a summons to appear at the Maintenance Office of the Johannesburg Magistrate's Court that Friday. *So quick*, he thought. *Though Anele had a friend at the Magistrate's Court and she could have manipulated the whole thing.* "Fuck, Anele! Gold-digger!" he cursed as he closed the tap, his voice reverberating through the empty house.

Leaving the bathroom, Kimathi made his way over to his private bar. Opening a bottle of seventy-year-old Mortlach whisky, he poured a double tot into a handcut crystal glass and swallowed it in one gulp. He had planned to only open the expensive bottle in a few weeks' time, when the multi-million-rand tender was awarded to Mandulo, but he couldn't wait any longer.

Kimathi's stomach started to rumble after he had swallowed his second whisky. He picked up his cellphone and looked for the number for Debonairs Pizza. *Two large pizzas will be fine*, he thought. He gave the delivery guy the address while pouring another double tot. Then he dropped the phone and took his whisky glass to the bathroom. As he stripped and plunged into the water, his mind was carefully sorting and rearranging the events of the last few days in his head. His thoughts kept shifting between Anele, the letter and Senami.

After forty minutes in the bath, Kimathi still had no convincing conclusions. The whisky had also done nothing to exorcise the unsettling spectre of Senami. He pinched his left arm to make sure he was awake. As the pain travelled through him, he tried to remember all the comrades he had met in exile, but his memory was cloudy and indistinct and he was unable to picture anyone who look like Senami. He grimaced as if in agony. "Go away, Senami!" he shouted as if he was talking to her in person and took another gulp of whisky.

Kimathi's thoughts were interrupted by the sound of a motorcycle pulling up in his driveway. As he peeped through the blinds, he remembered the pizzas he had ordered. When the doorbell rang, Kimathi went to open the door with only a towel around his waist and without drying himself properly. After paying the delivery guy, he switched off his phones. He was not in the mood to talk to anyone. He went to the bedroom and started to eat his pizzas with great appetite. Once he had finished eating, he passed out on the bed.

Chapter 15

Mafukuzela camp, Kwanza Sul province,
Angola

Comrade Pilate left Comrade Idi and the others to attend to the injured and count the dead. As he entered what used to be his office, he was greeted by a scene of utter destruction. He kicked with his boot at some of the smouldering papers that littered the floor – all that was left of the camp's records. *What am I going to tell The Movement? They will probably think that Idi and I are not fit to run this place*, Pilate thought while tilting his nose in the air. It was as if he was sniffing the scent of the recent violence. *I need to find the spy that set us up, and must do so immediately*, he concluded as he turned to leave the office.

Outside, the comrades were singing a struggle song. All those who had survived the raid had regrouped around their fallen comrades. There was anger in their eyes as they sang:

Ayasab' amagwala	(The cowards are scared)
Dubula dubula	(Shoot shoot)
Ayeah	
Dubula dubula	(Shoot shoot)
Ayasab' amagwala	(The cowards are scared)
Dubula dubula	(Shoot shoot)
Awu, yoh	
Dubula dubula	(Shoot shoot)
Aw, dubul' ibhunu	(Shoot the Boer)
Dubula dubula	(Shoot shoot)
Aw, dubul' ibhunu	(Shoot the Boer)
Awe, Mama, ndiyekele	(Mother leave me be)
Awe, Mama, iyeah	(Oh, Mother)
Awe, Mama, ndiyekele	(Mother leave me be)
Awe, Mama, iyo	(Oh, Mother)

Mounting two empty oil drums, Pilate and Idi tried to address the angry comrades. Idi waved his hands to get the attention of the singing crowd without success. Pilate shot his AK into the air. The singing stopped.

"Bopha, comrades!" started Idi. "Silence! We have experienced the greatest tragedy today. The Movement –"

"We have to fight those Boers!" someone shouted, interrupting him. "We want to take back our country the Castro way!"

"Bopha, comrade! Be rational! The Boers are far too advanced militarily for us to just –"

"We don't care!" another person from the crowd cut in. It was Comrade Makana, who was standing next to Lady Comrade Mkabayi and Comrade Bambata. "All we want is to fight them. There must be a war. We have to fight for our land. The Boers must be driven back into the sea. They are not human beings."

"But comrades, there is nothing we –"

"Yes, don't tell us about the modern weapons, comrade," Lady Comrade Mkabayi said angrily. "King Dingane kaSenzangakhona defeated hundreds of invading Boer Voortrekkers under Andries Pretorius at the Battle of Blood River eNcome. And his warriors only had spears and shields."

"Yes," Comrade Bambata added, "King Cetshwayo kaMpande's army conquered the invading British under Lord Chelmsford at the Battle of Isandlwana, also with spears and shields. The British had modern rifles but were crushed like ants."

"It's about the will, comrades," Lady Comrade Mkabayi shouted. "We have AKs and we know how to use them. Let's not be cowards, comrades. Let's fight these Boers. Amandla, comrades!" Lady Comrade Mkabayi raised her right fist.

"Awethu," the crowd responded.

The crowd started clapping as Pilate tried to speak. Then Comrade Makana began another song:

> Mshin' wam, mshin' wami   (My machine gun)
> Awuleth' umshin' wam   (Give me my machine gun)
> Wena uyangibambezela   (You're holding us back)

Pilate fired his AK-47 into the air again to get the crowd's attention.

"Comrades! We are all angry, I understand, but we must act rationally."

Lady Comrade Mkabayi raised her hand and spoke at the same time. "Did the Boers act rationally when they killed our comrades?" she asked, pointing at the bodies laid out in the centre of the camp. "You can do as you will, but I want to fight the Boers!"

"Okay, comrades. Let's first hear from The Movement and if –"

But nobody was listening anymore and Pilate's voice was drowned out by yet another song:

Ziyabulala, lezinja	(These dogs are killing)
Dubula dubula	(Shoot shoot)
Ay iyeah	
Dubula dubula	(Shoot shoot)
Ziyarhepa, lezinja	(These dogs are raping)
Dubula dubula	(Shoot shoot)
Ay iiiyo	
Dubula dubula	(Shoot shoot)
Aw, dubul' ibhunu	(Shoot the Boer)
Dubula dubula	(Shoot shoot)

Chapter 16

Kimathi woke up at four in the morning, troubled by dark, bloody dreams. He changed position and hugged the pillow, but sleep did not return. He pulled up the duvet and covered his chin, but still he could not sleep. The house felt empty and silent; the only noise was the blinds knocking against the slightly opened window. Getting up he staggered towards the wall to switch on the lights. The floor next to the bed was littered with slices of half-eaten pizza. He stepped over an empty pizza box as he went to the bathroom to take a piss.

Coming out of the bathroom, Kimathi made a detour to the bar and poured himself a double tot of Mortlach, which he carried back to bed. He sat on his bed listening to the messages on his cellphones while drinking. Sleep returned only at about half past six.

At about nine, Kimathi was woken by the sound of a car stopping outside. When he peeped through the window, he saw Sechaba's silver Range Rover Sport parked behind his X5. George's white Toyota Tazz was outside in the street. He quickly put on sandals and tracksuit pants. By the time he opened the door, Sechaba and George were already standing there.

Sechaba was carrying the daily newspapers that had been left on Kimathi's lawn by the delivery van that morning. Kimathi ushered the two men to his bar, where they normally sat whenever they had a meeting at his house. Sechaba put the newspapers down and watched as Kimathi walked towards the Mortlach bottle. It was less than half full.

"We have been looking for you, comrade. We left many messages on all your cellphones. Where have you been?" asked Sechaba as Kimathi poured himself a tot and fumbled for some ice.

"I'm very sorry about that. I have been away in the Eastern Cape at a relative's funeral and I only came back at dawn," Kimathi lied.

"You should have at least informed us, or answered our calls, you know," said

George. "That's what business partners do. What you did was irresponsible and unacceptable."

There was a brief silence as Kimathi cupped his hand over his glass of whisky and ice. He stared at both Sechaba and George.

"You know how rural areas are with the network, comrade," said Kimathi, taking a sip of whisky and putting the glass down on the bar. "You have to climb a tree to get a signal."

Some of the whisky trailed down Kimathi's chin and he dabbed at it with his hand. His eyes felt bloodshot, and he wondered if George and Sechaba could see that he had not slept well.

"Okay, let's talk serious business, then," said George. "I'm sure you heard the terrible news . . ."

"Like I said, I just came back three hours ago and I'm clueless about everything else," responded Kimathi as he swabbed his nose with his hand. "Please, fill me in."

George and Sechaba looked at each other as if deciding who would break the news.

"Ludwe is no longer with us," started George, alternating his gaze between Kimathi and Sechaba. "He was found dead this morning at the Hyatt."

There was an abrupt silence. Kimathi put his glass down without taking a sip. He looked at Sechaba and George intently for a long time without saying a word. Then, interlocking his fingers, he leaned forward and rested his elbows on the counter. He turned his eyes away from Sechaba, opened his mouth and slowly ran his tongue over his lips.

"What? Dead? No way! Are you sure?"

"Yes. It happened, comrade," confirmed Sechaba. "Remember we were supposed to meet with him yesterday afternoon to finalise everything?" He paused and waited for Kimathi to nod. "When you didn't show up, and did not answer any of your phones, we all agreed to postpone the meeting until further notice. At around eleven that night, I received a call from the hotel saying that he had been found dead by the room service staff. Apparently he did not leave the hotel when the rest of us did."

"What happened?" Kimathi finally asked.

"That's the question we are also asking ourselves," said George. "The newspaper reports are pretty much all we have to go on."

"Check the newspapers," said Sechaba, pointing at the bundle he had picked up from the lawn. "The story is there."

In a daze Kimathi ripped the plastic covers off of the newspapers in front of him. He scanned the *Sowetan* until he landed on the mugshot of his friend on page three. He read the article silently.

> Ludwe Khakhaza, Director-General of the Department of Public Works, was found dead in his hotel room at the Park Hyatt in Rosebank last night. "He stayed with us last night, and I can confirm that he was found dead at about three o'clock this morning," the general manager said.

The general manager of the hotel, Mrs Lisa Steyn, could not give details of when Ludwe had checked in or whether he had any injuries to his body when he was found. She also could not shed light on the cause of death. All she could say was that the police were dealing with the matter. The article added that an inquest would take place. *The Star* claimed that Ludwe had been murdered by powerful entities uncomfortable with his method of awarding government tenders. It alleged that he was about to award a tender to a company chaired by one of his friends. The article also declared that a rival company would benefit massively from his death. *The Citizen* reported that Ludwe had been with a girlfriend when he died, and hinted that his death was a politically motivated murder.

Kimathi stopped reading and tried to speak. It was evident from the look on his face that he was at the bottom of a pit of despair. He tried to place his left elbow on the counter, but missed and nearly fell over.

"Impossible!" he said bitterly as he regained his balance. "I mean, about twelve of the missed calls that I have are from Ludwe. He sounded fine."

"Unfortunately, it is the truth," affirmed Sechaba, searching Kimathi's face. "His wife Unathi also called to confirm before his body was taken to the government mortuary in Randburg. In fact, we called you together, but you didn't answer."

There was another moment of silence as Kimathi's mind replayed the indistinct voice of a crying woman in three of the messages he had received. He had deleted the messages, as he could not attach the voice to anyone he knew. The woman did not leave her name, and Kimathi hadn't felt like caling her back.

Sechaba stood up, found himself a glass and poured himself a tot of whisky. Kimathi stared at the bottle, feeling as if something was being drained from inside him. He had not thought it possible that so many different kinds of misfortune could befall him in such a short space of time.

"What a blow to our bid," Sechaba finally concluded, sounding completely deflated. "We were so close, but now we have to work hard again to please his deputy, Ms Vokwana. She is a witch of a woman."

Kimathi did not react as Sechaba expected. Instead, a wave of grief and guilt rose inside him, and he wept silently. He felt very light, but the pain had gone deep.

"But how did this happen? I mean . . ." Kimathi said to no one in particular.

"That's still a mystery. According to some of the newspapers, he had booked a hotel room with some unknown girl," said George cautiously. "The next thing, he was found dead, as the article says."

"Indeed, he who dies with most secrets wins," said Sechaba. "We will never know the truth until that girl surfaces."

At the mention of a girl, Kimathi put his hands over his eyes as if he was afraid of something. He felt tormented.

"Do you have any leads on this mysterious girl?" he asked.

"No. She has disappeared. Just for his wife's sake, I asked the hotel manager to deny that Ludwe was with a girl," said Sechaba, shaking his head. "You know she likes us, and that is why I'm one of the first people she contacted. I called them this morning to see if they had traced the girl, but they haven't. The security cameras failed to capture her face. It seems she covered it with a cap."

"But we should at least try to identify her," reasoned Kimathi, looking displeased.

"You see, com," Sechaba took a sip from his glass and then put it down, "Comrade Ludwe was a great customer of the Hyatt and, as usual, he had instructed them to let the girl into his room without any questions. That's why they didn't bother to find out anything about her. The man was big in South Africa and he was married."

Kimathi's mind raced as he stared up at the vibrant blue-and-lilac painting on the wall behind the bar. It was Pablo Picasso's *Nude, Green Leaves and Bust*. He had bought it in China a few years earlier while on a business trip. He'd had the painting framed in mahogany and hung next to the window. His ego swelled every time visitors to his private bar commented on it. Which they all did. No one seemed to care that it was a fake. In fact, the only person who hadn't ever commented on it was George. He'd never said a word about the Picasso.

Kimathi knew nothing about art. He had bought the painting after overhearing the president talking to someone about Picasso. However, he liked referring to the painting as Mary, his mistress, whenever he talked to his friends about it. Every time, Kimathi would pretend to caress the breasts of the nude woman in the painting, but today Mary scared him. The Picasso reminded him of Lakeisha, the prostitute from Oxford Road. The image, too, of the mysterious Senami kept intruding into the secret gallery of his mind.

"I think the girl might have been bought by an enemy agent to poison him," Kimathi finally concluded with a note of real unhappiness in his voice. "They also want to win the tender, and they knew that we were Ludwe's preferred bidders."

"According to his wife, he had left the previous evening, telling her that he was off to some business meeting," Sechaba said.

"I'm very scared by this whole thing," said Kimathi as he sniffed and wiped his nose with the back of his hand.

"And yes, just so you know, Comrade Ganyani has betrayed us and joined the other bidding team," said Sechaba, trying to keep the irritation out of his voice. "I'm by no means implying that he is responsible for Comrade Ludwe's death, though."

"He did what?" asked Kimathi, with a surprised look. "Why did he leave us? Did he tell you?"

"I thought he had called you already," said George. "He called me yesterday."

"That son of a bitch!" Kimathi cursed. "He owes me a revolutionary favour and now he thanks me with a plate of shit." He paused and looked at both Sechaba and George. "Honestly, Comrade Ludwe and I took care of that arsehole while we were in exile."

"We have to devise a new strategy for the presentation in two weeks' time," George concluded as he walked towards the door. "And you'd better make sure that your phones are on."

"Let's talk tonight, comrade," said Sechaba as he also stood up to leave. "By the way, a memorial is being planned by Ludwe's department. I'll give you the details when we talk later, but I suggest you call his wife, your cousin."

"Thanks, comrade," Kimathi replied. "I know you guys might not share my level of confidence, but I assure you that we are going to win this tender."

As soon as Sechaba and George had gone, Kimathi went and sat at the bar by himself. He was stunned by what he had heard. As always, the house felt big and empty as soon as his guests had left. With a glass in his hand, he staggered to his bedroom. Opening the chest of drawers, Kimathi took out a grey pinstripe bra with pink trim and a matching G-string. After putting the two items on the bed, he picked up the bottle of Lancôme Trésor Midnight Rose and sprayed the fragrance on them. He had bought the lingerie for Anele on Valentine's Day 2001. On that special day, he had taken her to the Magaliesberg for a magical retreat at the Mount Grace Country House and Spa. After a rejuvenation session, where Anele was pampered with skin and body treatments, Kimathi had presented her with the lingerie. *She'd looked so sexy in it*, he thought as tears began to form in his eyes.

Chapter 17

Mafukuzela camp, Kwanza Sul province, Angola

Nantsi indod' emnyama, Verwoerd!	(Verwoerd! Here comes the black man!)
Nantsi indod' emnyama, Vorster!	(Vorster! Here comes the black man!)
Nantsi indod' emnyama, Botha!	(Botha! Here comes the black man!)
Basopa nantsi indod' emnyama, Verwoerd!	(Verwoerd! Be warned! Here comes the black man!)

Two days after the raid, Mafukuzela Camp was still littered with spent cartridges and other debris. However, this didn't stop the comrades from singing as they gathered in front of the burnt-out administration building. Comrade Pilate and Comrade Idi stood on the makeshift stage made out of two oil drums.

"Comrades!" started Pilate. "It is very important that we maintain our discipline, commitment, dedication, sacrifice and selflessness to our movement..."

There was a murmur of disappointment from the crowd. Several shots were fired into the air by five comrades wearing olive-green Cuban army fatigues.

"We cannot sit here doing nothing while we die from tsetse flies, UNITA ambushes, Boer raids and malaria," said Comrade Bambata as soon as the firing stopped.

"Comrades! The leadership understands your feelings," Pilate countered. "Give us some time to think about it and we will respond accordingly."

"There is no time," Lady Comrade Mkabayi chimed in. "We want to be deployed to South Africa, to fight over there."

Idi's patience seemed to be wearing thin. He shaded his eyes with his hand and scanned the crowd until he found Lady Comrade Mkabayi.

"Comrades, this is an order!" he said, frowning. "Anyone who is a true revolutionary and cares about The Movement will surrender their weapons. If you don't, we'll assume that you're an enemy, and that you're the one that is working with the Boers."

About fifteen comrades marched to the podium with their AKs raised in the air. Reluctantly, they dropped their weapons next to Idi and Pilate. Among those comrades were Comrade Bambata and Lady Comrade Mkabayi.

Siyobashiya abazali ekhaya	(We will leave our parents at home)
Siphuma sangena kwamanye amazwe	(We come in and out of other countries)
Apho kungazikhona umama nobaba	(Where mother and father don't know)
Silandela inkululeko	(We are following the freedom)

Chapter 18

At eight o'clock in the morning, Kimathi entered the waiting room of the Maintenance Office at the Johannesburg Magistrate's Court. He was wearing fine-framed designer glasses, which gave him the appearance of an educated man. In his left hand was an A4 envelope with a copy of his identity document, statement of income and expenditure and supporting documents for his expenses. He had been advised to bring these along so that the court could assess the affordability of Anele's maintenance claim. She was demanding nine thousand rand per month for their daughter.

As he opened the door, Kimathi tried hard to avoid the eyes of the people crowded into the waiting room. They all seemed to be looking at him. There were already about twenty people sitting on the wooden benches waiting for the court clerk to call their names. Most of them were women, and some had brought their children. He could hear them laughing and swapping stories as he walked to the end of the room.

Anele entered soon after him, and Kimathi watched as she scanned the place through the blue lenses of her wide, oval Pucci sunglasses. Two women at the end of the bench began whispering to each other as soon as they caught sight of her; although he didn't know exactly what they were talking about, it seemed that they were admiring the way she was dressed. And though he could not tell Anele, Kimathi also appreciated her appearance. The black scarf, bead necklace, cream dress and cream wedge-heeled shoes that she had picked out suited her perfectly. Kimathi also loved her new Mohawk-braid hairstyle, with cornrows towards the front and middle of her head.

Kimathi pretended not to be looking when Anele stopped in the middle of the room, her eyes searching for a place to sit. She ignored him too, her gaze settling on a young woman in cheap black net stockings holding an unhealthy-looking baby – its mouth was dripping saliva and mucus was running from its nose. The woman was supporting her baby with one arm and holding some papers in her other hand. Seeing Anele observing her, the woman nodded at her to express her solidarity. Kimathi watched as the woman shifted to create room on the bench between her and the woman sitting next to her. With a wave of her hand, she invited Anele to come and sit down in the space.

Kimathi kept staring at them. With two nods, Anele thanked the two women silently as she sat down between them.

As soon as she sat down, Anele opened her handbag, took out a tissue and removed the baby's mucus. Although Kimathi somehow felt pity for the woman with the baby, he had already concluded that the baby's untidiness was a trick to substantiate the woman's claim for maintenance.

After watching Anele wipe away the mucus, Kimathi returned his attention to his own maintenance claim. He tried hard to avoid thinking about the past. However, the memories kept coming back. He reflected on the awful day that Anele had found him with their domestic worker, the day that had brought an abrupt end to their six-year relationship.

Kimathi took out his phone and started scrolling, just to kill time. He stole a furtive glance at Anele, and when their eyes met, he felt a mixture of anger, anxiety, betrayal and distrust. As he looked at her, he felt an irresistible and inexplicable urge to confront her in front of the other women. He wanted her to explain why she had resorted to the courts to solve their domestic problem. He wanted to remind her that he was a person of high social standing, never mind all his other problems at the moment. For about ten seconds, Kimathi considered how to say all this to Anele, but in the end he decided to say nothing. Instead, his attention shifted to two women sitting at the end of the bench who were nudging each other playfully and laughing at whispered jokes.

At nine twenty-five, both Kimathi and Anele were called before the clerk, who introduced herself as Ms Manganyi. She wanted to talk about Zanu's informal needs, so she said. They sat on the two chairs in front of her. Kimathi removed his glasses and held them in his hands, while Anele put hers on the clerk's table.

"I have called you two here to verify the amount of the claim," the clerk said, looking at the forms that had been signed by Anele. "I want to make sure that the monies that we are talking about here are agreed upon before we even go to the court."

Both Kimathi and Anele nodded as the clerk gave them a searching look. She referred to the form again as if she was reading through it one last time, then she put it away and rubbed her eyes.

"Ms Mngadi, you are the claimant in this case, am I right?" asked the clerk, with her eyes fixed on Anele.

"Yes, ma'am," responded Anele.

"You have mentioned the expenses of your daughter as follows: school fees, travel, food, accommodation and clothing." As she spoke, the clerk counted the items off on her fingers.

"Yes, I did."

"You said your ex-husband has not been supporting your daughter for about four months now?" said Ms Manganyi, her eyes shifting from Anele to Kimathi, and then back to Anele.

Anele looked at Kimathi and nodded before she answered. "That's right, ma'am."

The clerk turned to Kimathi. "Why are you not supporting your daughter, Mr Tito?" She paused, and then continued, "Is it because you are disputing that she's yours, perhaps?"

"No, I know she's mine," affirmed Kimathi, shaking his head. "There's no question about that."

"Then, if paternity is not the issue here, why are you not supporting her?" Ms Manganyi's elbows were on the table now, on top of the papers.

"I can no longer afford it. The amount she is claiming is very high," said Kimathi, his right hand playing with his glasses, "and my company is not doing well."

"He's lying!" Anele blurted out. "He's never in arrears when paying for his two flashy cars."

"How do you know that?" Kimathi said. "You left two years ago."

"Shhhh!" said Ms Manganyi as she tried to control the two of them. "That's for the court to investigate."

They both were quiet as Ms Manganyi retrieved a form from the file in front of her. She looked at Anele and again at the form before she pushed it away. "On your application, Ms Mngadi," she started, looking at Anele once again, "you said that your daughter needs school fees amounting to the total of five thousand and fifty per month, and you also gave us the receipts from the school."

"Yes, ma'am." Anele nodded.

"You also cited transport money and aftercare expenses to the tune of two thousand per month. Your food, clothing and other stuff like medication are also to the value of two thousand for your daughter, is that so?"

"That's right."

"The whole amount of support you're claiming from the father is nine thousand per month."

"Yes, ma'am."

Ms Manganyi looked at Kimathi, her displeasure clearly visible. "Do you agree to pay this amount, sir?" she asked, with a pen in hand as if ready to write something down.

Kimathi stroked his upper lip. "It's too much for me." He shook his head. "I cannot afford it."

"How much can you afford, Mr Tito?" Ms Manganyi asked.

"Two thousand." The words came out of Kimathi's mouth automatically.

"But that only covers her transport and aftercare," said Ms Manganyi, tapping the pen against her forehead.

"As I said, my business is not doing well at the moment. I'm in the process of securing some good money from the Department of Public Works. But, as you know, the bureaucratic wheels turn very slowly in this country." Kimathi paused and looked at Ms Manganyi. "So I don't expect greater efficiency soon on the part of that government department. They might take longer to make the funds available."

Ms Manganyi wrote something down. "Okay, I'll have to refer you to the public prosecutor, then. Both of you must follow me."

Ms Manganyi stood up, took the forms and walked towards the door. Kimathi and Anele followed her. As Anele walked out of the door, Kimathi suspected she was pregnant, and he felt angry.

The queue in the waiting room had swelled, snaking out of the door. A child was crying as they passed.

They walked up to the first floor to an office marked *Prosecutor S Kekana*. Ms Manganyi knocked only once before a female voice called her in.

The other side of the door was a short, dark woman with a pimpled nose that was a little off centre. She was sitting at an oak table, scribbling something in a book. Ms Manganyi cleared her throat and the woman looked up, nodded and motioned Anele and Kimathi to the two chairs in front of her desk. Ms Manganyi stood by the table as she talked to the prosecutor. After a brief conversation, she dropped the forms on the table and left the room.

Kimathi's heart began to beat faster as the prosecutor paged through the forms that had been deposited on her desk by Ms Manganyi. He was thinking about how to avoid a trial. At the same time, he was aware that prosecutors had a lot to do and were always eager to mediate and keep the congestion on their roll to a minimum. His lawyer had advised him that each prosecutor had to deal with roughly twenty-five maintenance cases every day and that they would probably opt to try and convince him to pay the amount. If not, it would mean that the prosecutor might have to face Kimathi's attorneys in court. Most prosecutors hated this scenario, feeling intimidated by well-prepared lawyers.

Ms Kekana pushed the forms aside and looked at Kimathi. He noticed her sparse lashes. "If I were you, sir, I would pay this money in order to avoid the formal enquiries by the court," she said, smiling.

"It's not that I don't want to support my daughter. It's just that I cannot afford the amount," Kimathi answered.

"This might be a tricky case for you, sir." She paused and picked up one of the forms in front of her. "Say you lose the case, for example. The court might order you to sell some of your assets, like your cars, so that you can afford to pay. I don't think you want that to happen."

"Is that so?"

"Yes. I know of such cases. One father was ordered to sell his Mercedes-Benz," she put the form down, "so as to lower his outgoings. This allowed him to then make his papgeld payments. I'm only saying this because I'm told you have two luxury cars and a house, the repayments on which, you claim, are part of the reason you cannot afford to pay your daughter's maintenance."

Kimathi looked at the ceiling and tried to communicate with God by talking softly to himself. Sweat broke out on his forehead while Anele tried to suppress a smile.

"Are you being serious?" Kimathi finally asked, rubbing both hands slowly over his face.

"Yes, I am being serious. Also, the court will investigate your life cover and other insurance policies," the prosecutor continued, "and might order you to reduce the number of your policies so that your earnings are channelled towards child support."

"But that is so unfair."

"I'm not sure what you've been told, but those are the powers of the court when it comes to the best interests of the child. We can also force you to cancel your DStv and cellphone contracts, my brother."

Kimathi thought momentarily about getting his lawyer involved, but rejected the idea. If he went the legal route, the court might also find out that he hadn't paid any taxes for the last three years. He decided to strike a bargain.

"Look, madam, I will try to pay seven thousand and not nine," he offered.

"I know you can afford nine thousand, Mr Tito," said Ms Kekana. "And remember, sir, that there are serious consequences if you default on your payment. The sheriff will attach and remove your property in order to enforce the maintenance order. Do you understand that?"

"I do."

"So, will you start paying nine thousand at the end of this month?" Ms Kekana asked.

"I'll try," Kimathi said doubtfully. "But I don't promise."

"Don't try. Just do it, babuTito. Us women always respect a man who is willing to sink," Ms Kekana said sarcastically.

"Fine, I'll pay the nine thousand."

"Fantastic."

Anele smiled broadly as the prosecutor gave Kimathi a commitment form to sign. Her heart felt like bursting with happiness and gratitude.

Chapter 19

Mafukuzela camp, Kwanza Sul province,
Angola

Later that day, after all the weapons had been surrendered, Comrade Pilate and Comrade Idi looked at peace with the world. Swinging their arms like they were taking part in a military parade, they led six comrades over to the eucalyptus trees by the entrance to the escape trench. Comrade Makana and Comrade Bambata were part of the party, each of them dragging two bound comrades behind them. The comrades had been arrested earlier that morning on suspicion of spying on The Movement.

As they approached the trench, one of the prisoners twisted himself out of Comrade Makana's grasp and ran.

"Leave him alone!" ordered Idi as Comrade Makana started to run after the prisoner. "He's not worth wasting your breath on."

Stepping forward, Idi raised his AK. Before the escaping prisoner could take two more steps a shot rang out, its sound shaking the hills around them. The prisoner dropped silently as the bullet hit him in the back of his head.

"If any of you still think you can run faster than this bazooka, you're free to try it," Idi said to the remaining prisoners, who had all stopped, their mouths shaped into paralysed ellipses. "But I guarantee you that you'll be on the ground with a bullet in your head before your heart takes another beat."

Unable to control himself, one prisoner bent over and vomited.

Idi gave him a disgusted look. "Let's go, you piece of shit!" he said, shoving the prisoner forward.

The prisoner tried to walk, but tripped over his own feet and fell to the earth. Pilate gave him a hard kick in the back, making him bellow with pain and squirm helplessly like a goat tied up for slaughter.

Upon reaching the entrance to the escape trench, Idi instructed Comrade Makana to tie each of the three remaining detainees to a tree. They were then stripped naked.

"I'm sure you will all talk after this," Idi said as he began to walk up and down the line of men. "There is no way the Boers could have known where our camp is. One of you dung-eating baboons leaked the information."

One prisoner swallowed his fear and started talking. His eyes were blinking rapidly with uncertainty. "We . . . we love The Movement. We could never do anything like that," he said, still trying to absorb the reality of the moment.

"Speak for yourself, traitor," ordered Pilate. "I'm sure your friends have mouths too."

"I'm not a traitor. The Movement is my home and family," the prisoner said, his lower lip starting to tremble. "I hate the Boers. They killed my father and my grandmother in the Sharpeville Massacre." He paused for breath. "Why on earth would I work for them?"

Pilate dismissed the prisoner's statement with a wave of his hand. "You're a liar!" he shouted, curling his hands into claws. "A fucking liar, that's what you are!" Narrowing his eyes, he spat into the prisoner's face.

"I'm asking you one more time, who amongst you is a spy?" said Idi with a frown on his face. "You knew that the Boers were coming to attack, didn't you? Answer me, you bastards!"

Seeing that no one was giving him the answers he wanted to hear, Idi removed his pistol from its holster and pressed it against the head of the nearest prisoner. The captive screwed his eyes shut in anticipation of death.

"Bloody apartheid agents!" Idi yelled at the prisoners. "Did you really think you could get away with betraying our noble Movement? You ungrateful, dung-eating bastards! Who do you think you are? Huh?"

The captives remained silent, but their eyes pleaded with Idi not to harm them.

"Talk! You bloody agents of destruction!" Idi screamed. "Talk! Or I will kill you one by one."

Instead of talking, the captive who had Idi's gun to his temple pissed himself. Seconds later, there was a loud bang as Idi shot the man. Brains and blood splashed all over the prisoner tied to the nearest tree. His screams filled everyone's ears as Idi and Pilate left the scene.

The following day, all the comrades suspected of betraying The Movement were rounded up. After interrogation, they were all transferred to a new prison camp called Amilcar Cabral.

Chapter 20

Kimathi stood in front of the bedroom mirror admiring the purple Prada suit he had bought at Desch, an exclusive fashion house in Sandton. It was his friend's memorial service and he was going to dress appropriately. He was going to meet many of the country's most important people at Ludwe's farewell, which was to be held at Museum Africa in Newtown at nine that morning, and he needed to look his best.

Dissatisfied with the Prada suit, Kimathi put it back in the wardrobe. He took out his lime Giovanni Gentile for a few minutes, but put it back again as if unable to make up his mind. He finally settled on the orange Eduard Dressler, with a white Fabiani silk shirt, Gucci belt and purple Roberto Botticelli shoes.

Before he opened the door to leave, Kimathi looked at himself in the mirror again and smiled with a sense of self-congratulation. He was sure that he would make an impression at the memorial.

As he came out of the house, Kimathi decided to park his BMW inside the double garage. He would deal with the dent later, he thought. This done, he got into his black Mercedes-Benz SLS 63 AMG gullwing.

As it was Saturday morning, the traffic on the M1 North to Johannesburg was smooth. "Mannenberg" by Abdullah Ibrahim was playing on his CD player, and Kimathi whistled along with his left hand strumming the steering wheel.

Kimathi arrived at Newtown twenty minutes later and parked his car in the Market Theatre parking lot. As he got out of the car, two parking attendants approached him and asked whether they could wash his toy for thirty rand. Without hesitation he gave them the go-ahead, but told them to use only liquid soap, or just plain water.

Kimathi passed Sechaba's silver Range Rover Sport in the parking lot, near the building that used to be Kippies jazz club. Glancing at his Rolex, he realised that it was still only eight thirty-five. He had twenty-five minutes to chat with other important mourners, one of who was bound to be Comrade Ganyani. He was hoping that Ganyani would be willing to negotiate with him on the Public Works tender bid, and was willing to compromise as long as Ganyani stayed on their team.

In front of him, the flea market in Mary Fitzgerald Square was already buzzing with customers looking for bargains. Kimathi passed a CD stand near the entrance to Museum Africa and climbed the steps to the main door. Just before he could enter the museum, he saw a toothless blind man playing a guitar. Kimathi stopped and listened to his rendition of Oliver Mtukudzi's "Todii". As he played, the man's sunken eye sockets were raised up as if he was playing for an invisible audience in the sky. Kimathi reached in his pockets, took out a handful of coins and threw them into the metal cup on the step in front of the blind man. Upon hearing the sound of the coins, the man thanked Kimathi in a high-pitched voice in between the Shona lyrics of the song. *What happened to the Great Zimbabwe?* Kimathi thought to himself as he entered the museum. *Zimbabwe's biggest export nowadays is its citizens.*

Kimathi stood at the back of the museum's lecture theatre and scanned the crowd for a friendly or familiar face. He spotted his cousin, Unathi, sitting with some women in the front row and went to greet her.

There was a decent turnout for the memorial service, but, to Kimathi's surprise, not many politicians attended. Although the flag of the country and The Movement's colours were displayed in all corners of the museum, the president and his ministers were absent. *What a disappointment*, Kimathi thought. He had expected the president or his deputy and at least five ministers to come and talk about the contribution that Comrade Ludwe had made to democracy. However, it was the absence of Comrade Ganyani that made him feel deserted and angry.

The service started at five minutes past nine. They had chosen a young lady from Public Works, Mrs Seema, to be the MC. She had bright lipstick on her moist lips and was wearing a white silk blouse that clung provocatively to her pointed breasts. After a prayer, she called on someone from the family of the deceased to speak. Unathi had asked Kimathi to be on the programme but he was only due to speak after Ms Vokwana, Ludwe's deputy at the Department of Public Works. As the designated representative of the friends of the deceased, he had decided to tell the mourners the story of how he had first met Comrade Ludwe at SOMAFCO in Mazimbu, Tanzania, in 1986.

"I still remember how much we used to love sitting under the mango tree during our lunch break, watching Comrade Ludwe as he tried to teach us songs and dances from South Africa," Kimathi started, scanning the faces in the crowd. "This was a very important part of The Movement's curriculum in SOMAFCO and it would never have happened without Comrade Ludwe..."

Kimathi looked down at his speech for his next line, but when he looked up again his eyes locked with those of a woman who had just entered the theatre. Dressed in a camouflage army uniform, she slowly descended the steps as if she was looking for an empty seat in the front row. But she did not take a seat. Instead she sat down on the bottom step. Kimathi's nervousness intensified as she ran her fingers over her scarred left cheek. He rubbed his face as if to bring some sense to what he was seeing, but this made him forget the rest of his story.

"There is a rumour that Comrade Ludwe was seen with an unidentified woman at the hotel before he died," Kimathi said, to the surprise of everyone in the theatre. "I swear on my father's grave in Mazimbu that I will find the girl that killed my friend and..."

An embarrassed Sechaba stood up, cleared his throat and started a revolutionary song before Kimathi could finish his sentence. It was obvious that this was done to drown out Kimathi's words.

> Hamba! Hamba kahle, Ludwe. We, Ludwe, qabane lesizwe. Thina maqabane sizimisele, ukuwabulala amabhunu!

Most of the mourners stood up to sing along, except for some white people. Although the song was loosely about the preparedness of comrades to kill the Boers, George clapped to the rhythm of the song along with the others. To him, it meant nothing.

As if manipulated by some unseen puppeteer, Kimathi began to pace about the stage aimlessly. The mourners who weren't singing began to comment on his strange behaviour as he pointed again and again at a row occupied by fashionably dressed young women and prosperous-looking men.

"You!" Kimathi pointed his finger at the lady in the camouflage uniform. "Leave me alone! You hear me?"

The almost hysterical torrent of words stopped abruptly when Kimathi collapsed and banged his head against the edge of a video projector. As he fell to the floor, his world became a blind, black and boundless abyss.

Chapter 21

**Amilcar Cabral camp, Kwanza Norte province,
Angola, 1988**

>   RE-Educate
>   RE-Orientate
>   RE-Habilitate
>   RE-Dedicate
>   RE-Deploy

With an unlit cigarette lodged behind his right ear, Comrade Pilate strolled between the buildings of Amilcar Cabral. The camp, situated near Quibaxe village, consisted of five grimy, flea-ridden warehouses eaten away by damp. Pilate was wearing a green army fatigue uniform for his morning inspection. Alongside him, similarly dressed, were Comrade Idi and four guards, all carrying AK-47s.

In front of each of the five blocks were five keywords, written in red paint on a huge white sign. The prisoners were expected to recite the keywords each morning. Comrades suspected of having betrayed The Movement, the so-called mutineers, were sent to this secret camp. The Movement felt that Amilcar Cabral was an ideal place to re-educate, re-orientate, re-habilitate and re-dedicate those who had strayed from the straight and narrow. There were two hundred and forty-four prisoners in total, divided into five very different groups. The only common denominator was that all of them had been deemed disloyal to The Movement.

Comrade Bambata, who had been assigned to unlock the doors during each routine inspection, was walking in front of Pilate and Idi as they approached the first building. Each block had a concrete stoep lined with pillars that held up rusty sheet-steel roofing and Comrade Bambata shivered as he stepped out of the sunlight and fitted a large iron key into the door. The architecture somehow seemed to whisper the secrets of past torturers. Rumour had it that the place had been used centuries earlier to house slaves before they were sent away across the Atlantic.

All the prisoners stood up as Pilate and Idi entered Block One. This was the home of the so-called Native Spies. These were UNITA rebels who had been captured and then employed by The Movement to gather information on UNITA. When these spies could not deliver, they were recaptured and brought to the camp.

The stench in Block One rose and thickened as the heat washed in from outside. Just like the other sections of the camp, this block was segregated, with the male and female prisoners held on different sides of the building.

Inside, it was damp and dark. There were no blankets or mattresses, only the concrete floor. The toilet was blocked and urine covered one corner of the men's quarters. Comrade Pilate and his men held their noses as all thirty-three male prisoners stood up. "Re-educate us, re-orientate us, re-habilitate us, re-dedicate us, re-deploy us," they recited as if deep in prayer, "for we have sinned."

Chapter 22

No one had imagined that it would take long for Kimathi to recover, but after five days he was still in hospital. He had missed Comrade Ludwe's funeral – the burial had been held in Khwezi, outside Umtata (also known as the Holy City because of its potholes) – as the doctors could not discover what was wrong with him. He was alive, but was not consciousness of his existence. Unathi, Anele and Zanu had come to visit him on three occasions, but he could not speak to them. In fact, for the whole time that he had been in the clinic, Kimathi had not opened his eyes once. Soft darkness had hidden the whole world from his sight, but in his dim and troubling nightmare he'd had a vision of a familiar woman. Hers was the kind of beauty he could not help but remember. The scar on her left cheek had stuck in his mind. He was sure he had seen her somewhere, but could not recall where. She was sitting cross-legged on the chair beside his bed, wearing metal-rimmed glasses with heavy lenses.

"What is your name?" he asked, looking directly into her face.

Before she answered him, the woman removed her glasses to show Kimathi her gleaming eyes. She looked at him long and hard, as if trying to help him make some discovery about her.

"It seems your memory betrays you, comrade." She smiled briefly and became serious again. "I must help to refresh it for you."

"What have I done to you?" Kimathi asked in a frightened voice as he twisted and turned on his bed. "Why do you keep following me?"

"There is no hiding place when you have hurt someone, comrade." She watched him with contempt.

Kimathi sprang up off his bed as if her words had ignited a spark of malice. He tried to seize her by the throat, but he was too late. The woman had ducked towards the table and Kimathi found himself holding a pillow with an owl-feather print on it. With a gasp, he lurched sideways and collapsed into his bed again. He was sweating and breathing heavily as the woman stared at him.

"Are you trying to harm me again, comrade?" the woman asked.

"Who are you, really? And why are you stalking me?"

"Consider me another life that you have wrecked," she replied curtly.

"But why me?" Kimathi asked in a sleepy voice.

"Because it's time for you to pay for your sins, comrade."

Kimathi lay on his bed. He gazed at the ceiling, and all at once a thought darted through his brain that he was mad.

"Why me?" he asked again.

"You must learn to remember your enemies by the scars you inflict on them," said the woman, pointing at the scar on her left cheek.

"What do you mean?"

"It is your choice that charted my path of tragedy," she answered. "If you deliberately choose to forget the past, you'll lose both eyes."

The mention of the word "tragedy" somehow piqued Kimathi's curiosity, and he narrowed his eyes as if in deep thought. Then he stared at the door; there was a faint streak of light coming in under it.

"But why?" he asked again. "What have I done to you?"

"Your past deeds are so shameful that only by forgetting have you been able to live with them."

"I don't understand you," Kimathi said, weakened and disoriented.

"Just take a journey into your past, and you'll have all the answers you want."

The woman's words seemed to speak directly to his heart. Kimathi exchanged a wordless glance with her.

"Oh God, if you're alive, this is your opportunity to make an appearance to save me," he whispered to himself.

"You have no right to talk to God," the woman said with bitterness showing on her face. "Not after you brought me to such a premature and unpleasant end."

"You are mistaken!" Kimathi shook his head. "We have never crossed paths."

Chapter 23

Amilcar Cabral camp, Kwanza Norte province, Angola

After checking on the women's section of Block One, Comrade Pilate and his men made their way to Block Two, where Comrade Bambata once again produced the key and opened the door.

In many ways Block Two was similar to Block One – it was another dilapidated Portuguese colonial building – but the inmates were completely different. Block Two was occupied by the Internal Spies. These were mainly members of the SADF who had been placed in key positions to gather information and had betrayed The Movement by failing to alert it to imminent raids on its camps (particularly those in Lesotho and Botswana). As soon as the forty-five prisoners in Block Two had recited their daily mantra, Pilate and his men left for the next block.

The third block was for the Double Spies. These were spies that had initially been recruited by the apartheid government before being captured by The Movement. They were seen as very useful tools – if they could be persuaded to work for The Movement – but when the information that they delivered was deemed substandard they were recaptured and put in Block Three.

Were it not for his dedication to his work at Amilcar Cabral, Pilate would not have bothered going to Block Four. This block housed the Doomed Spies. As the name suggests, these were originally The Movement's own secret agents, who had been deliberately given false information to report to UNITA and the apartheid government. However, they had failed to lure The Movement's enemies into its traps and had often also had their cover blown.

As soon as Pilate and his men unlocked the door, they were greeted by a stagnant blast of air, fouled by unwashed bodies and suppurating infections. As always, the cells were in complete disorder and the noise level inside was almost as unbearable as the stench. Some of the prisoners were undoubtedly mad, while others were teetering on the brink.

"Quiet!" ordered Pilate.

No one responded. In fact, it seemed that no one was taking any notice of them at all.

Comrade Idi tried to say something to Pilate, but he couldn't make himself heard over the noise.

Finally, Idi took out his pistol and fired a shot through the window. The din stopped temporarily, but, as most of the inmates in the Doomed Spies block were suffering from cerebral malaria, there was little hope of getting them to remember their own names, let alone the camp's slogans. Nearly every night, the whole block would scream deliriously and the place would resemble a mental hospital. It was not unusual for them to bury one or two prisoners from the Doomed Spies block every weekend because of the malaria.

Chapter 24

Kimathi's eyes flicked towards the door of his hospital cubicle. He dropped his head back against the pillow and ran the tip of his tongue along his dry lips.

"Yes," affirmed the woman, as if reading his thoughts. "I'm still here with you. Dont worry, I'm not going to leave you alone."

"But you're alive, and I'm talking to you now," Kimathi said in a conciliatory tone. "Dead people don't come back to life."

"Indeed, they rarely return, and only when it's necessary."

"Are you the one that killed my friend Ludwe?"

"No, comrade. Guilt and shame for his past deeds finally crept from the shadows, and he found the climb to be too steep."

"I don't understand."

"Comrade Ludwe was afraid of the truth, but you're not. And that is a smart move."

Kimathi eyed the woman thoughtfully for several seconds as if he was busy working something out in his empty head. The woman looked at him, her face metamorphosing first into that of Senami, then Lakeisha and then the woman he had seen at Ludwe's memorial.

"But . . ." The words would not come out of his dry mouth.

The woman looked at Kimathi without a word before walking out of the room.

"Please," Kimathi said. "Please. I don't remember. I don't know who you are and I don't remember . . ."

He heard footsteps outside, as well as some voices, but the woman did not return.

"Please!" Kimathi shouted. "Please! I don't remember!"

"Wonderful! He is conscious!" a female voice exclaimed jubilantly outside the cubicle. "He's awake."

When the doctor entered Kimathi's cubicle, she found him embracing his pillow like a lover. A thatch of whiskers had sprouted from his chin over the preceding five days, and grief had made his eyes larger. The doctor stood by his bed, a file in her hand. He looked at her expectantly.

"From the look of things, I think you're suffering from the aftereffects of some kind of past trauma." The doctor paused and ran her fingers through her blonde hair. "I think you must confront whatever it is."

Bewildered, Kimathi stared at her. The doctor gazed back at him, her expression unreadable. She had large light-brown eyes that were flecked with green.

"How did this happen?" Kimathi asked, raising a questioning eyebrow. "And how do I confront it?"

"Well, I suggest that you go for therapy."

"Therapy?" Kimathi frowned, trying to process the word.

The doctor looked at Kimathi with a hint of pity; he seemed to be engaged in some kind of internal struggle.

"Yes." The doctor gave him a polite smile, her eyes assessing him. "You should think about it." Then she put his file on the table and left.

Kimathi had an overwhelming desire to sleep. As he closed his eyes, he heard someone talking to the doctor outside. He tried hard to stay awake, but fit wasn't long before darkness clamed him.

When Kimathi opened his eyes again, the bed was surrounded by the gleaming faces of Sechaba, Ludwe's widow, Unathi, Anele and his daughter Zanu, who was carrying some flowers for her father. Sechaba was tastefully dressed in a blue Eduard Dressler suit and a black pure-cotton shirt. He was carrying a bottle of Veuve Clicquot Ponsardin Rosé champagne. Anele looked beautiful. Her hair was layered with curls, with loose tresses falling down over her shoulders. She wore a velvet dress with a matching scarf, snakeskin shoes with gold trim and Barton Perreira leopard-print glasses. Her brown Louis Vuitton handbag hung on her left shoulder and she also wore a pearl necklace and a silver bracelet on her right wrist.

Kimathi caught Anele staring at him. She was now visibly pregnant. He knew that she had not forgiven him for what he had done with Moliehi, their domestic worker. Anele's look was enough to convince Kimathi that she still thought he was a bastard. *She would not have bothered to come if it were not for Zanu*, he thought.

Kimathi looked at Anele again. As if letting the feeling of his betrayal sink to the bottom of her stomach, she switched her gaze from him. In response he turned his attention to Zanu, who was standing close to the bed and playing with his hand.

"What is today's date?" asked Kimathi to no one in particular.

Instead of answering him immediately, Sechaba gave him a broad smile of brotherhood. "I'm glad you're back from the dead, comrade," he said. "It's going to be our D-Day in four days. That's when we are doing our tender presentation to the department. Money is coming our way again, comrade. I can smell it! Currency!"

"Where is the venue?" asked Kimathi while rubbing Zanu's hand.

"In Pretoria, at the department headquarters."

"Why Pretoria?" asked Kimathi, sounding disappointed. "I thought they had booked a different venue. Remember, we were told that it was going to be held in the boardroom at the Hyatt?"

Sechaba shook his head. "There have been some changes since the passing away of Comrade Ludwe. Some people he worked with betrayed him even in his coffin by saying he was corrupt. Now the government is under pressure to do things properly, they claim. So, the whole board has been replaced, and we'll be facing this new bunch of monkeys in the interview."

"When did this happen?" asked Kimathi.

"Three days ago. There were some newspaper reports claiming that Ludwe stood to gain from the awarding of this tender and that a relative of his was associated with one of the bidding companies. Although the name of the company was not mentioned, they were obviously referring to us. There is also talk of change everywhere, even in the higher levels of government."

"Shit! That's bad news," said Kimathi.

All of a sudden he felt Zanu's little hand withdrawing from his, and this attracted his attention. He looked at his daughter's surprised face.

"Daddy, you said a bad word," said Zanu. "When you get home you must wash your dirty mouth, sit in the naughty corner and face the wall."

Laughter rippled around the room.

"Oh, did I?" Kimathi responded, smiling apologetically at his daughter. "I'm sorry, my princess. I won't mention the bad word again, my dear, clever princess."

Zanu smiled at the endearments. As Kimathi retrieved her hand and caressed it again, her mouth opened to display two gleaming rows of even teeth. But even as he looked at his daughter's perfect smile, Kimathi felt like his life was shrinking and was leaving him with nothing. The changes at Public Works would certainly make winning the tender very difficult.

"Yeah. And, as you know, the saddest part is that Comrade Ganyani has left us," said Sechaba. "But don't worry, comrade, we'll make it. We're still a strong team without him."

Kimathi's brain froze, stunned into inactivity. "That man is a traitor," he eventually said angrily, the thought coming involuntarily into his head. "He didn't even bother to come to Comrade Ludwe's memorial service."

"And he even had the nerve to call me three days ago to say that he had been offered fifteen per cent by our rival bidder," added Sechaba. "Though he wouldn't give me the name of this rival when I pressed him."

"That man owes us a revolutionary favour for everything we did for him in Angola," said Kimathi. "Comrade Ludwe took him in like his own brother, and against everybody's wishes he made him a junior guard at the camp. This is not the way to repay people's kindnesses."

"Don't stress about that one, com," said Sechaba. "Our presentation plans are right on track. I'll show you once you're out of here. But at this moment we must celebrate the fact that you are alive."

Kimathi nodded dumbly as he looked around him. His business conversation with Sechaba seemed to have isolated them from the others. Both the women and Zanu were now paging uninterestedly through old magazines. Sechaba decided not to continue with the talk, and instead opened the bottle of champagne to celebrate his friend's return to life. They all applauded vigorously as the cork went off. Zanu came around the bed with a broad smile and extended her arms to hug her father; her small eyes were twinkling.

"I think we need to arrange to speak to Ganyani. He can't just leave us," Kimathi said after taking a sip from his glass. "We've got history with that monkey."

Chapter 25

Amilcar Cabral camp, Kwanza Norte province, Angola

The last assignment of the day was to inspect and interrogate the inmates in the fifth block – the solitary confinement cells. However, Comrade Pilate and Comrade Idi preferred to conduct these interrogations alone. There was no risk like there was in the communal cells, they thought. So, having released Comrade Bambata, Comrade Muzi and the other two comrades, their first stop was Lady Comrade Mkabayi's cell.

Pilate had recently given Lady Comrade Mkabayi a new name: Delilah. According to him, this fitted her sins well – in the Bible, Delilah betrayed her man, Samson, and similarly Lady Comrade Mkabayi had betrayed The Movement to the enemy. He and Idi had beaten her up the previous week using the soles of their boots. Her crime? That she had insisted on being called Lady Comrade Mkabayi, the name she had been given in Mafukuzela (where many of her comrades had likened her courage to that of King Shaka Zulu's aunt).

Lady Comrade Mkabayi and the rest of the group from Mafukuzela had arrived at Amilcar Cabral in August 1988. Upon her arrival at the camp, she had initially found herself in the overcrowded Internal Spies block. However, she was soon placed in solitary confinement. The reason for this was that she had refused to make her body available to Pilate and Idi. They had promised to release her and secure her tickets to fly to East Germany if she slept with them. When she refused this clumsy offer, Pilate accused her of disrespecting The Movement and its capable leaders and had her moved to solitary.

Idi unlocked Lady Comrade Mkabayi's dimly lit cell and they both entered. Pilate scanned the cell. The Party slogans appeared in bold letters on all of the four damp walls, but the words were no longer decipherable in many places as much of the paint had peeled off. The cell itself was the length of one human body, and Lady Comrade Mkabayi was sitting on the cold floor, staring unblinkingly at the cement slab on which she slept. Her body was skeletal due to lack of food and her left cheek was still swollen from the beating they had given her the previous week.

Pilate cleared his throat to attract Lady Comrade Mkabayi's attention, but she ignored his presence. Instead, her eyes followed a small gecko that was crawling across the floor. Her mouth was wide open, and a green fly settled on her lower lip as if exploring the small cut in it.

The nauseating odour of shit – issuing from a twenty-five-litre plastic container that stood in the corner of the cell – penetrated Pilate's nostrils, and he felt like vomiting. He cleared his throat again, but before he could say anything Lady Comrade Mkabayi started talking to herself as if addressing an invisible audience. Pilate and Idi were aware that she had been down with a bout of malaria and that she could be hallucinating. They stood there without a word, hoping she might snap out of it, but the moment she stopped speaking she returned to motionlessness as if waiting for her brain to reboot.

"We don't have the whole day for you, Delilah," barked Idi finally. "You'd better wake up and talk to us."

"What do you want to hear from me?" she whispered. It was evident that she was having some difficulty breathing. "Ever since you brought me here my most important daily thoughts are deciding not to commit suicide."

"You have created this atmosphere yourself."

"I feel let down by you and The Movement," she said without looking at them. "I just can't understand why you, Comrade Pilate, of all people, are accusing me of being an enemy agent. I killed the paratrooper who was about to shoot you on the day of the raid."

"Shut up, you temptress Delilah!" shouted Pilate in a sudden fit of rage. "We don't care how you feel. You know exactly what you did. Why did you disobey the orders to go and fight UNITA?"

"First of all, I'm not Delilah!" Her energy seemed to have returned. "Call me Comrade Mkabayi."

"We don't care who you are, or what you call yourself anymore," retorted Idi. "All we want to know is the reason you let The Movement down. First of all, you and the other spies leaked information of our whereabouts to the Boers in Mafukuzela, and then you refused to carry out The Movement's orders and fight UNITA."

"It's not like we don't want to fight UNITA." Lady Comrade Mkabayi hesitated.

"But we really want to fight the apartheid government back home in South Africa. Look how many people they killed during the raid. A lot of comrades have fallen. We must fight the real enemy, which is the Boers, not Savimbi." She paused and then continued, "Savimbi and his UNITA are the MPLA's problem, not ours."

"Shut the fuck up!" Idi snapped, clenching his hands into fists as if he was about to strike her. "You are a naive, half-baked, dung-eating coward! Where do you think you are, huh? Heaven? Who do you think gave us the land for our camp if not the MPLA? Who do you think is supplying us with weapons to fight the Boers? Who do you think is feeding our comrades, huh?"

"But we want to fight the Boers, not Savimbi, comrade," Lady Comrade Mkabayi insisted. "If we fight UNITA we will die here in Angola. I want to die inside South Africa, fighting our real enemy."

"You and your friends in the Amadelakufa Division always had an attitude," growled Pilate. "You are not disciplined! We will not tolerate that in The Movement." He looked at her accusingly. "Tell us, which enemy camp are you working for: UNITA or the Boers, or both?"

"I left home hating the Boers after they abducted and killed a lot of my schoolmates at Pace Commercial High School in Soweto," Lady Comrade Mkabayi said. "You know this, Comrade Pilate. Both of you know this. How could I possibly work with someone who has stolen my dignity and my right to live as a human being?"

"You are a spy! I asked you whose agent you are?" said Pilate, leaning towards her as if talking to a deaf person. "Answer me, damn it, bitch!"

"I might be guilty of not wanting you. But I'm a dedicated member of The Movement. How can you accuse me of such a horrible thing?"

"Shut up!" shouted Idi. "You and your friends are the ones that informed the Boers of where our camp was. You have to pay the price."

"Where is your evidence?" Lady Comrade Mkabayi asked defiantly. "There isn't any, is there? This is all simply because I refused to sleep with both of you."

"You had better change your attitude, Delilah," said Pilate as he and Idi turned to leave. "Otherwise we'll be forced to find other ways of making you confess."

Chapter 26

Two days before their Public Works tender presentation, Kimathi and Sechaba once again arranged to meet Ganyani at the Hyatt hotel. Kimathi had fully recovered. The prospect of winning the tender encouraged them to buy overpriced tots of whisky but they were also eager to declare their mutual loyalties and drown any differences in alcohol. Ganyani's presentation was also scheduled for two days' time, immediately after that of Mandulo. His new business partners, a German-owned company called DMM, had booked him into the Sandton Hilton for four days. Kimathi and Sechaba had asked to meet him in the hope of convincing him to rejoin their venture. They were sitting in the corner of the hotel bar drinking whisky as they discussed business. George had not been invited.

"It's never too late to reconsider, comrade," Sechaba said as he put down his double tot of Johnnie Walker Blue. "We've come very far together."

"I know. But why should I bet on a limping horse, knowing that it's not going to finish the race, comrades?" asked Ganyani, moving his eyes between Kimathi and Sechaba. "I can't do that, not even when I know the owner of the horse. No hard feelings, comrades, but this is a business decision."

Sechaba's smooth brow became furrowed. He had expected that they would easily convince Ganyani to rejoin their team if they became nostalgic.

"But you have to show your loyalty to the struggle and your comrades," Kimathi persisted. "Do it for Comrade Ludwe, if not for us."

Ganyani laughed politely and snapped his fingers. "There is no loyalty and honour amongst thieves and murderers, comrade." He paused and looked Kimathi in the eye. "We are all in this to make money, not so?"

"In point of fact, we are doing this for the betterment of our people's lives," said Kimathi, "and that is why the masses love to be governed by us."

"Don't tell me about the masses." Ganyani paused and lifted his glass, and then continued without taking a sip, "They are a useless bunch of lazy monkeys who still vote for us even when we embezzle their tax monies, even when we employ our friends and relatives, even when we use their taxes to buy expensive houses and cars and sleep with their wives." He drained his glass. "Come election day, the masses will still vote for us. So don't tell me about the masses."

There was a moment of silence as Ganyani put his empty glass down.

"We have come a long way, comrade," said Sechaba, looking straight into Ganyani's drunken eyes.

"Well, Comrade Sech, I think you have already learned that in politics and business there are no eternal friends," said Ganyani, massaging his empty glass and slurring his words, sounding like a drunk. "I also learnt it the hard way myself when you guys offered me that pathetic seven per cent during our negotiations. And, like they say, if a man does not keep pace with his companions, perhaps he is hearing a different drummer. I went to the other drummer and he showed me respect."

"But, comrade, think of our Elim days," said Sechaba. "You'll understand then that the drummer you're hearing is a fake, not a friendly one."

There was a ring of nostalgia in Sechaba's voice when he talked about Elim. He had left the country for exile with Ganyani in 1984. Prior to that Ganyani had been a teacher at Shirley Primary School in Elim, a village outside Makhado in Limpopo. Shirley School was said to be the same institution that Frelimo leader Eduardo Mondlane taught at after completing his teacher's course at nearby Lemana College. Ganyani used to boast to Sechaba that he had been influenced by Mondlane.

Sechaba and Ganyani had known each other from an NGO called the Akani Rural Development Association, which was a hideout for guerrillas and a recruitment point for The Movement's new military underground fighters. Sechaba had come from Zamdele township near Sasolburg as a new recruit. The Movement's underground commanders had posted him to Akani for four months and he and Ganyani had become friends while training at the underground military centre, which was in the Magangeni bush near Lemana College. After four months, they were transported to Mozambique via Komatipoort. They were then sent to Lusaka at the beginning of 1985. From Lusaka, the two were posted to different camps. Sechaba was sent to Malange in southern Angola and Ganyani found himself in Mafukuzela and Amilcar Cabral, near Luanda.

At that moment, Ganyani caught sight of a waiter. He snapped his fingers at him, and the waiter approached their table.

"Look at my glass. It has been empty for the last ten minutes. Do I have to fill in a form just to order a double tot of Johnnie Walker Blue?" Ganyani asked.

The waiter shook his head.

"And bring a separate glass of ice with that," he ordered.

Sechaba and Kimathi also placed their orders. When the waiter had gone, Ganyani lit a cigarette. He took three drags, letting the ash grow on the cigarette before flicking it into the glass ashtray.

"What you don't know, comrades, is that when he died, Comrade Ludwe was under investigation." Ganyani paused and studied their reaction. "Disciplinary action has already been taken against some executive members of his department." He paused again, and continued, "I wouldn't bank on knowing him if I were you. That would be counting the chickens before the eggs are hatched."

"How do you know all this?" asked Kimathi, sounding surprised.

At that moment the waiter placed their drinks on the table. Ganyani ignored Kimathi and dropped two ice cubes into his glass. He paused and lowered his nose to the rim of the glass and breathed in the whisky smell before taking a sip. His eyes were closed as he drank and he had a satisfied, childlike smile on his face.

"All I can tell you at this stage is that a ten-person commission was appointed to investigate the allegations against his department." Ganyani finally said. "Some people were found guilty of spending on non-core items which add little or no value to service delivery."

"What are those?" enquired Sechaba, his face tight with anxiety.

"Things like the purchasing of calendars, catering, promotional items and expensive overseas trips. Do you remember, comrades, that Ludwe was in Italy six months ago with his wife and kids?" Ganyani didn't wait for them to answer. "Apparently," he continued, "he used taxpayers' money for that personal trip."

"How do you know all of this?" enquired Sechaba.

"Every wall has an ear, Comrade Sech." Ganyani paused and twirled the ice in his glass before taking a sip. "It has also been discovered that he appointed six of his friends and relatives to well-paid positions within the department."

"The only time people are brave enough to spread such malicious rumours is when they know a person won't be able to defend himself," remarked Kimathi angrily.

Ganyani consulted his watch – Montblanc, with a black leather strap – and rose from his chair. It was nearly half past nine in the evening.

"I'm sorry, comrades, I have to go. I have an important meeting tomorrow morning," he said, trying hard not to slur his words. "I guess we'll see each other soon, and thank you for the good whisky. The round is on you, comrades, and it's for the valuable information that I have just given you about how unlikely it is that you will win this tender."

"You are betraying us, comrade," said Sechaba, staring at him. "That's not the way to treat your friends."

"No, comrade, I've given you my reasons for not backing your bid," said Ganyani, looking straight into Sechaba's face without flinching. "You cannot call that a betrayal . . . And I have also given you inside information so that you will be prepared when those two ugly guys come knocking on your door."

"What guys are you talking about now?" asked Kimathi suspiciously. "Are we under some kind of investigation that we are not aware of?"

"No, comrades. All I'm saying is that when those two ugly men – *trouble* and *misery* – come knocking on your door, you can't turn them away by merely saying that you do not have chairs for them to sit on in your dining room," said Ganyani, standing up. "If you do, that will be stupid of you because they will tell you that they have brought their own."

The remark angered Kimathi, at least partly because he knew it was true. Ganyani tossed his car keys in the air and caught them. As he walked towards the door, Kimathi lifted his glass of whisky. Halfway to his mouth, his hand shook and the whisky sloshed. He put it down without taking a sip. Leaning forward, he rested his elbows on the table. He looked despondent, and Ganyani's words kept echoing in his head like a drunkard's song in an empty shebeen. He blamed himself for imagining that he could get Ganyani to change his mind and rejoin the team.

"If Comrade Ganyani can do this to us, then I'm convinced that our struggle has been sold to the highest capitalist bidder," said Kimathi finally, plucking a cigar from the pocket of his jacket.

Chapter 27

**Amilcar Cabral camp, Kwanza Norte province,
Angola**

Comrade Pilate opened the door to Lady Comrade Mkabayi's cell. He had an enamelled mug of steaming tea in his hand. Comrade Idi followed with a bowl of bean soup and a piece of brown bread on a tray. They stopped in the doorway and looked down at Lady Comrade Mkabayi. Her eyes were focused on some ants that were industriously carting a dead fly across the floor of her cell.

Idi coughed to get Lady Comrade Mkabayi's attention, but she remained quiet, refusing to acknowledge their presence. She stayed this way until Pilate went and stood right in front of her.

"Delilah, are you ready to talk now?" Pilate asked, putting the mug down.

"But I've already told you that I'm not a spy," she answered, without looking at him. "What more do you want me to say to you?"

"Prove that by doing what we have asked you to do," said Idi.

"I will not sleep with you, if that is what you want me to do," Lady Comrade Mkabayi said weakly. "I have come here for a great cause, the revolution, and not to make babies with comrades."

"Then your life will be much more miserable than it is now," said Pilate.

"On what basis am I being punished here?" she asked.

"Well, I'm sorry for bringing you some bad news, but some of your comrades have already confessed to us that you were part of a plot to topple The Movement's leadership," said Pilate.

"That's a lie," Lady Comrade Mkabayi said, without blinking. "Who told you such a lie?"

Pilate looked at Idi as if he was seeking some kind of approval. "Should we tell her, comrade?" he asked.

"Why not?" Idi replied. "It's no longer a secret, anyway."

"Okay then, listen. It was your beloved friend, Comrade Bambata, that betrayed you," said Pilate.

Chapter 28

It was ten o'clock on a cold Friday morning and the Pretoria sky was filled with heavy clouds – it looked as if it was going to rain. George, Sechaba and Kimathi were sitting in the corner of the State Theatre's Capello restaurant in Church Street with a laptop open in front of them. They had just finished eating their breakfast. Although Pretoria was less than sixty kilometres from Johannesburg, they had decided to leave early to avoid the Friday morning traffic. They also wanted to go over their presentation to the Department of Public Works. Kimathi had chosen to go first with the introduction of the team, George would go second with the real mining stuff and Sechaba was supposed to conclude the presentation.

After paying the bill, all three men got into their cars and drove in convoy to the corner of Church and Bosman. They parked their cars in three empty visitors' spaces and entered a building that bore the inscription *SOUTH AFRICA WORKS BECAUSE OF PUBLIC WORKS*. Sechaba and Kimathi wore expensive clothes that spoke of status and the culture of a person who has risen from rags to riches. Kimathi had donned his black GG suit, a pure-cotton blue shirt and a red tie, as well as a pair of black, sharp-nosed Roberto Botticelli shoes. Sechaba was in his cream tailored Prada suit, a pure-cotton white shirt and a pair of pointed brown Fabiani shoes. George had opted for a pair of brown corduroy trousers, a white tie with a plaid shirt, a brown jacket and some black Bronx lace-up shoes. Sechaba and Kimathi joked about George's dress sense while they were in the toilet before the start of the presentation. Kimathi whispered to Sechaba that George's clothes were a serious fashion crime, and their total value did not exceed six hundred rand. Kimathi boasted that, with the clothes he was wearing, he could buy a brand-new Toyota Tazz, which was what George drove.

They started at eleven o'clock sharp, with Kimathi handing a copy of the Mandulo presentation booklet to the five members of the Construction Industry

Development Board (CIDB) and the Acting Director-General of Public Works, Ms Vokwana. The design of the booklet was impeccable; it even had a catchy quotation from Nelson Mandela on the cover: "A good head and a good heart are always a formidable combination".

After the members of the panel had introduced themselves, it was Kimathi's time to shine. His desire to win the tender had injected new life into him. As he looked around, though, he realised that he did not know anybody on the panel except for Ms Vokwana. It was evident that there had been a serious rearranging at Public Works.

"Thank you all for this rare opportunity and for choosing my team to come and present to you," Kimathi said and cleared his throat before launching into his carefully prepared presentation. "Allow me to use the words of that wise man, former President Nelson Mandela: 'a good head and a good heart are always a formidable combination'. This team is indeed a formidable combination." He paused and pointed at his business partners. "Let me start with myself. I am a true son of the revolution. I was born in exile in Tanzania, and studied at the Underground People's University of Siberia, where I received my Master's degree in Fine Arts."

Kimathi paused and drank some water.

After trumpeting his achievements to the panel, Kimathi started his PowerPoint presentation. He mentioned all the comrades that he knew from exile, and how most of them were the incumbent ministers and deputy ministers in the government. Then he introduced his business partners.

"George Tsongas, ladies and gentlemen," said Kimathi, pointing at the screen with his red-dot pointer, "is a world-famous Greek-American who has been based in South Africa for the past decade." He looked at George, who was sitting next to him. "Besides his degree in engineering, he comes from a family of scientists in Iowa State, Midwest of the United States of America. His grandfather worked with the genius himself, the father of modern science, Albert Einstein, on the Manhattan Project."

There were puzzled looks and all eyes turned to George, who looked embarrassed by Kimathi's exaggeration.

"Yes, ladies and gentlemen," continued Kimathi with a forged smile on his face, "in fact, George was just telling me before this presentation that his grandfather actually drafted that famous letter to President Franklin Delano Roosevelt." He looked around to see if everyone was following him. "I am, of course, talking about the letter written by Einstein to warn Roosevelt that Hitler was busy with a nuclear project, and that the United States must do something soon." He paused and pointed at George. "So, without this gentleman's grandfather Germany would have won the war, and, who knows, maybe we would all be speaking German in this presentation." He gave a smile and a nod, but no one returned the gesture.

George shook his head in disbelief. He wanted to say that his late grandfather and father had had nothing to do with the war or the atomic bomb. They had merely worked as scientists at the Ames Laboratory, but it was too late.

One of the panellists from the CIDB, a fat man with an egg-shaped body, had his hand up. He reminded George of a picture of King Dingane that he had come across before he moved to South Africa. The man looked as if he had swallowed three large watermelons.

Kimathi stopped talking, and looked at the fat man, imploring him to speak or ask a question. The man breathed through his mouth before he spoke.

"I just wanted to know, who is this Albert Elstar you are referring to?" asked the fat man.

He was very dark and clean-shaven, and his nipples were like a little girl's breasts inside his white shirt. Kimathi wondered whether the fat man had a wife and how he made love to her.

Kimathi dabbed at his face with a handkerchief. "Albert Einstein is the man credited with the creation of the atomic bombs Fat Man and Little Boy," Kimathi said, looking directly at the man as he said the words "fat man". "I'm talking about the bombs that ended the Second World War after they were dropped on the Japanese cities of Hiroshima and Nagasaki and killed thousands of innocent Japanese civilians."

"Thank you," said the fat man, nodding vigorously.

"Okay, let's continue," said Kimathi. "Sechaba More here is also a true man of the soil. He studied in Siberia, same year as me. He has an MA in Literature and his thesis was on *The Gulag Archipelago* by Aleksandr Solzhenitsyn. He lived in the former East Germany for a while before coming back to South Africa. He was there when the Berlin Wall was demolished in November 1989. That's my formidable team, ladies and gentlemen."

Kimathi scrolled to his closing sentence, a quotation from civil rights leader Ella Baker.

"'Give light and people will find the way'. With that, ladies and gentlemen, I would like to hand over to Mr Tsongas to continue with the presentation."

George rubbed his face as if trying to remember what he was about to say.

"The coal mining industry is very destructive, ladies and gentlemen," he finally said. "And that is an honest truth. But, the fact is, it doesn't have to be. Mitigating the environmental impact of this project depends on choosing the right team to do the job. But firstly let me show you something."

Opening a map of the Soutpansberg and the Vhembe region, George told the panellists how rich the area was and outlined how the mining would be done. He then took them through the figures, concentrating on how South Africans in the area would benefit in terms of job creation and how the economy would be enlarged. His presentation took twenty-five minutes as he also touched on the issue of the 2010 FIFA World Cup. When he noticed that the fat man was asleep and breathing heavily through his mouth, George decided to conclude.

"Ladies and gentlemen, my team and I are not prepared to go where the path may lead," he said. "Instead we are prepared to go where there is no path at all and leave a trail. That place is in the Soutpans."

As soon as George sat down, Sechaba stood up and continued the presentation. His portion did not take more than fifteen minutes; he started by quoting John Muir.

"'Climb the mountains and get their good tidings'. Ladies and gentlemen, that is what we are prepared to do. Given your blessing, we are prepared to climb those mountains in the Soutpansberg and bring all of the natural resources we can find back to our people," Sechaba said, pointing at the map that George had left open on the computer.

After mumbling for about ten more minutes, Sechaba summed up the whole presentation. "A creative man, ladies and gentlemen, is motivated by a desire to achieve, not by a desire to beat others. We are doing this for the love of our people, so that forever we can stay in the light."

Sechaba sat down to allow the panellists to ask questions. Ms Vokwana, who was sitting next to the fat man, took the floor.

"Mr Tito." She looked at Kimathi and then at her notes. "I understand that your company was paid one point five million to fix the potholes in Bassonia. Is that right?"

"Yes, and we fixed them," Kimathi replied with confidence.

"But according to the records, your company did not have the technical capacity for the contract at that time." She paused and poured some water into a glass.

"What do you mean?" Kimathi asked, sounding confused. "Please explain."

Ms Vokwana leaned forward. "What I mean is that your company was only registered on 10 June 2001 and the bids were due to be submitted on 13 June." She paused and looked at him.

"I see no problem with that because we definitely submitted on time," said Kimathi.

"Of course there is a problem, Mr Tito," Ms Vokwana continued. "You had no track record at that time, and the tender strictly required technical experience and capacity for a successful bid. Can you explain how it was awarded to you?"

Kimathi shrugged his shoulders. "Those are merely allegations, Ms Vokwana. We had a qualified civil engineer and a quantity surveyor. Their names were Mr Shezi and Mrs Ngubo. I can give you their contacts if you want."

"But, Mr Tito, the winning team should have also included engineers and project managers with experience in the design and construction of roads. That was unequivocally specified in the tender document." Ms Vokwana paused and searched Kimathi's face as if looking for signs of disapproval. "Although Mr Shezi is a civil engineer," she continued when his face remained blank, "he only graduated from the University of Cape Town in 2000."

"What I don't know is why we should dwell on the past when dealing with today's tender," said Kimathi arrogantly. "Unless this is personal, of course."

"I'll tell you why clarity is important on this point, Mr Tito. And I hope the rest of your team take note of this." Ms Vokwana paused and looked first at George and then at Sechaba. "In your submission you included Mr Ganyani Novela as a member of your team. We were confused as Mr Novela is bidding with another company, one that will present after you today. When we needed clarity on this matter he indicated that he is not part of your team. It seems to me you are misrepresenting the capacity of your team in order to get this tender, as you did previously. I guess it's now clear to you why we are questioning your past practices. It's nothing personal."

"But Mr Novela only told us today that he is not part of our team, when we were already on our way here," Kimathi lied. "All along we had thought that he was still with us."

"I think you should have at least indicated that to us in your presentation. Also, we received a letter from him about a week ago, stressing that he was not part of your team. How come he did not communicate this to you?"

"I really don't know. I wish he was here to answer that question himself," replied Kimathi.

"Okay. We understand that the former DG, the deceased Mr Ludwe Khakhaza, was also indirectly part of the committee that awarded you the tender to fix the potholes." Ms Vokwana paused again and looked at her file. Without waiting for his answer, she continued, "Mr Khakhaza did not declare any possible or potential conflict of interest in terms of the law. He did not even excuse himself from the process."

Kimathi smiled cynically. "I don't know about that," he said.

"Do you have equipment ready to do the job?" asked the man sitting next to Ms Vokwana, whose name – according to the sign on the table in front of him – was Mr Lethoko.

"Well, we are in negotiation with Umcebo Mines in Emalahleni to lease their equipment for five years," Sechaba answered. "The negotiations are near conclusion, and we'll be more than ready by the time the tender is announced."

"Umcebo Mines? Isn't that the very same company that is being sued for not complying with the National Water Act?" the man asked.

Sechaba shook his head and shrugged his shoulders. "I have no idea about that, Mr Lethoko."

"But surely you are aware of the state of their business if you're planning to have a relationship with them?"

"I know that the company was issued with a mineral licence by the Department of Mineral Resources," insisted Sechaba.

"I agree with you there. But they had to apply for other licences, from Water Affairs and Forestry and Environmental Affairs, for example."

"Well, that's news to me. But we are only interested in their equipment and not their problems, Mr Lethoko. I'm sure they can sort out their troubles with the lease money that we'll pay them," answered Sechaba.

There was a moment of silence as Sechaba poured water into his glass.

"Mr Tsongas," said another member of the panel – a gentleman with a goofy tooth. "What engineering experience do you have, apart from what has already been presented?"

"I worked as a senior mining engineer at a uranium mine in the Democratic Republic of Congo for five years. Before that I worked as a senior mining engineer at a copper mine in Zambia for two years."

George had spoken so fast that the fat man had had to watch his lips in order to catch what he was saying. It was as if he was lost in admiration of George's achievements.

"Mmmm. Impressive," said the woman sitting next to Ms Vokwana. She had been thumbing through the presentation booklet. "But seeing that you are two black males with degrees in arts, and a foreign white male with engineering qualifications, how are you going to deal with issues of women empowerment?"

Kimathi was not expecting this question, but he was obliged to answer. "Well," he cleared his throat, "actually we have Mrs Sindi Yeni as an executive chairman. Unfortunately she could not be with us today because of pressing family commitments. There are also two hard-working black ladies that are about to join us on the management team very soon." He paused. "One of the ladies will be replacing Mr Ganyani Novela, who left us without warning."

Kimathi was then asked how he would make sure that Mandulo achieved its delivery targets before the start of the World Cup. His company was also accused of not properly fixing the potholes in Bassonia, one of the panellists claiming that they had used cement only. Kimathi denied this, and assured the panel that the targets would be reached before 2010.

Once Kimathi had answered all the panel's questions, they all rose to their feet in unison and left the boardroom. It was twenty past two in the afternoon.

As Kimathi, George and Sechaba made their way out of the building, George yawned and excused himself, saying he had to pick up his kids, Alexis and Antaeus, from school in Kensington. Kimathi and Sechaba agreed that they would go and reflect on the whole ordeal over a late lunch at Melrose Arch. Seconds later, while they were laughing at the question posed by the fat man during the presentation, they saw a new black Porsche Cayenne 4x4 without number plates pulling into the parking slot that George had just vacated. Their laughter trailed off as the driver's door opened and out climbed a man in a grey suit. It was Ganyani.

Kimathi's blood instantly began to boil and he clenched his fists as if he was squeezing out his anger.

Ganyani came towards them, grinning as if Kimathi was his dentist. He extended his right hand, but Kimathi twisted his lips and ignored it. Instead, he cleared his throat and spat at Ganyani's car. They all watched in amazement as the blob landed on the Porsche's windscreen.

"That is your fifteen per cent share, you fucking traitor," shouted Kimathi, pointing at the saliva flowing down the window.

"What do you fucking think you're doing? Do you have any idea how much that car is worth?" Ganyani retorted as Kimathi pushed past him.

"Who cares, you fucking ugly monkey," snapped Kimath, climbing into his Mercedes-Benz AMG gullwing.

"Oh, you want to fight me?" asked Ganyani with rage. "I will teach you people today."

Loosening his tie, Ganyani cleared his throat, summoning all the mucus and saliva he could, and spat at Kimathi's car. The spit landed on the car's windscreen. "That's a forty per cent stake for your company and your whores, loser," Ganyani yelled.

"Fuck you!" cursed Kimathi, using the car's wipers to remove Ganyani's spit from his windscreen. "You must know that from now on, you're on my shit list. I'm watching you closely."

With his left fist still clenched in anger, Kimathi drove off.

Chapter 29

Had it not been for Sechaba, who had insisted on leaving, Kimathi would still be sitting at Pigalle in Melrose Arch, absorbing enough whisky to exorcise the unsettling image of his fight with Ganyani. He had not eaten as he was too full of bitterness to put anything in his stomach, but, despite this, the whisky had still done nothing to calm his nerves.

It was ten minutes past nine when Kimathi looked at the dashboard clock. While waiting for the robot to turn green at the M1 bridge by Corlett Drive, he remembered his medication. The lights turned green, and he swerved the car towards the M1 South freeway. But instead of immediately joining the road, he decided to stop the car. Pulling over, he put on the handbrake and searched for the pills in the glove compartment. When he found the container, he swallowed three pills with some still water. Billie Holiday was serenading him through the speakers. He turned up the volume and sang along drunkenly:

> Southern trees bear a strange fruit
> Blood on the leaves and blood at the root

The voice from the speakers was like a lullaby to him, and it took his mind on a long sweet journey to Mazimbu, where his mother, Akila, was singing a song to him. In his dream, the whole world belonged to him. His mother was standing on her grave and talking to him, warning him about enemies like Ganyani. She advised him that Ganyani didn't want him to succeed in the vicious arena of South African politics, and that he was out to get him. Kimathi assured her that he was already the king of the Soutpansberg.

The focus of the dream shifted to the Soutpansberg and the coal riches beneath its trees. Ganyani was hanging from one of the trees, his hands tied behind his back. His throat had been cut deeply from ear to ear, but he was still alive, and was begging for mercy and forgiveness. Kimathi ignored him, took out a cigar and lit it. A helicopter passed above them, carrying Sechaba and Senami. It dropped three hand grenades, blowing off Ganyani's arms and legs.

All of a sudden, Kimathi saw Akila again. She was singing "Strange Fruit" to him. He saw images of sweating, hard-working miners. They were labouring painfully with picks and spades, and their faces were painted black from the coal. The labourers were holding spadefuls of coins and coal. Kimathi was happily swinging from one tree to another while giving orders to his workers. Most of the workers were white, and they were under the supervision of Kimathi's trusted Indian foreman. He savoured an image of the white miners desperately trying to obey the foreman's order to chase all the monkeys and baboons from the Soutpansberg.

When the monkeys climbed the trees and laughed at his white workers, the workers asked for Kimathi's help. Ignoring them, Kimathi told the foreman to inform the monkeys that King Kimathi was reclaiming his crown as he was now nationalising the Soutpansberg. His coal-painted white workers tried to talk to the primates again, but the monkeys laughed mockingly from the tops of the trees while revealing their blue and green testicles. Laughter rang out through the dense forest, and suddenly there was a helicopter hovering above the trees. The monkeys ran away. The tree branch that Kimathi had been hanging on to broke, and he fell into a burning pit of coal.

Rubbing his eyes, Kimathi awoke to find himself glaring at a torch flickering beside his Mercedes. A person wearing a reflective jacket was leaning against his car, and his lighted cigarette looked to Kimathi like a distant orange star. He ran his hands over his face as if to convince himself he was not dreaming, but it was only when he saw the cars driving past him at high speed on the freeway that he realised he was not in the Soutpansberg but had been sleeping by the side of the road. He rolled his window down slightly. The air outside reeked of exhaust.

"Do you want some help, sir?" It was an Indian guy who had parked his breakdown van in front of Kimathi's car.

"No, thanks," Kimathi answered, feigning a smile. "I'm fine. I was just appreciating the value of loneliness and doing some introspection."

"Are you sure, sir?" asked the Indian man, unconvinced.

"Yeah." He hesitated. "Tell me, though. I'm facing Joburg south, right?"

"Absolutely."

The Indian walked back to his breakdown van, flicking away the ash from his cigarette. He got into the van and drove off. Kimathi followed with his window slightly open to let in a cool breeze. The laughter of the monkeys that he had heard in his dream still reverberated in his mind as he passed the bridge that separated the East and West campuses of Wits University. His cellphone rang, but instead of answering, he lit a cigar and continued to sing along with Billie Holiday, whom he had put on repeat play.

It was only when he reached Oudeberg Main Road that Kimathi realised he was actually not far from home. Turning into his street, just a few metres away from his house, he groped in the side pocket of the car for the remote for the gate. But as he steered the car into his driveway, he realised that the gate was already open. He didn't give it a thought, though, as he knew he had left in a hurry that morning. Turning off the engine, he stepped out of the car and pocketed the car keys.

Still humming "Strange Fruit" and steadily chewing at the end of his half-smoked cigar, Kimathi walked towards the main door. A couple of steps before he reached it, the automatic floodlight that overlooked the swimming pool suddenly came on, emitting an eye-searing burst of light. What nearly gave him a heart attack was the sight of a young woman sitting on the veranda of his house. The cigar dropped from his mouth onto the ground and he unwittingly crushed it under his right foot.

The woman was somewhere between seventeen and twenty years of age. She was barefoot and had thick make-up on her face. *Shame, probably to hide her acne-ridden cheeks,* Kimathi thought as he walked towards her. As he approached, he could see that she had pierced ears, though she wasn't wearing earrings. Her eyes were watery and had long, thick lashes.

"Hey, what are you doing in my house at this time of the night?" Kimathi asked as soon as he had regained some composure. "And who are you?"

"I-I-I . . ." she stuttered. "I tried ca-calling you on your cell, but you di-did not . . . di-did not answer."

"Calling me for what?" Kimathi asked impatiently. "And, by the way, I don't think I know you. Who are you, and where did you get my number from?"

"My name is D-Dee," the young woman answered, blinking rapidly as if her eyes were hurting her.

"What do you want here, Dee?" Kimathi asked. "And how did you get into my yard?"

"The g-gate . . ." Dee pointed towards the street. "The g-gate was open, so . . . so I thought that instead of sitting on the cold street and looking like a thief, I thought . . . I thought I should enter before it rained and wait for you here."

Kimathi shook his head drunkenly – he was getting impatient with the stuttering girl. His nose caught a disgusting smell coming from her armpits. *Indeed, bad condition and time do not favour beauty*, he thought to himself as he took a step back.

"I've been sent b-by my sister," Dee said, holding out a letter to Kimathi. "S-she was a domestic worker here. Her name . . . her name is Moliehi. S-she said if I talk to you, you might give . . . might give me a job."

"Your sister sent you here?" Kimathi looked puzzled.

The woman nodded as Kimathi took the letter from her. It was only then that he noticed that Bassonia ants were crawling all over her hands.

Kimathi opened a dirty envelope that had crumbs of pap stuck to the seal. As he removed a letter from the envelope, a picture of a baby boy fell to the ground. He picked it up and scrutinised it. The baby was about eighteen months old, and was clothed in a nappy made from a white plastic bag. He shook his head and began to read the letter, which, strangely, was written in red ink. It talked about his son, Kalushi. His mother, Moliehi, had named him after Kimathi's favourite comrade, Solomon Mahlangu, the letter said. Moliehi had overheard him at a party saying that he and his friend Comrade Ludwe loved Solomon Mahlangu. Moliehi had decided to call their son by his favourite struggle hero's Ndebele name. The letter also pleaded with him, saying that the boy was suffering and that Moliehi had decided to send her sister to Kimathi for help. Perhaps he could give her the domestic worker's job? *Say hi to Madam Anele, and tell her I'm sorry for sleeping with you behind her back*, the letter concluded.

Kimathi folded the letter and offered Dee a slight, meaningless smile. She gave him a broader one in return.

"I can't have you here," Kimathi said, staring at Dee's long nails, which were black around the edges. "There is nothing I can offer you."

Dee began to cry and her teeth started to knock against each other as if she was cold. Kimathi felt for her.

"Why are you not wearing any shoes?" he asked.

"Because I-I-I've got . . . I-I've got the ancestral calling and I-I-I'm not supposed to wear shoes," she said, looking down at her cracked feet. "I-I sweat a lot and my feet . . . my feet swell if I wear shoes."

"If Moliehi is your sister, how come she didn't mention you when she was working here?" Kimathi enquired, not looking convinced. "In fact, she told us that she didn't have a family."

"I think . . ." Dee paused. "I think that was after the family had fought," she said. "There was a rift in the family and s-she . . . s-she ran away to Joburg. Now she relies on my father's pension for survival."

"So, where is she now?"

"In Qwaqwa, sir. Where . . . W-where we come from."

"You mean she's not from Lesotho?" Kimathi looked surprised.

"N-no." Dee shook her head vehemently. "But the area is not far from the Lesotho border."

Silence fell. Dee looked at Kimathi with pleading eyes, but he avoided her gaze and instead looked at a distant point over her left shoulder.

"Listen, you can sleep here tonight in the domestic quarters while I decide," Kimathi finally said, pointing at the cottage behind the house.

"Thank you, sir." Dee nodded appreciatively.

"I'm not saying you can live here, though," Kimathi added quickly. "This offer is only for tonight because it's already late. But tomorrow you must leave, understand?"

"I understand, sir." Dee nodded again. "Thank you, sir. You're so kind."

"For now, you can use the bathroom in the domestic quarters and take a bath. It is open, and you may use anything that is there," Kimathi said. "Have you got any luggage?"

"No, sir." Dee shook her head.

"Have you eaten?"

"I have, sir. Thank you."

Kimathi looked at his watch. It was already five minutes to midnight. Fishing his house keys out of his pocket, he made his way over to the house, unlocked the front door and stepped inside. In the bar, he opened a new bottle of Glenfiddich. He looked out at the pool, where the glaring automatic floodlight had turned the night into day. He saw an owl sitting on the wall next to the swimming pool, and this frightened him. A huge rat scampered along the wall and disappeared behind an overflowing rubbish bin next to the cottage. A black cat appeared out of nowhere and stood on the wall separating Kimathi's garden from that of his neighbour. It waited there for a while as if trying to figure out where the rat might have gone. The owl looked on from a distance, but flew away when the cat approached.

Kimathi turned away and poured himself another drink. He had downed the first in one go. He looked outside again for any sign of the cat and the owl, but they had disappeared. Instead, Kimathi saw Dee standing by the swimming pool dressed in a white gown. As he rubbed his eyes and opened them again, Dee was already taking off the gown. She stood naked at the edge of the swimming pool, facing away from him, as if ready to swim. Kimathi stood by the window and scrutinised her. She had slim legs, a flat butt and big shoulders. Definitely not his type, he thought. As he watched her, she plunged into the pool.

Kimathi had just poured his fifth glass of Glenfiddich when he heard Dee scream for help from the swimming pool. The glass dropped from his hand and smashed on the floor and he ran out of the bar to the pool. Her face was chalk-white by the time he dragged her from the water. There was a fresh gash on her left cheek next to the eye; he assumed she had banged her head against the edge of the pool. Screaming her name out loud, Kimathi tried to resuscitate her, but she was already dead.

Chapter 30

Sechaba was sitting alone in his Northcliff mansion watching one of the DStv news channels. His wife, Cornelia, had left that morning to go to Lichtenburg, a small platteland town in the North West, to visit her ailing father, Johannes, a well-known maize farmer in the area. Cornelia had been reluctant to make the journey, but had given in after her mother, Wilhelmina, had insisted that her father could die any day. According to Wilhelmina, Johannes had expressed a wish to see Cornelia and her brother, Herculaas, before he died.

Cornelia had left their three-year-old son, Castro, behind. As a staunch member of the AWB, Johannes had always been clear that no black person could be a member of his family. On the day that Cornelia had insisted on marrying Sechaba, it is said that Johannes went to the Lichtenburg Town Hall and prayed for three full hours in front of the twice life-size statue of his hero, General Koos de la Rey. After that, he had called his daughter a "traitor to the volk" and disowned her.

Although Wilhelmina had also failed to attend her daughter's wedding, she had at least sent their domestic worker, Meisie, and Seun, their farm labourer, to show her support. Herculaas had defied his father's orders and attended his sister's wedding, which had been held in Mangwanani River Valley, Hartbeespoort, in 2002. It was on that day that Herculaas had met Kimathi, Sechaba's best man. Herculaas had brought his friend George Tsongas to the wedding, and had introduced him to Kimathi and Sechaba. This was how the three had become business partners.

Cornelia's relationship with her father had deteriorated further when Johannes heard that she had named her son Castro, after a man Johannes regarded as the "worst terrorist on earth".

Wilhelmina had also tried to talk her daughter out of the marriage "for the sake of the family", but without success. Cornelia did not budge, and had been married to Sechaba for the past five years. They had met while she was doing her PhD at RAU in 2000. Sechaba was still working at The Movement's headquarters in the city centre when Cornelia called to interview him for her thesis, "Exiles and Inxiles: The Emergence of Affirmative Tenderpreneurship in South Africa", which she published in 2002. Sechaba had taken her to numerous rallies, where she was able to interview most of The Movement's leaders. After a few months, the two had started dating, and eventually Sechaba proposed.

Sechaba picked up the remote. He was getting tired of watching the news – it was all about the upcoming local government elections. Most political commentators were busy predicting that the ruling party might lose Cape Town metro to the Democratic Alliance. *Bullshit, the ANC will rule until Jesus comes*, Sechaba thought before he changed the channel.

Putting the remote down, Sechaba poured a glass of Taittinger Brut to wash down the takeaway lamb shank and vegetables he had picked up at Pigalle earlier that evening. But before his lips could even touch the champagne glass, his cellphone rang on the coffee table next to the remote control. He looked at the caller's identity and saw it was Kimathi.

Sechaba ignored the call four times, but when the phone continued to ring he reluctantly answered. It was sixteen minutes past one in the morning.

"Comrade," he answered, faking tiredness in his voice.

But it was not Kimathi. The caller had an Afrikaans accent and Sechaba panicked as he tried to place the voice on the other end of the line. "Sorry to disturb you, sir, but . . ." said the caller.

"Who's this?" Sechaba asked, loosening a piece of lamb from between his front teeth with a fingernail.

Sechaba was only too aware that Kimathi had a nasty habit of drinking with strangers at his home as he would often call and introduce him to people he didn't know. However, the caller did not seem like the kind to hang around and drink with Kimathi. Sechaba listened.

"Hi, sir, I'm Willem Steinmans, Mr Tito's neighbour here in Bassonia," the caller said calmly.

Sechaba breathed a sigh of relief and picked up the remote to reduce the volume on the television set.

"Is everything all right with him?" Sechaba asked.

"You'll have to come and see for yourself, sir," said Steinmans.

"Where are you?"

"I'm at his house, here in Bassonia. Let me give you the directions."

"On my way," Sechaba said and dropped the call.

Sechaba did not waste time. Five minutes later he was in his Range Rover on the N1 South. He tried to chase from his mind the horrible pictures of what might have happened to his friend, but the resulting blank space felt awful too. The hole that had opened in his consciousness continued to grow until he arrived at Johannes Meyer Drive.

Kimathi's house was on a hill overlooking The Glen shopping mall and the rest of upper-class Bassonia. The neighbouring suburb of Glenanda looked both more prosperous and more settled from here.

Sechaba could not use Kimathi's driveway as there was an ambulance parked there, so he left his car in the street. He was scared at first, but relaxed when he saw his friend conscious, though obviously confused, on the stretcher. Two paramedics, a guy and a woman, were lifting him into the ambulance. Before Sechaba could ask anyone about Kimathi's injuries, a well-built white male of about fifty-five approached him. The man had a bushy moustache, and was a dead ringer for Pik Botha. He was followed by a woman of much the same age, whose well-applied make-up failed to mask the fine wrinkles and liverish blotches on her chalk-white face. Sechaba had guessed she was the Pik Botha lookalike's wife even before he introduced her as such.

"Hi. You must be the gentleman I called thirty minutes ago?" the man said, extending his hand.

"Willem, I presume?" Sechaba replied, shaking the man's hand. "I'm Sechaba More."

"I didn't know who to call, so after I called the ambulance I dialled the last person he had spoken to on his cell," said Willem after releasing his hand from Sechaba's and introducing his wife, Jacoba. "That's when you answered."

"You did well," acknowledged Sechaba with a nod.

At this point, the male paramedic came to join them. He took some details from Sechaba.

"Is he going to be all right?" Sechaba asked as the paramedic scribbled the information he had given him on a clipboard.

"Yes," said the paramedic, placing a consoling hand on Sechaba's shoulder. "We are just going to check that the water did not damage his lungs, since he had been drinking when he nearly drowned." He paused and looked at both Sechaba and Willem. "Who's coming to the hospital? Is it you, Mr More?" he asked, referring to Sechaba's name on his clipboard.

"I'll follow you after locking the house up," said Sechaba, pointing at the open kitchen door. "Which hospital is that, by the way?"

"Milpark, sir."

"Shall I bring his clothes?"

"Please do."

The ambulance was idling in the driveway and there was no time for Sechaba to ask further questions. He watched as the paramedic left them to join his colleague in the vehicle. His eyes followed the ambulance until it disappeared down the hill towards the shopping centre. He turned to Willem.

"What happened to him?" Sechaba asked, trying to confirm what he already suspected. "Did he fall into the swimming pool or something?"

"Well, it was Jacoba who first noticed something strange was going on. She saw him from our bedroom window." Willem pointed at window of an upstairs room in the house next door. "She saw him standing outside naked, reading the Bible. He was reading it very loudly."

Jacoba looked at both Sechaba and her husband as if she knew something that they should know about. She pushed her brown hair back from her face and cleared her throat dramatically. She had a long nose that looked like a parrot's beak.

"Ja! I was surprised to see he had been swimming on such a cold night and that he was carrying a Bible," she said. "He was also holding a bottle of whisky and kept calling the name Dee." She paused and looked at Sechaba. "Did his wife die or something? He sounded drunk and he was busy pleading with Dee not to die. You should have seen him." She paused again. "He acted as if he was talking to someone, and yet he was by himself. Poor thing!"

"No. In fact, they are divorced. And her name is Anele," Sechaba said, "not Dee."

"Shame! It must be very hard for him to live alone in this huge house," Jacoba said sympathetically. "No wonder he is absent-minded these days. He has developed a habit of leaving his car in the street at night, and he does not lock his gates. He seems to have forgotten that South Africa is a very dangerous place."

"How often does he do that?" asked Sechaba curiously.

"Quite often," answered Willem.

"And, ja," said Jacoba, looking at her husband, "the curtains of his house are always either half-drawn or not drawn at all. And his letters are always piled in the mailbox." She paused and pointed next to the wall. "It will attract criminals, you know. Look at the lawn; it is overgrown. It is different from the time his domestic worker and wife were here. But what worries me most is that he no longer takes his rubbish out." She looked at Sechaba for a response, and then continued, "The rats are starting to breed in his yard and ours."

Sechaba felt that the couple were exaggerating. He was aware that they were not on good terms with Kimathi as a result of two embarrassing incidents. The first had occurred the week Kimathi and Anele moved into their multi-million-rand mansion in 2002. They had decided to give the house a new look by repainting it – the previous owner, a Mr Redelinghuys, who had moved to Perth, had had very conservative taste. According to Kimathi, Willem had seen him and two other guys painting the house one weekend, and had assumed that he was Mr Redelinghuys's employee.

It seemed that, by selling the house to black people, Mr Redelinghuys had broken the pact that he and Willem had agreed upon some fifteen years earlier, during the transition from the apartheid state to the rainbow nation.

Assuming that Kimathi was just an employee of Mr Redelinghuys, Willem had approached him and told Kimathi that he had a painting job for him. He asked Kimathi to come and give his daughter's room a new look after he was done at the Redelinghuys place. Willem said that his daughter, Natasje, wanted bright yellow, as she was writing her matric exams that year. Willem and Jacoba were convinced that the colour would help their daughter's mind absorb things more easily. Although they did not agree on a fee, Kimathi had accepted the offer. In Kimathi's words, he had wanted "to spite Willem, and show him that he should not judge people by the concentration of melanin in their skin".

A day later, dressed in his overalls, Kimathi had gone to his new neighbour's house and completed the painting work. Willem had given him three hundred rand for a job well done, but Kimathi had politely declined the money. Willem only found out days later that Kimathi was actually the owner of the mansion next door when he saw him drive out in his BMW, wearing a very expensive suit.

The second incident had occurred shortly after the first and had ended up in court. Kimathi had organised a party to celebrate winning the tender to fix the potholes in Bassonia. A sheep had been slaughtered to thank the ancestors, and the noisy party had gone on into the wee hours of the morning. Willem had lodged a complaint with the authorities, claiming that the slaughtering had been traumatic for his family, especially for his daughter Natasje, who was about to write exams. Although she had passed her matric, Willem and Jacoba had argued that Natasje could have received more distinctions had it not been for the slaughter of the poor sheep. He had therefore decided to sue Kimathi.

The matter was eventually thrown out of court due to lack of evidence and on the principle that people should be allowed to practise their customs and traditions freely. However, Kimathi had been given a warning by the court that his rights must not infringe on other people's rights, and that he should take this into account in future. In effect, this meant that Kimathi had to apply for a permit to slaughter an animal on his own property. Since then, his relations with the Steinmans had not been good.

Sechaba walked along the edge of the heart-shaped swimming pool towards a white plastic lounger. On it were Kimathi's clothes, and not far away he spotted a bottle of Glenfiddich single malt. He remembered Kimathi boasting about it a few weeks earlier. As he picked up the bottle, Kimathi's words echoed in Sechaba's mind. Kimathi had claimed to have bought the bottle for twenty-eight thousand rand, and had boasted that there were only three in the whole country. Sechaba and Kimathi had agreed that they would open the bottle after they won the Soutpansberg tender.

Next to the bottle were two glasses, both containing whisky. Sechaba wondered who his friend's guest might have been.

"Are you sure he was alone?" Sechaba asked as he examined one of the glasses. "To me, it looks like he had some company."

Jacoba shook her head. "When I saw him from my house he was alone," she affirmed, but doubtfully. "But someone could have been here earlier."

"I'm asking because I see two glasses here."

"Well, after we tried to resuscitate him, I did help myself to half a glass of that stuff," confessed Willem, rubbing his moustache and smiling apologetically. "The kitchen door was open, so I got myself a glass."

"Oh, I see."

On the other side of the pool, Sechaba spotted a Bible. Walking over, he picked it up. A red pen had been used to underline a passage in Judges – the story of Delilah and Samson. The pages were wet, but he could still see the underlined passage:

> Then she said to him: "How can you say 'I love you' when your heart is not with me? You have mocked me three times now and have not told me what makes your strength so great." So he told her his whole secret, and said to her: "A razor has never come upon my head; for I have been a Nazarite to God from my mother's womb. If my head were shaved, then my strength would leave me; I would become weak, and be like anyone else."

After reading the passage, Sechaba became frightened. *Something is not right with Kimathi*, he thought. He had never heard him speak of the Bible before. Sechaba was convinced that the only passages of Scripture his friend knew were the Lord's Prayer and the Ten Commandments.

Looking at his watch, Sechaba realised it was quarter to two. He thanked the couple for their help and gave Willem what was left of Kimathi's Glenfiddich. Willem poured out copious thanks as he admired the bottle. His wife smiled sympathetically at Sechaba as he strode towards his Range Rover.

"Let us know if there is anything we can do," said Jacoba. "May the good Lord be with your friend!"

"Can you just keep an eye on the house for the time being, just until I get someone?" Sechaba responded as he opened the Range Rover's door.

"Will do," said Willem. "Please keep us posted."

"Sure will."

"Thanks for the drink," said Willem, holding up the bottle.

Sechaba drove off, leaving a cloud of fumes behind.

Chapter 31

Amilcar Cabral camp, Kwanza Norte province,
Angola

"Comrade Bambata would never say such a thing. Besides, it's not the truth."

"Fortunately we have a written affidavit," said Comrade Idi.

"I can't believe you want to punish me on hearsay evidence. It's as unfair as what the apartheid government is doing to our people back home."

"Unfortunately we have to eradicate the spies in our midst."

"I'm not a spy."

"That's not what Comrade Bambata said to us," Comrade Pilate said. "He confessed that you were both spying on The Movement. We know that this is a sin that deserves a death sentence, but we have pardoned him in return for his full co-operation. His sentence has been commuted. You are on your own."

"Even if he had confessed, I think I deserve justice. You can't force one comrade to say something and then use that to punish innocent people. It's like burning the whole house to cook just one pig."

Idi and Pilate looked at each other and laughed.

"I'm glad you understand the law and that you're a pig," said Idi. "But you seem to forget what the law of common purpose says. At least, as the apartheid government back home uses it. For your information, the law of common purpose states that if a group of pigs connive and agree on a course of criminal action, and that action is carried out, then all the pigs are guilty to an equal degree. It does not matter which pig did what."

"But I am innocent."

"We don't care," said Pilate. "Our counter-intelligence has reliable evidence that you stole documents from The Movement and passed them on to your handlers."

"But you told us that all the documents had been destroyed in the raid."

"According to Comrade Bambata they did not all burn," insisted Idi. "You stole some of them before the raid."

"You know that is a lie."

"Like I said, we don't care."

Lady Comrade Mkabayi stole a glance at the two men. Her expression was beyond hurt and she looked scared. Everyone in the camp knew what Pilate and Idi were capable of.

"I want my freedom," she said finally. "And I want it now."

"When you're here, Delilah, you must only think of us and the five keywords." Pilate paused and bent towards her. "Re-education, re-orientation, re-habilitation, re-dedication and re-deployment are the words. That's the only way of avoiding death. Otherwise you must forget about your so-called freedom."

Lady Comrade Mkabayi tried to remain calm, but she was afraid of the two men. She began to bite her fingernails. They were black with dirt under the edges. She knew that they meant what they were saying. They had been given absolute power by The Movement to investigate, arrest, interrogate, prosecute and execute anyone they considered a threat to the revolution. She knew her fate was out of her hands.

"But I have done nothing wrong, and you know it," Lady Comrade Mkabayi insisted. "If you still have conscience left inside yourselves, you'll let me go."

"What? So you can continue carrying out your acts of sabotage against The Movement?"

Pilate pulled some mucus through his nostrils and spat it on the floor. It was a sign that he was in a bad mood.

"Let's go, comrade," said Idi, "before this smell in here makes us ill like her."

"But I'm innocent," Lady Comrade Mkabayi persisted as the two left her. "I hope one day you'll realise that what you're doing is very wrong."

Chapter 32

The sun was high in the sky, shining warm and bright through the trees around Milpark Hospital by the time the doctor left Kimathi. It was the second time he had been admitted to the hospital in less than a month and the doctor was concerned that he was on the verge of a breakdown. She had given him some mood stabilisers but they'd also had a long talk, during which she had once again recommended that he see a psychologist. The doctor had also sternly warned him not to mix alcohol and his medication.

With a *Saturday Star* tucked under his right arm, Sechaba arrived at the hospital at about half past twelve, just before Kimathi was discharged. The first thing he noticed upon entering Kimathi's room was that his friend looked thin and haggard. His cheekbones were showing and his beard needed trimming.

"What happened to you, comrade?" asked Sechaba, putting the newspaper down on the table. "You have changed."

"I threw up all night," Kimathi answered, without making eye contact.

"You see what happens when you refuse to eat," Sechaba said, smiling. "You were busy with the whisky at Pigalle yesterday instead of eating."

Kimathi remained tight-lipped, as if his ears had not registered what Sechaba had said. Rubbing his eyes, he stood up and walked to the window to get a clear view of the day. He could still smell the whisky and cigars on his breath. Standing by the window, his brain flooded with images of the girl he'd seen at his place the previous night. He started to sweat and shake, and his stomach grumbled. His heart shot up into his throat and he felt like vomiting.

"Comrade, I see dead people," Kimathi said as if talking to himself. "They are following me everywhere. They come into my head uninvited and demand residence."

"What are you saying, comrade?" Sechaba asked.

"I'm not sure if you'll believe me," Kimathi paused and looked at Sechaba to see his reaction, "but there is a ghost that is making me do things. My head is so full of horrible images." He forced a weak smile.

"I'm sure it is," Sechaba said, "otherwise, how on earth do you explain what happened yesterday by the pool at your house?"

"What happened yesterday?" Kimathi asked as if the whole thing was new to him.

"Enough to make you spend time in a mental hospital, comrade," Sechaba answered.

As he sat back down on the bed, Kimathi's eyes said it all. He was not the kind that expressed emotions openly, but this time he looked scared. He kept tapping his right foot impatiently.

"I received a call last night from your neighbour, Willem Steinmans," said Sechaba. "Apparently you were trying to swim at night. You were drunk and naked in the cold water, comrade."

"You have to believe me, comrade. I was trying to save her," Kimathi said, surprised at the impatience in his own voice. "She's the one that was drowning, not me."

"Who is this she that you are talking about?" Sechaba asked.

"She said her name was Dee. She died in my swimming pool."

"Listen, comrade, we are all concerned about you. I asked Anele about this Dee person and she swore she knows nobody by that name." Sechaba paused and looked at Kimathi seriously. "You have to come clean, comrade. If this Dee person is not one of your girls, then seeing dead people, as you put it, might be the only equation that makes sense."

Kimathi shrugged sadly as images of the previous night and his visit to Senami's home kept invading his thoughts.

"Pride is a deadly sin, comrade," warned Sechaba. "You have been ignoring this for a long time now."

"Perhaps you're right, comrade, otherwise why do I keep meeting evil?" Kimathi said mournfully. "I have these strange and incomprehensible dreams at night."

"It is evident in the way you have been behaving lately – first at Comrade Ludwe's memorial, and now this. You have been in hospital twice already this month. Maybe your ancestors are trying to tell you something."

"Well, comrade, I guess every person must follow their fate. I cannot change what has already been decreed by my ancestors."

Kimathi's eyes were cast downwards as if he was looking deep into his soul. "I think I'm going to thwasa and be a sangoma. I presume that's my destiny." Kimathi paused as if trying to think of a way of rephrasing what he had just said. "I keep dreaming about my ancestors in Tanzania and Dimbaza, and maybe they are telling me something. I suppose I was not introduced properly to my Xhosa ancestors when I came back into the country. Or maybe my parents want me to erect tombstones for them in Mazimbu, or bring my father's bones and spirit back home. I don't know, but I must do something."

"Yeah," Sechaba nodded, "you could be right, with all of this bad luck following you. You know, in this world, comrade, scientists, medical doctors, traditional healers and churches, they all tell different stories. I think you have exhausted the medical and scientific world, if you ask my opinion." He paused. "So, what would your next step be?"

"I think I must go see a traditional healer for the answers," Kimathi said, sucking in his breath and blinking. "Do you know of any that I can consult?"

"I can ask around for you." Sechaba paused. "How soon do you want this?"

"I want it yesterday, comrade," Kimathi said as if the thought of speaking about his misfortune hurt his chest. "All I wish for is just to live like a human being again."

"Come to think of it, I guess I have one in mind." Sechaba paused again and scratched his head. "He lives not so very far from here in Zuurbekom. I once experienced something similar to what you're going through. When my grandmother died some seven years ago in Zamdele, we made the mistake of cutting down a grape vine at the back of her house. We had overlooked the fact that it was apparently her favourite plant. I swear that she used to come back to the house at night as a ghost and haunt us. When we went to this traditional healer in Zuurbekom, he performed a ritual and asked us to replant the vine. After that, my grandmother's ghost left us in peace."

"What is his address?" asked Kimathi impatiently. "I want to go as soon as they discharge me today."

"His name is Makhanda," Sechaba said, taking in the look of pain that Kimathi was trying to conceal. "He is well known."

The traditional healer's name made Kimathi's face glow, but he hid his excitement. "You are a true comrade, man." His eyes were wet and he wiped them quickly before Sechaba could see. "I truly appreciate."

"That's it, comrade," Sechaba inhaled and rubbed one corner of his mouth, "friendship should be measured by what men do for one another in the bad times, not by what they share in the good times."

"Do you think our medicine man will succeed where the white doctor has failed, comrade?" Kimathi asked doubtfully. "I mean, both the CAT scans and MRI have yielded no answers."

"You never know, but it's worth it to try," Sechaba answered. "But, comrade, tell me, who's going to look after your house when you go and see Makhanda?"

"Hopefully it won't take that long," Kimathi said earnestly. "But if it does, if it's not too much to ask from you, comrade, I'd appreciate it if you could make those arrangements for me."

"Don't worry, I'll do that," Sechaba said without hesitation.

"I really appreciate your help in these times of need, comrade."

There was a moment of silence.

"Have you checked out the newspaper today?" asked Sechaba, handing it to Kimathi. "Things don't look so good."

Kimathi wet his thumb with his tongue and turned to the second page. There was an article about Greenpeace Africa with pictures of activists protesting in front of the Eskom headquarters in Megawatt Park and at the Department of Public Works in Pretoria. There was a picture of people holding placards standing in front of a heap of coal. Behind them was the sign *SOUTH AFRICA WORKS BECAUSE OF PUBLIC WORKS*. One of the placards read *1 COAL POWER STATION = 17 MILLION TONS OF COAL PER YEAR = HEAVY DESTRUCTION*, while another one demanded *CLEAN UP YOUR ACT AND STOP COAL*. Kimathi read the article, which quoted one of the activists:

> Our action highlights the true cost of Eskom's addiction to coal: environmental destruction at every step, the pollution of scarce water supplies and the destruction of people's health and wellbeing. South Africa does not need coal investment. We should move straight to a future powered by clean, safe and renewable sources of energy such as sun, wind and water. We condemn the proposed coal-fired power stations. Eskom must make the transition away from coal towards a clean and greener future by replacing fossil and nuclear fuels with renewable energy. Eskom should be

investing in people and green jobs, and averting catastrophic climate change instead of locking South Africa into dirty energy . . .

Kimathi finished reading the article, looked at the pictures of the heap of coal and the protestors again and shook his head.

"Bullshit," he exclaimed involuntarily. "These monkeys are mad. Where do they think over three million households will get electricity from? These people are unpatriotic. Do they want Africa to stay a dark continent even though we have resources?"

"It happened yesterday, so I thought I should bring it to you," said Sechaba as if he was answering Kimathi indirectly. "The protestors used three trucks to dump five tons of coal at the headquarters and block the entrance."

"They must all be arrested and put into jail for a very long time," said Kimathi angrily. "Don't these monkeys know that coal is the cheapest and most abundant option we have as South Africans?"

"You know what it means for our tender bid, right?" said Sechaba. "It means that the bloody UN climate change idiots will convince the fucking monkeys in our government that South Africa is the only African nation among the twenty countries that emit nearly ninety per cent of the world's greenhouse gases because of its dependence on coal. This will fuck up our tender bid for the Soutpansberg, comrade. Fuck these goddamn bloody agents of neo-colonialism!"

"All we need is a leader with vision," reckoned Kimathi. "Someone who will not be afraid to tell the climate change monkeys to go fuck themselves and their solar energy."

"You're spot-on, comrade," Sechaba concurred. "But wothout such a leader this will have a serious impact."

Ten minutes later the doctor arrived and told Kimathi that he had been discharged. As soon as he was checked out of the hospital, Sechaba and Kimathi got into the Range Rover and drove off. They had agreed that they should pass by Kimathi's house to collect some things he might need before heading to see Makhanda.

The song "Beasts of No Nation" by Fela Kuti was playing in Sechaba's car. Slowly, Kimathi's heartbeat synchronised with the rhythm of the song until by the time they reached his home in Bassonia he could not tell one from the other.

Chapter 33

Sechaba parked the Range Rover in the driveway.

"I suggest you take only the necessary things," he advised Kimathi as they climbed out of the car. "I won't recommend a suit for you, comrade. Our ancestors don't believe in fashion, but bheshus."

Inside the house, Sechaba proceeded to the bar and settled himself on a barstool. Kimathi entered the bedroom, sat on the bed and stared at the framed picture of himself and Anele. They were both dressed in white and smiling. In front of them was a huge wedding cake, and their hands held the knife together as they prepared to cut it.

Kimathi folded his arms and cast his eyes downward. He put his face in his hands and began to sob quietly. Getting up, he walked to the bathroom and looked at himself in the mirror, examining his eyes closely. They were bloodshot, as if reflecting the pain of his tortured soul.

Going back to the bedroom, Kimathi closed the door behind him and sat on the bed. *Nostalgia has never been so painful*, he thought to himself. He was reflecting on how he and Anele had got engaged at the top of the Eiffel Tower in Paris. It was 29 August 2001. Anele had nearly fainted with happiness and surprise, as she had no idea that he was going to propose. As they'd reached the top of the tower, an announcement had been made in both French and English from the speakers that Anele Mngadi from South Africa had won a prize. Kimathi was standing with her against the railing where a signpost pointed back to South Africa. At that moment a chef from the restaurant downstairs had appeared. All eyes were on them as the chef handed Anele her prize, which was a gold plate that was covered with a lid. When she removed the lid, she saw a glistening diamond ring. Everyone on the observation deck had clapped as Kimathi had gone down on one knee.

"Anele, my love," he had said, "will you marry me?"

"Yes," she had replied, wiping the tears from her eyes.

There was more clapping.

They had wrapped up their night with dinner on a boat on the Seine. That was where she had told him that he was the most romantic man on earth.

Kimathi tried to blink away the memory. Standing up, he opened one of the dresser drawers and looked at the neatly folded garments inside. He came out with a deep blue, taupe and pink bra with a matching G-string. He took the Lancôme Trésor Midnight Rose and sprayed the lingerie before inhaling from it. After sneezing three times, he heard footsteps approaching along the passage.

When Sechaba opened the bedroom door, Kimathi looked at him briefly, then returned to inhaling the scent from the G-string. Sechaba lingered by the door.

"Are you ready, comrade?" Sechaba finally asked, looking at the lingerie in Kimathi's hands.

"Yes, we can go now."

"Are those the items you have chosen to take with you?" Sechaba asked jokingly.

"No," Kimathi forced a smile, "I'm just trying to understand women with these."

"I know. Divorce is always nasty, isn't it, comrade?"

"Not really. It is marriage that is nasty. I should not have been married."

"What I can advise you is that women are meant to be loved, not understood, comrade," said Sechaba, smiling.

"Is that right?"

"Absolutely, comrade. What is there to understand about them? They wear fake hair, false nails and fake lashes, and they buy fake tits, fake lips and get Botox. On top of all that they want a real man."

They both laughed.

"I should have thought about that before I married Anele," said Kimathi.

"Don't cause yourself headaches over them. As long as you know that their G-spot is located at the end of the word 'shopping' you'll be fine, comrade."

"You should have given me romance advice like this before Anele left me," said Kimathi as he stood up. "Now it's too late."

"Comrade," said Sechaba as they walked towards the car, "romance is a fallacy created by lonely poets to make people think that they are cleverer than everyone else. There is no such thing as romance."

As they drove away, Kimathi stared out of the window for a long time. Sechaba followed his gaze.

"You seem to be talking from experience, comrade."

"You don't need experience to know that a woman's idea of an ideal man is a guy who does not get drunk, smoke or flirt," Sechaba said as he twisted the wheel and accelerated. "In fact, their ideal man does not exist in this world, but women keep searching for him because they are big dreamers. All you can do is to coexist with their dreams."

Ali Farka Toure's "Amandrai" was playing softly as they passed Freedom Park settlement. A sign in front of them read *Kimberley 479*.

"Women think that the perfect husband is all they need for a perfect life, comrade," continued Sechaba. "But the problem is that they want commitment before they become loyal to you. What they don't know is that men want loyalty first, and after that they might consider commitment."

"But I was committed to Anele," said Kimathi.

"Maybe that was not enough," Sechaba replied.

"What do you mean?"

"Maybe you should have sent her flowers every now and then." Sechaba laughed. "They like flowers. And you should have tried to go to the mall more often and held her hand in public."

They burst into peals of laughter.

"Is that what you do with Cornelia?"

"Yes. Women always need reassurance. But what they are not aware of is that men talk to women so that they can have sex with them. But women, on the other hand, have sex with men so that men will talk to them. Women always forget that men don't know how to talk after sex."

"At least your marriage has inspired you to new levels of creativity, comrade. Mine was dull." Kimathi could not keep the hurt out of his voice. "The only thing that came out of her mouth during our marriage were problems for me to solve."

"Like they say, comrade: he who has the longest sword will survive the marriage."

Kimathi said nothing. The last statement hurt him, although he did not show it. Instead, he opened his hand and examined his short fingers. He had once been told by a prostitute that short fingers were a sign of a small dick. This had bruised his ego and left him with very low self-esteem when it came to sexual matters.

"You must have the heart for marriage," continued Sechaba. "Otherwise it is a game that you will never win."

Kimathi yawned to indicate that he had lost interest in the topic. Sechaba read the sign well and stopped talking. There was silence as they passed Avalon Cemetery. As Sechaba switched the Ali Farka Toure disc for Winston Mankunku Ngozi's *Yakhal' Inkomo*, Kimathi remembered the last time he had visited Avalon Cemetery. It was 4 February 1995, when he had attended the funeral of Joe Slovo, the long-time leader of the South African Communist Party and the only white man to be buried at Avalon. He had come with Ludwe and other comrades. He had been eager to see the place as his father had told him that most of the students killed by the police in June 1976 were buried there.

As they passed the Soweto and Lenasia off-ramp, Kimathi started wondering about his own death, and whether he would be buried in Dimbaza or Avalon.

"Comrade!" started Kimathi as if trying to free his mind from the perils of introspection. "There is something important that I need to tell you."

"Sure. What is it?"

Instead of continuing, Kimathi peered out the window for a moment as if in deep thought. His mouth hung slightly open for a while. Sechaba glanced at him and said nothing, but maintained a look of curiosity.

"When I was in the hospital, the last time, I talked with the doctor about what is happening to me . . ." Kimathi's voice was empty, dead, like that of a torture victim.

"And what did he say to you?" asked Sechaba, flipping down the sun visor before studying Kimathi's face.

"She told me that maybe I'm suffering from the aftereffects of some kind of trauma. She suggested that I go for therapy."

"What?" Sechaba let out a sound of surprise and looked at Kimathi briefly. Still open-mouthed with astonishment, he turned the CD player off.

Kimathi was silent for a while as if he was replaying the conversation with the doctor in his head. He ran both hands over his face.

"It sounds like some white man's disease," said Sechaba.

"That's what I thought. I decided that I'm not going to some damn therapist who will tell me things that I won't be able to understand. That's why I chose to come to the healer."

"I see. But, do you think you have the symptoms?"

"Not really, but I am scared that she could be right about me. Just yesterday I slept on the roadside and thought I was at home."

"Scary shit," said Sechaba, concentrating on the road.

Kimathi wiped his eyes and stared straight ahead. He fought to suppress the fear, but something made his stomach queasy. He lifted one eyebrow and coughed.

"They say it is precipitated by a stressful episode, an earlier life trauma. There is this dream that always comes to me, and it's very frightening. It's about the exile days, comrade."

"Seriously?" Sechaba's eyes narrowed. "You didn't tell me about that."

"The thing is that I no longer know whether it's a dream or whether it really happened."

"So, what are you going to do now?"

"Simple. I have to confront my past," Kimathi concluded with real sincerity.

They were now approaching Zuurbekom. A big sign – *Western Deep Levels, AngloGold Ashanti* – pointed ahead, and in the distance they could see tall mineshaft headgear rising above the houses.

Chapter 34

Soon after they turned off the N12, Kimathi and Sechaba spotted a plume of smoke billowing upward from a large white house. As Sechaba guided the Range Rover slowly into George Sachs Street, a stab of anxiety pierced Kimathi to the core. He coughed explosively, before suffering a fit of hiccoughing which lasted for several minutes. After making sure that a train wasn't coming, Sechaba crossed the Westonaria-Johannesburg railway line. Their eyes were fixed on a white cloth that hung like a flag from a tall pole outside the large white house.

"That's where we are going, comrade," Sechaba said. "How do you feel?"

"I can't tell a lie, comrade. I'm nervous," confessed Kimathi and coughed again. "But I have to do it; it's a matter of life and death." For the first time in a long while, Kimathi felt imbued with purpose. "All I want is my life back. I don't care what it takes," he said, his voice suddenly low and hoarse.

"You'll be fine, comrade. Don't worry," Sechaba said. "I remember feeling the same when I first came here. But the most important thing is that you must be healed. I want you to start seeing money instead of dead people and ghosts."

Sechaba steered the Range Rover to the left onto another gravel road. He drove for about a hundred metres and stopped outside the yard of the large white house. It was only when they got out of the car that they heard the loud drumming and singing. About ten male and female novices were singing and dancing to the izangoma spirit song.

Wethonga lami ngilamlele   (Fight for me, my ancestor)
Wedlozi lami ngilamlele
Mina angizenzanga   (I did not bring this upon myself)
Ngenziwe abaphansi   (It was given to me by my forefathers)

The novices were dancing barefoot on the dusty ground and singing while they circled a smouldering fire. Three women drummed on gourd bowls with their bare hands as the female novices thrust forward their busts while the men wiggled their butts.

As soon as Kimathi and Sechaba came through the gate, however, the spirit dance changed. The novices switched to a fast, twirling dance that made Kimathi's head spin. One female novice leapt away from the circle carrying a flywhisk made of long hairs from the end of a buffalo tail. Without a word, she took both Kimathi and Sechaba by the hand and led them towards the indumba, a dome-shaped healing hut erected behind the main house. The hut was built of wood, and there were cacti flanking its entrance. Behind the indumba was a neglected swimming pool, with muddy water and neck-high weeds.

"I'm Gogo Mpiyakhe," said the novice, still holding their hands. "What you have is something that cannot be explained in rational, empirical or linear terms. That is why you have come here to seek the cure for your body and soul."

"Siyavuma, Gogo," replied Sechaba.

Kimathi looked at Gogo Mpiyakhe for a few seconds. She was between twenty and twenty-five years old, yet she had introduced herself to them as "gogo", meaning "grandmother" or "ancestor". She wore beads on her left wrist, a white vest and a red-and-black ceremonial skirt.

"We are not here to convert you," Gogo Mpiyakhe said, reading the doubt on Kimathi's face. "We are only here to help those who want help. That is why you must only come here with respect and faith."

"Siyavuma," Kimathi replied, nodding.

Gogo Mpiyakhe instructed Kimathi and Sechaba to remove their shoes before entering the indumba. As they did so, a small black snake crossed in front of them. Kimathi cringed with fear.

"Don't be afraid, they won't bite you," said Gogo Mpiyakhe, taking their hands again. "It's a sign that you're welcome here." She offered a brief smile, and for the first time Kimathi and Sechaba noticed that she had a wide gap between her front teeth.

"Siyavuma," Kimathi said in a relieved tone.

"And you are not to harm them either," Gogo Mpiyakhe said as she released their hands. "They are the spirits of our ancestors."

"How many are there?" Kimathi sounded amazed and afraid at the same time. "It sounds like you've got lots of them."

"There are a few of them," Gogo Mpiyakhe said. She paused and started to count on her fingers then nodded as if in agreement with herself. "Perhaps ten or more..."

Before she could finish the sentence, an albino python slithered very slowly into the indumba. Kimathi jumped, breathing heavily and holding his chest.

"That python is a sign that someone is bewitching one of you," Gogo Mpiyakhe said with confidence. "You have come at the right time and you are in the right place."

"What does that mean?" asked Kimathi, his heart pounding in fear.

"You'll soon understand what I'm saying to you," Gogo Mpiyakhe responded as if the topic did not interest her anymore. "By the way, which one of you has come to see the healer?"

After Kimathi had identified himself as that person, Gogo Mpiyakhe asked him to kneel on the ground and crawl into the indumba.

Kimathi peeped into the hut while rolling his trousers up to the knees. He had expected darkness and was glad to be greeted by mellow candlelight.

"Don't forget to put five hundred rand on the mat first to open my gobela's mouth," said Gogo Mpiyakhe. "You'll get all the answers you want later."

"I'll be in the car, comrade," said Sechaba as he walked away with the novice. "Good luck with the snakes."

As soon as he entered the indumba, Kimathi heard a throat being cleared, followed by a male voice ordering him to sit on the grass mat in the middle of the hut. It took a few seconds for his eyes to adjust to the candlelight but as soon as they did Kimathi realised that he had entered a completely different world. There were medicines hanging in every part of the hut and he was sitting facing a sizeable mirror that was leaning against the wall, half of it covered with a red sheet. Makhanda was standing next to the mirror, wearing only a red cloth around his waist. Hanging on the wall behind him was a bicycle without tyres and some buffalo horns.

Makhanda began to walk around the hut, uttering something in a language that Kimathi could not understand. He was carrying a small drum and he would hit it with one finger, say some words and then spit on the floor. His head was painted red and he had wool tied across his forehead like a bandana. A large white bean dangled between his eyes. He also had wool around his neck, with a gall bladder pendant over it.

"The oracle foretold that I would see you again," said Makhanda in a deep voice immediately after Kimathi tossed five hundred-rand notes on the mat. "I have seen you before, but you're not aware of it."

"Siyavuma! Thanks for having me here, Makhosi!" said Kimathi, sounding nervous.

He wanted to ask where Makhanda knew him from, but decided against it. *Maybe he saw me in his dreams, just like I see dead people*, he thought.

"I saw you coming from far, very far," Makhanda said slowly without looking at Kimathi. "You have a huge problem."

"Makhosi!"

"You're seeing things and hearing things that you're not supposed to."

"Siyavuma! Makhosi!"

"You are from far away, but somebody is following you."

"Siyavuma!"

"My ancestors are telling me that you are having visions and hearing voices."

"Siyavuma."

Makhanda burnt impepho in a small clay calabash, before putting it in front of Kimathi. He then removed the red sheet that covered the mirror and wrapped Kimathi in it. After that, he asked Kimathi to inhale the impepho for good luck. Kimathi sneezed several times.

"Makhosi! So, can you help me?" Kimathi finally asked.

"This requires the utmost dedication and commitment on your part," answered Makhanda. "It's not me who is going to help. You are going to help yourself."

"Siyavuma! Just mention it and I will do whatever it is."

"If you want to be healed, you must remove the fear first," Makhanda said as he removed the sheet from Kimathi's body.

Kimathi tried to look brave as Makhanda put two more clay calabashes in front of him. He put a piece of umkhuhlu bark, about the size of two fingers into one of the calabashes. Striking a match, Makhanda set light to the bark. He then asked Kimathi to gargle a mouthful of ibhuma that had been mixed with water.

Makhanda poured water into a steel bath before placing the large mirror inside it. When this was done, he told Kimathi to spit the mixture he had been gargling into the bath.

"I want you to be strong, and not be afraid of the things you're going to see. Whoever you speak to while facing this mirror, you must not look or sound afraid of them." Makhanda put his hand on Kimathi's shoulder. "Make sure you're brave. If not, they will take advantage of your weakness. Also, make sure that you don't remove your eyes from the bath when speaking."

"Makhosi!"

Makhanda left the indumba promising to return shortly. As soon as he had gone Kimathi started to spit the muti into the bath as instructed. In the mirror, he saw a huge albino python swallowing a piglet. He could see only the head of the piglet as it disappeared into the mighty jaws of the python. Kimathi managed to control himself and conceal his fear, but the python was not fooled.

"Are you afraid?" asked the python, rolling its eyeballs.

"Yes. I mean, no." Kimathi paused. "Are you going to swallow me too?" he asked with a fresh surge of fear.

"Maybe," responded the snake. "It depends."

"Please don't kill me," Kimathi pleaded. "I still want to live."

"Don't worry. You'll soon appreciate that dying is more attractive than living and suffering."

"I don't understand."

"The answers lie deep in your subconscious," the snake said. "And you are the only person that has access, I'm afraid."

"I want to be happy and live a normal life like other people," sobbed Kimathi. "Please leave me alone."

The python smiled at Kimathi. The smile was composed of one part contempt, one part surprise and one part mischief. While Kimathi was still making this out, the snake's features suddenly metamorphosed into those of a woman. She had a scar on her left cheek, and Kimathi was sure that she was the same woman he had seen at Ludwe's memorial service.

"Would you please stop trespassing in my mind, whoever you are?" Kimathi demanded, growing angry.

"If your fate does not make you laugh at yourself, comrade, then you simply don't get the joke," the woman said.

"What is going to happen to me now?" Kimathi asked.

"You are seventeen years late with that question, comrade," the woman said. "The spirit guides have already turned away from you."

"You must stop it, I'm ordering you," Kimathi replied, trembling with rage.

"I can't."

"But why me?"

"Because evil has to be fought, comrade. Otherwise the world will go down in darkness."

"Whoever you are, you are enjoying this, aren't you?" Kimathi shouted, starting to sweat and twitch.

The woman gave him a wink and disappeared.

Chapter 35

As Makhanda re-entered the indumba, bile rose in Kimathi's throat and he vomited into the steel bath. Trembling, he told Makhanda what he had seen in the mirror, and narrated everything he had been through since he had met with the ghost that first night.

When Kimathi had finished, Makhanda made him drink a bitter concoction made from dried green umaguqu berries, before making some incisions on his left cheek. Then he fetched four wooden effigies from beside the door and asked Kimathi to remove one nail from each with a hammer. Finally, Makhanda dipped a paintbrush into a container of syrupy bangalala herbs, whose roots had been boiled in milk, and proceeded to paint over the holes where the nails had been removed.

"Son, there is a hostile spirit attacking you, and it wants you dead," said Makhanda once he had completed the ritual. "It is a dead woman's spirit, and I think I know who she is. I have done a ritual at her home and now she has sent you to me."

Kimathi's heart started racing. He looked at Makhanda, whose expression was neutral.

"Siyavuma," Kimathi said. "I know the hostile spirit is my ex-wife. She is bewitching me so that I will give her more money for the maintenance of our daughter."

"I don't know your wife, but the spirit attacking you is a Ndau spirit. That's what the albino python and the vomiting indicate to me." Makhanda paused and looked at Kimathi's confused face. "Was your wife Ndau, perhaps?"

"No, she is actually Zulu, and she is still alive."

"But this is definitely a Ndau spirit," Makhanda asserted. "In the tradition of the Ndau people, every individual has to drink a liquid derived from the mvuco plant. This is a powerful medicine that makes the individual that drinks it stronger. When that person is murdered, the killing is avenged by his or her spirit if the proper burial rituals have not been observed."

"Siyavuma."

"You must have done something that led to this person's death." Makhanda paused and looked at Kimathi again. "It might have been intentionally or by accident."

"Makhosi! I'm not sure about that."

"Think carefully. It is very important that you remember," said Makhanda as if he was trying gently to elicit a confession from Kimathi. "Have you ever killed someone?"

"In the line of duty, I sometimes had to do distasteful things while in exile." Kimathi paused. "I'm not proud of it, but during the war against apartheid, yes, I killed Boers for our freedom and democracy as well as UNITA rebels."

"Were there women who fought alongside or against you?"

"Many of them."

"Can you remember some of them, like the one that talked to you just now?"

"Not really. There is so much I don't remember from those times. But there was this lady who begged me to finish her off after she was badly wounded by the apartheid forces during a raid on our camp." Kimathi spoke with exaggerated pain in his voice. "A bomb had chopped off her legs and she was bleeding profusely. I felt too much in love with her to stand by and see her in pain."

"And where was this?"

"In a camp in Angola." The words came automatically.

"How did it happen?"

"There were just too many wounded during the raid, and we could not leave our comrades on the battlefield in such agony. The commander instructed me to finish off those who could not be saved. I had to follow his instructions and decide who was going to live and who was going to die. I don't know how many people I shot that day. Some were conscious and some were not. There was this young lady among them who had been terribly wounded by a bomb. There was no hope for her."

"Do you remember her name?"

"I don't remember her birth name, but words can never describe how badly she was wounded." Kimathi paused. "When she looked at me, I realised that there was no hope for her. I had to shoot her. I had nightmares for several months after that, and I still have them now."

"What did she look like?" enquired Makhanda as if he was trying to match the picture of the lady with someone in his mind.

"She was young and beautiful, about seventeen or eighteen years old," Kimathi replied.

"Where did she say she was from?"

"I guess she was from somewhere in Soweto." Kimathi scratched his head, trying to remember. "I could be wrong, though."

"Has anybody in your family died recently, after you saw the ghost of this woman?"

"No." Kimathi shook his head thoughtfully. "Why?"

"The spirits sometimes extend their revenge to members of your family, who may have to pay for your past behaviour if you do not act fast."

As Kimathi nervously considered his future, Zanu came into his mind. For the first time, he concluded that God had set him up. He was convinced that the universe was based upon the wheel of fortune and he was spinning downwards.

"I recently lost a close friend called Ludwe," said Kimathi. "We were in exile together and he also knew the lady that I am talking about."

"You were together at the camp?" asked Makhanda as if his mind was starting to piece things together. "When did you first realise that you were seeing dead people?"

Kimathi thought of Senami for a while and grimaced. He no longer wanted to talk about her; she had long ceased to be a beautiful memory in his mind.

"As I told you, I followed a ghost into a house in Soweto," he said.

"Okay, I see now. Can you still remember the house?" asked Makhanda.

"I think I can remember." Kimathi looked up at the thatched roof as if it would help him to recollect. "It's not far from the Protea North police station."

"We must go there tomorrow, before anything else happens to you. I know the house well, and I have performed rituals there, but I want you to show me the place yourself." Makhanda paused and looked directly at Kimathi. "I don't know what this has to do with you yet, but what is clear is that the lady did not make a smooth transition to her next life."

"Siyavuma!"

"Your ancestors are very strong because the spirit is out to kill you. You must do the right thing."

"Siyavuma."

"Tell me more about the lady you were speaking about. I want to know how you buried her."

"She was buried just like any other fallen comrade. We dug a grave for her next to the camp. There were no coffins or decent burials in exile."

"Do you remember which direction her grave faced?"

"No," Kimathi said, a surprised look on his face. "Is that important?"

"The thing is that when someone with a Ndau spirit dies, their grave must face the east, as they are also worshippers of the sun. Though in some traditions, they face the west." Makhanda paused and tried to correct himself. "What I'm saying here is that this could be another reason her spirit is very angry."

"Siyavuma," Kimathi said with a worried face. "I'm sorry, I can't remember those details."

Makhanda gave Kimathi a feather, telling him to carry it with him until the transitional rites had been performed. He then took a razor blade and made some more small incisions on Kimathi's cheeks, wrists and chest before rubbing a muti he called umzilanyoni on the fresh wounds. He told Kimathi that the muti was to hide him from the ghost.

A few minutes later, Makhanda asked Kimathi to take a short walk with him behind the indumba. Once they were outside, he unrolled a white goatskin on the ground and instructed Kimathi to sit down. One of the novices came with warm water in a plastic bowl and washed Kimathi's hair with Sunlight bath soap. Then he started to shave it with a razor blade.

After the shaving, which lasted for less than fifteen minutes, Makhanda asked Kimathi to dig out a plant, which looked like a large white daisy, from the ground next to the swimming pool. While the roots of the imbhabazane were boiling behind the hut, Kimathi buried his hair at the spot where he had uprooted the plant.

As they turned to go, dust rose up from the spot. The dust coiled upwards like a snake, slowly moving past the fireplace, where the novices were still singing and dancing, and made its way out of the yard.

"We have temporarily managed to chase the evil spirit away," confirmed Makhanda. "But you must not go back to your house tonight. If you do, you will die. I suggest you sleep at your friend's house."

"Siyavuma."

"The evil spirit is very angry, and it is going to wait for you at your house. You must go through a ceremonial purification, otherwise you will die," Makhanda warned again. "You hear me?"

"Siyavuma."

They went back into the indumba and Kimathi watched as Makhanda mixed the boiled imbhabazame root with coarse salt. After Kimathi had drunk a cupful of the concoction, which produced some irritation on his body, Makhanda blew some powdery muti he called "umnqandane wezimpisi" onto Kimathi's face. He then instructed him to return the following morning with two live white chickens and a goat.

"Are you sure you didn't come back with a snake?" Sechaba asked, trying to lighten the mood as they rejoined the N12.

"I came with more problems, comrade," said Kimathi as they drew to a halt at a red traffic light at the R559 intersection.

"Tomorrow I have to come back with two live white chickens and a goat," Kimathi continued as the robot turned green, "and I don't know where to get them."

"Is that what they feed the python?"

"Who knows? I can't even go to my house until the ritual is complete."

"You can come crash by my house for a while," Sechaba offered. "My wife is still away."

"No thanks, comrade, you have already done so much. I'm thinking of booking into a hotel and hiring a car. In fact, drop me at Milpark Garden Court."

"Sure." Sechaba nodded. "There are some livestock farms I know around Walkerville, in the south. How about I come pick you up tomorrow morning, say around five, and then we can buy the goat and chickens there."

"Thanks, comrade, that sounds like a great plan."

Chapter 36

Amilcar Cabral camp, Kwanza Norte province, Angola

The following morning, Comrade Idi and Comrade Pilate dragged two men from the Double Spies block. They buried them alive, neck deep in the hot soil, until only the men's shaven heads could be seen.

"Give us some water, please," one of the men pleaded. "I'm thirsty."

"You should have thought about that before you tried to escape," said Pilate. "You fucking spy."

"I beg you, comrade."

"Okay," said Pilate, feigning concern, "but you must bear with us because the rule in this camp is that we only keep drinking water for human beings and not dogs like you. But I'll try to get you something as you sound so very thirsty."

Walking over to the two, Pilate placed his foot on the head of one of the men and unzipped his trousers. He aimed his penis at the other man's face and urinated. Idi stood there laughing as the urine hit the man's head.

"That's enough water to last the whole day," said Pilate as he zipped up his trousers again. He kicked the man in the mouth before spitting at him.

The man's front teeth were smashed and bloody. For the duration of the punishment, Pilate and Idi enjoyed some mahango beer, which they had bought nearby, in Bondo village. Later that day, the two men died.

Chapter 37

Bingelela, gogo, umhlab' uyalingana (Greetings, grandmother, the world is the same)

Bingelela, gogo, mhlab' uyalingana
Sanibonani, boGogo mhlab' uyalingana
Sanibonani, boGogo mhlab' uyalingana (Greetings, grandmothers, the world is the same)

The next morning, Kimathi was once again met with the sound of drumming and singing as he delivered two white chickens and a goat to Makhanda's place. Sechaba had left him there; Kimathi had agreed to call him once the rituals were complete.

Kimathi was called inside the indumba, where two novices were waiting for him. The novices sang along to the rhythm of the drumbeat as they began to undress him. As soon as Kimathi was naked, Makhanda used a razor blade to make small cuts on his shoulders and buttocks.

Makhanda examined the torn flesh for a moment, then pushed him on to his hands and knees and rubbed some brown herbs into the cuts. Kimathi groaned and clawed at the leg of one of the novices to ward off the pain.

"This should be the last ritual," said Makhanda, still holding a bloody razor blade in his hand. "After this, we are done until Angola."

"Angola?" Kimathi said, gritting his teeth as the herbs penetrated his body.

"Yes, Angola," said Makhanda. "The only way to free you from this spirit is to perform the proper rituals and bury Senami as tradition demands. Otherwise this spirit will continue to haunt you. And those you love will not be safe."

Once again, Kimathi's thoughts turned to Zanu. He couldn't risk his daughter's life.

"Okay," Kimathi finally said. "I will do it."

After about thirty minutes, Makhanda and the two novices came out of the indumba and left Kimathi on his own. It was only then that Kimathi realised that the hut had been cleaned out – all the medicines had been removed and even the bicycle with no tyres had gone.

Makhanda and his novices walked over to the fireplace, where each of them picked up a piece of burning wood and returned to the indumba. Surrounding the hut, they set it alight, with Kimathi still inside. The female novices were then instructed by Makhanda to rescue Kimathi by hauling him out of the flames. Kimathi emerged coughing hard.

As Makhanda led Kimathi to the main house to take a bath, the novices began to sing another spirit song around the fire.

Mthakathi, uvusa abangoma balele	(Sorcerer, you wake up the spirits)
Mthakathi, uvusa abangoma balele	
Inkunzi yomthakathi	(The greatest sorcerer)

After about forty-five minutes, Kimathi and Makhanda drove in Makhanda's van to the house in Protea North that Kimathi had talked of the previous day. It didn't surprise Makhanda when Kimathi directed him to Napo and Lola's house.

As soon as they were in what used to be Senami's room, Makhanda began a ritual, dipping his flywhisk into a bowl of water and then sprinkling drops around the room as he talked to the spirits. The water had been mixed with pieces of aloe. He explained to them that it was for removing bad luck.

"We didn't sleep yesterday," said Napo. "There were crying noises in here the whole night."

"It started with a gust of wind that broke the window in the evening. When we opened the room, everything was upside down," added Lola, pointing at the broken window. "The wardrobe had been pushed over and the mirror had been broken."

After Makhanda had addressed the spirits, asking them to protect the Tladi family against evil, they all went outside. Makhanda took a spade and started digging a hole next to a peach tree. He removed some of Senami's clothes, which he had buried there when he had performed the first ritual at the Tladi home. Some bones and python skin had been buried with the clothes. The sight brought Kimathi's thoughts into merciless disorder.

Makhanda instructed Napo to call upon the names of his deceased relatives, to inform them of the state of the family. Kimathi looked on as Napo did as Makhanda had asked.

"Thank you for your protection and guidance, and please continue looking after my family," Napo concluded. "Tell Senami not to trouble us again. We have had too much grief already."

"And why is *he* here again?" asked Lola, pointing at Kimathi. There was distrust in her eyes.

"Do you still remember what I told you last time, that though she's dead, your daughter's spirit wants to return? This might be the man to help us locate her remains," Makhanda said. "He was in exile too, just like Senami."

Lola smiled briefly at Kimathi. "Did he know my daughter?" she asked hopefully.

"I think so," Makhanda answered. "And he has agreed to help detach Senami from the living, so that she can make a smooth transition to the next life as soon as possible."

"How can he help?" asked Lola.

"This man here might be the last person to have seen her alive." Makhanda paused as they all looked at Kimathi. "She might have been the woman he told me about yesterday." He paused again. "A woman he saw dying at the hands of the apartheid forces. She is now using him to inform you that her passage into the world of the dead has had many interruptions. If the funeral rituals are not correctly done, she may come back to trouble you again and again, like she has already. She is very angry now."

Tears started forming in Lola's eyes at Makhanda's words.

"What are we supposed to do now?" asked Napo, looking confused.

"We must bring her home from wherever she is," said Makhanda. "Firstly, you must slaughter a cow. Then you must go to Avalon Cemetery and speak to her ancestors. They must allow her to return home to rest, because at the moment her spirit is hovering around and will remain restless until this happens. She is becoming impatient with you."

"When must this home-bringing and slaughtering take place?" asked Napo.

"It must happen very soon. But the home-bringing ritual is a tricky one because it must be performed where she died and is buried. And if this man is right, she died in a foreign place."

"How are we going to know where she died and was buried?" Lola asked. "We have tried everything in our power to search for her."

"This man here has been sent by her spirit." Makhanda paused and pointed at Kimathi again. "Since he is affected by the same spirit, he will be our guide. This is a matter of life and death for all of you and there is no turning back."

A visible thrill of expectation shot through Napo. "Did you see my Senami die in exile?" he asked Kimathi.

"Yes, I think I did, sir," Kimathi said, his voice resonating in his mind as he spoke. "She was very brave. Unfortunately I could do nothing to help her as we were under heavy attack from apartheid forces. I still feel bad about it. But we managed to bury her in the camp the following day."

"I think you did your best, given the circumstances," said Napo, giving Kimathi a genuinely appreciative smile. "How did you know her?"

Senami's parents now seemed to have taken a liking to Kimathi and they both looked relieved at the imminent closure of a bitter chapter of their lives.

"Well, it's a long story. We received basic training together for six months at the University of the South."

"So The Movement also sent her to university?" Lola asked curiously.

"Well, not really." Kimathi shrugged. "I'm talking about the training camp called Novo Catengue in Benguela province, Angola. We just affectionately called it 'the university'. I mean, there were several camps in Angola: Gabela, Pango, Funda, Fazenda, Quibaxe . . ." He paused and tried to remember. "I think she had been transferred from Viana Camp when she came to Novo. I was coming from Caculama." He paused again. "After that, we both went to Mafukuzela, then later to Amilcar Cabral. That's where she died, during the raid."

"Was she happy before she died?" asked Lola. "Did she ever talk to you about us, her mother and her father? We miss her, you know."

Lola's questions struck Kimathi's mind like a sharp knife. "I guess she was happy," he said unconvincingly. "She would have played a major role in South Africa today if she had lived. She was a very intelligent young woman."

"All I want is to see my daughter's remains," said Lola, tears streaming down her face. "I don't care what it takes."

"But how sure are you that the person you are talking about was Senami?" asked Napo doubtfully.

"Well, the ghost I saw led me to your house." Kimathi paused and looked at Napo and Makhanda for a few seconds. "I don't remember that the woman I knew in exile resembled the girl in the picture you showed me the other day, but she brought me here, so it must be her," he continued. "Anyway, we will have to talk to the Angolan government and ask for permission to exhume the body. Only after performing a DNA test will we be sure."

"That sounds expensive, and I don't think I can afford it," said Napo. "I'm only a teacher, and my wife is out of work. She was retrenched last year."

"But it has to be done." Kimathi paused and thought for a second. "I will cover some of the costs myself, as this also affects me and my family. Get together whatever you can and I will pay the rest."

"Before I forget," said Makhanda, "is there anybody who is Ndau in your family?"

"No," said Napo, looking at Lola for confirmation. "We are all Sotho in this family, including Senami's grandparents."

"On the day that she left, did you take her to a sangoma?" Makhanda asked.

Napo shook his head. "No. We didn't even know that she had left until she didn't return home. Even then, we initially thought that maybe she had slept at a friend's home, but when we went to her school we were told by one of the students that she had gone into exile together with some of her classmates."

"Well, it is possible that she might have passed by a sangoma to give her strength before she left," concluded Makhanda. "I have dealt with many cases like this, where freedom fighters have come to me for cleansing. Many of them consulted a sangoma on their way into exile."

"As far as we know, she was deeply religious," said Napo doubtfully. "So the sangoma stuff is out of the question, unless her friends made it a condition when they left."

"Okay, then," Makhanda said, "there is a lot to be done here. We must help Senami's spirit take the first transitional steps to life after death. But I warn you that this might take a long time. Your cooperation will be needed. We must perform a ritual to catch the spirit as soon as possible."

Later that day, the four of them went to Senami's symbolic grave in Avalon Cemetery. Makhanda asked Napo, Lola and Kimathi to stand silently together on one side of the gravestone while he removed Senami's personal belongings from the grave and put them into a black plastic refuse bag. Then he asked Napo to take some of the earth covering the grave and put it in an empty jar. They proceeded home with assurances from Makhanda that Senami and her grandmother were accompanying them.

Back at the house, Kimathi, Lola and Napo were given charms to wear around their necks. Kimathi was also given a special herb to bath with, so that the ghost would not follow him anymore. He was still not allowed to sleep at his house, although Makhanda told him that he could now go there during the day. The ritual was not complete, however, as Napo's family still needed to brew traditional beer and slaughter an ox to appease the ancestors. However, this was all to be done once they returned from Angola.

Chapter 38

Amilcar Cabral camp, Kwanza Norte province, Angola

Ngomhla sibuyayo kokhala kuthi du!	(The day we return, there'll be silence!)
Kokhala uVorster!	(Vorster will cry!)
Kokhala uVerwoerd!	(Verwoerd will cry!)
Kokhala uBotha!	(Botha will cry!)
Kokhala imbayimbayi phezulu kwentaba!	(There will be the roaring of guns in the mountain!)

It was about midday at Amilcar Cabral and all the prisoners from the Native and Double spies blocks were standing outside. The singing gained in strength as Comrade Pilate and Comrade Idi walked in front of the assembled inmates, encouraging them. Their intention was to drown out the screams of Comrade Makana. Idi walked around holding an AK-47, a cigarette lodged behind his ear. He gave one prisoner an unpleasant look before hitting him in the stomach with the butt of his gun.

"Sing out loud, you monkey!" he shouted as the prisoner fell to the ground with a thud.

Standing up, the prisoner dusted himself off before he started clapping his hands and singing. Idi smiled cynically at the prisoner, retrieved the cigarette from behind his ear and lit it with a match. He threw the still-burning match into the prisoner's face.

"Let's go, you sellout monkey!" shouted Pilate. "You pretend to be sick when all you need is a little exercise."

In front of him, Comrade Makana crawled naked on the hot alkaline soil towards a mopani tree about thirty metres away. Industrious ants were swarming all over his body, which had been smeared with warthog fat. He screamed in pain.

"Let's go, Banda!" ordered Pilate as he strode over to Makana and kicked him firmly in the ribs.

Comrade Makana, an inmate of the Doomed Spies block, had been given the name Banda at Amilcar Cabral. The Movement believed that his sins equalled those of Malawian president Kamuzu Banda. According to the rumour at that time, Banda was a pathetic sellout who had connived with Botha and the apartheid government to kill Samora Machel, the beloved president of Mozambique, in a plane crash in 1986.

"Go faster, like you did when you betrayed The Movement to the Boers, Banda," Pilate commanded, "or I'll kick your monkey ass again!"

The Movement's counter-intelligence section had concluded its day-long investigation and all the evidence suggested that Comrade Makana was a spy. However, most comrades knew that his only sin had been to question the leadership at his former camp. Why were they letting comrades starve when there was plenty to eat? The leadership had good food and they slaughtered pigs, chickens and ducks. They also bartered bags of sugar for goats and sheep with the nearby community in Quibaxe. When Comrade Makana dared to tell them that they were living a life of luxury, it was taken as a criticism of The Movement's leadership. He was sent to the prison camp.

Comrade Makana coughed violently and vomited blood. He tried to speak, but pink foam erupted from his mouth. Pilate kicked him in the ribs again and Comrade Makana began to choke. For two minutes he twitched and gurgled, breathing in short wheezing spasms. Then, finally, there was silence.

Idi approached and threw his half-smoked cigarette on Comrade Makana's back. There was silence.

"Banda is in heaven," Idi said as he squatted next to Comrade Makana's lifeless body.

Chapter 39

A week after his consultation with Makhanda, Kimathi felt healthy again. He was sitting with Sechaba in their 7th Avenue offices in Parktown North sharing their favourite drink: Piper-Heidsieck champagne. It was Sechaba's idea to celebrate before his friend left for Angola.

Kimathi poured himself another glass of champagne while reading emails on his laptop. He had not checked them for a while and he had more than three hundred unread messages. The one that he was interested in at that moment was from his friend Mongezi, who was promising to take Kimathi to several exotic strip clubs in Luanda.

"This whole thing has exhausted me both physically and financially, comrade," Kimathi said as he read the email. "Look here! Comrade Mongezi says that I have to apply for an import permit for Senami's body through the Department of Health once the autopsy has been performed. I don't know why they can't do it there in Angola." He sipped from his glass and put it down on the table. "Eish, I hate this complicated bureaucracy."

Mongezi, now a South African diplomatic representative in Angola, had been a junior guard at the Amilcar Cabral camp until 1989, when the camp had been closed down. Kimathi had told him of the exhumation of Senami's body in the hope that he could help him speed up the process. All the expenses for the Angolan trip had been paid for the previous day, including the exhumation process, which was to be performed in the presence of Fito, an Angolan pathologist hired by Mongezi at Kimathi's request. Fito would supervise the location of the body. Kimathi had also hired a forensic archaeologist named Josina to plan, direct and execute the operation.

Sechaba pulled his chair towards Kimathi, who was still looking at the laptop screen. Their faces were close enough for Sechaba to see the red veins in the whites of Kimathi's eyes.

"If I may ask, how much has the whole arrangement cost you, comrade?" asked Sechaba, leaning towards the screen.

"It's cost me about a metre," Kimathi answered. He touched his chin and felt his stubble prickling his palm. "They say their currency in Angola is the kwanza, but I'm telling you that they are lying, comrade. They use American dollars for everything and that country is damn expensive. That is why I've spent close to a million rand."

"I hope Napo is helping you with the costs."

"What do you mean 'help'?" Kimathi sounded puzzled. "I had to help him buy air tickets and pay for his accommodation."

"I see."

Kimathi gulped his champagne again and smacked his lips. "You won't believe it, comrade, but I'm putting my house up for sale because of this."

"Your house? For sale?" asked Sechaba, sounding surprised.

"Yes. There is no way that I can go back there after everything that's happened." Kimathi paused. "And, besides, this whole Angola thing has bankrupted me."

"I get you, comrade," said Sechaba, but he looked puzzled. "How long will the whole Angolan thing last? I understand an autopsy can be a very long process."

"It is indeed a long process," replied Kimathi after giving a brief nod. "Fortunately Mongezi knows people in high places in Angola, so it will take approximately two weeks."

"Great!" said Sechaba, looking pleased. "So we'll see you back here soon."

The silence that followed was ponderous and cold. Kimathi looked away from his laptop as if he was still recovering from voicing his decision to sell his house. He had not gone back to Bassonia as yet. Instead, he was living in a rented townhouse in Little Falls.

"So, how much are you looking at?" asked Sechaba, smiling. "Not that I'm interested, but . . ."

"I'm selling it for two metres, comrade."

"Only two metres?" said Sechaba, staring at Kimathi. "Don't you think two million is too little for a big house with four bedrooms, a Jacuzzi, swimming pool, double garage, staff quarters, bar and so many other things?"

"I don't know, comrade. Whoever it was that said our happiness is inversely proportional to the size of our house was not a liar." Kimathi paused to drain his glass. "Anyway, the only victory that really counts for me at this stage is survival. That's why I have to do this Angola thing – in order to survive."

"Don't worry. You'll get over it, comrade. The only trick to survival is hope, and it lies behind the dark patches. Survival and hope are blood brothers. When we lose hope, it means we have lost control of our ability to survive."

"I can't say I'm with you on that one, comrade. More often, hope is the biggest lie." Kimathi paused and pondered. "It is the ultimate lie. People who live on hope always die fasting. This life is a wheel of fortune. And I guess everyone is indebted to someone and must pay their debts sooner or later. No free man exists anywhere and that's the truth of it."

"You reckon?" said Sechaba, sipping from his glass.

At that moment one of the cleaning staff brought in the day's post. Sechaba perused the letters while Kimathi read another email. It was from the five-star Hotel Presidente Meridien in Luanda, confirming his booking for an en-suite room. Kimathi was glad that Napo, Lola and Makhanda had booked themselves into a B&B called Residencial Miramar, on Feo Torres Street – they would be a long way from his hotel.

"Look what we have from Public Works," Sechaba said as he nervously opened a letter. "They remembered us."

"Let's hope this is good news, comrade," said Kimathi, though there was no hope in his voice.

Sechaba started to read the letter and his face suddenly changed.

"What are they saying?" Kimathi asked as Sechaba handed it to him.

> Dear Mr More,
>
> The Department of Public Works would like to thank you for your participation in the Soutpansberg tender process.
>
> It is with regret that we inform you that your bid was unsuccessful. We wish you every success in your future endeavours.
>
> Yours sincerely,
> Ms K Vokwana
> Acting Director-General
>
> **SOUTH AFRICA WORKS BECAUSE OF PUBLIC WORKS**

Kimathi put down the letter and sipped from his glass. He clicked his tongue in disgust and sank deep into depression. "Shit! This is all because of that bloody monkey, Ganyani," he said. "He has also bewitched me."

"Now I believe you," Sechaba concurred, nodding. "Since that man got his mouth to the government's milky tits, he has changed."

"Do you remember I told you that Ganyani was once sent on a mission back to South Africa?" Kimathi said thoughtfully as his fingers played with the champagne cork. "All the comrades he was with got caught and were killed. He was the only one that survived. How come?" He paused before concluding, "It's because that monkey worked with the enemy. I think we made a big mistake by maintaining contact with him."

"But what's the way forward now, comrade?" Sechaba asked, pushing his empty glass away from him.

"I don't know yet, but we have to find a way soon."

"We have already lost too much money on this bid," said Sechaba, removing imaginary perspiration from his forehead with the back of his hand. "Ludwe's kickback for the arrangement of this tender, the consultants, putting the tender together, going to and from the Soutpans . . ." He paused. "That's a lot of money, comrade."

Kimathi nodded in agreement while Sechaba consulted his watch. It was now eighteen minutes to five in the afternoon and two bottles of Piper-Heidsieck champagne stood empty in front of them. Sechaba wanted to leave. He needed to go home to his wife and son.

"Comrade, you must go home and rest," said Sechaba, rising from his chair. "Perhaps we can hook up again tomorrow before you leave for Angola. When you come back, we'll see what to do with the Public Works monkeys. I think we must lodge a complaint. That bitch Vokwana was biased against us because we were friends with Ludwe."

"You're right," said Kimathi as he switched off his laptop and stood up. "Going home is what I'm going to do, although I have to go to Bassonia to collect my passport and some clothes before the sun sets."

They went outside. The air felt heavy, signalling that the rain was on its way. Kimathi looked up at the sky.

"Oh, I nearly forgot, Ganyani is in town," said Sechaba before the two parted ways. "He has invited us to a party his company is organising at his hotel. He said I should tell you to come if you wanted."

Kimathi looked away without answering. He could not bear to think of Ganyani and his betrayal. While Sechaba was busy locking up the office, Kimathi's mind weighed the options of what he should do that night to appease his depression.

"Where is the party?" he finally asked Sechaba uninterestedly as he unlocked his car.

"It's at the Sandton Hilton. Do you reckon we should go and watch those monkeys celebrate their happiness?" Sechaba asked sarcastically.

"I don't think we should," said Kimathi, getting into his car. "Besides, I don't think that monkey and I can coexist anymore."

"After what he has done to us," said Sechaba, "our friendship is over."

"I think we made a bad mistake when we befriended that monkey," said Kimathi. "When we allowed him into our midst."

Chapter 40

Kimathi watched from the bridge at the Emmarentia Dam as the police surrounded the car and pulled Ganyani's dead body out of it. The whole dam had been cordoned off, making it difficult for him and other onlookers to see anything. Sechaba was there as well. A policewoman wearing a wetsuit dived into the dam and a few minutes later came out with the body of a little girl. The girl was about six years old and was still in her school uniform – yellow check dress, white socks and brown shoes. Three policewomen were restraining a pregnant woman who was crying uncontrollably next to Ganyani's body. As she cried, the woman pointed in Kimathi's direction, and when he looked at her again, he realised that it was Anele. She stared straight at him, her gaze unwavering, and then drew her finger across her throat as if threatening to kill him.

"Why did you have to kill her?" Anele asked Kimathi, sobbing. "She's my only daughter. You should have killed me instead, not her."

"I'm not the one that killed her. He did it," said Kimathi, pointing at Ganyani's corpse.

Surprisingly, the girl was still alive. One of the policewomen standing next to Anele pointed at Kimathi. Suddenly her face changed into that of Senami and she picked up the little girl and placed her on the stretcher next to Ganyani's body.

Senami looked at him and smiled. "You did it again," she shouted. "Congratulations! You must be very happy with what you have achieved."

"Oh no, please don't hurt her," Kimathi said. "She is my only child."

While Kimathi was still looking at Senami, Sechaba came from behind him with a long-bladed knife, ready to stab him. As he was about to plunge the knife into Kimathi's back, his mother, Akila, shoved Sechaba aside. The knife fell into the dam.

Kimathi slowly withdrew from the crowd. He started to run and the police and onlookers on the bridge gave chase. His legs felt heavy and he had the impression of treading water. The police and the crowd drew closer, even the heavily pregnant Anele gaining ground on him.

"It's him. He is the killer," he heard Anele and Sechaba saying simultaneously behind him.

"It wasn't me, it was Senami," Kimathi screamed. "It was Senami and Ganyani."

Just as they were about to catch him, Kimathi changed positions and rolled to the other side of his bed. He hugged the pillow and wrapped himself in the duvet. Suddenly, he opened his eyes and realised that he had been dreaming. He was sticky with sweat. When he looked at his Rolex on the bedside table, he realised it was three forty-three in the morning.

Unable to get back to sleep, Kimathi switched on the bedside light and sat up. A tremor of fear floated across his face as he looked around his bedroom. Everything was blurred and stirred up. Standing up, he tried to stretch while yawning. He thought of going to the bar, but remembered that he was at his townhouse, not his mansion in Bassonia. As he stood there, his mind began to race as he tried to make sense of the nightmare he had been having. He thought of Zanu and of Anele's love that he had betrayed and lost forever. He felt lonely, ashamed and sorrowful.

* * *

At eight in the morning, Kimathi decided to give Anele a surprise call. He was not sure if she would answer. The last time he had seen her was when she had come to the hospital with Zanu to see him. Today he wanted to make up with her. The phone rang four times before Anele answered.

"I've realised that running away from my problems is a race I'll never win," Kimathi started cautiously. "I'm leaving for Angola tomorrow in the morning and I'll be gone for a while. I was thinking of paying Zanu's outstanding school fees for the rest of the year." He paused. "How much is still owed?"

"As you know, I'm paying five thousand and fifty per month. You can calculate that by four as we still have four months left."

"Okay . . ." He paused and then continued, "I'll transfer forty thousand to your account today." He paused again and listened for her reaction. When he heard nothing, he continued, "I would love to fetch her at school today, if you don't mind. I just want to spend a few hours with her before I leave tomorrow. I'll drop her at your place later."

"Well," Anele hesitated, "I'll have to phone the school to let them know that you're coming. Otherwise they only know Thami, who has been fetching her for me now I'm on maternity leave."

"I see."

"But I don't think there will be a problem. As long as you bring her here before six and don't run away to Angola with her."

"Trust me, I'll definitely bring her over. And you can call the police if she's not there at one minute past six. Besides, I don't have her passport." Kimathi paused. "One last thing, I'm thinking of selling the house. We can share the proceeds."

"Listen, I'm not interested in your money. Just take care of your kid, that's all I'm asking you to do. Be responsible."

"I know. What I'll do is create an account for her and deposit the money from the proceeds of the sale."

"Whatever you decide," Anele said. "I'll call Mrs Thompson at Zanu's school to let her know that you are coming. She knocks off at half past two, so be there at least by quarter past."

"Thanks. I really appreciate it."

"Please let me know if you decide not to go and pick her up so that I can ask Thami to fetch her."

"I will. And thanks again."

As soon as the call was over, Kimathi switched on his laptop and made an electronic transfer of forty thousand rand to Anele's account, to cover Zanu's school fees.

* * *

At about two o'clock that afternoon, Kimathi guided his car into the parking lot of the Montrose Primary School in Parkmore, Sandton. He eyed the schoolchildren running ahead through the trees by the school gate as he walked towards the reception. His mind was filled with speculation. He wondered what Zanu's class teacher, Mrs Thompson, would think of him when he introduced himself as her father.

When Kimathi reached the reception, the young coloured woman behind the desk offered him a white-toothed smile before calling Mrs Thompson on the phone. As he sat on the pink sofa waiting for Mrs Thompson, Kimathi paged through an old copy of *Fairlady*. The image of the murdered girl at the dam kept intruding on his consciousness until he put the magazine aside.

Five minutes later, Mrs Thompson emerged from the corridor wearing a floral dress and brown platform heels. She had green eyes and freckles on her neck and chest.

"Mr Tito," she said, "I'm Mrs Thompson. Pleased to meet you. Ms Mngadi told me that you were coming to pick up Zanu today." She paused. "She will be out of class in ten minutes. Can I offer you coffee or tea so long?"

As she spoke, Kimathi wondered how far down her body her freckles went.

"No thanks," he said politely.

"Well, if that is the case, let me take you to the class, then."

"No. No. No," protested Kimathi, shaking his head. "I don't want to disturb their lesson."

"Don't worry, they are in the Aerobics Hall at the moment. I just thought I would show you their classroom before she comes."

"Oh, yes, I would like that," said Kimathi as they walked along the corridor.

"I've never seen you fetching Zanu before," Mrs Thompson said, not looking at him. "Are you related to Thami, the man who sometimes comes to fetch her from school?"

"No, no, he is her stepfather," said Kimathi. "I'm her biological father. Zanu's mother and I have been divorced for two years now."

"I'm sorry to hear that."

"Well, I guess it is part of life." He paused and tried to change the topic. "Anyway, how is she doing in school?"

"She is a brilliant learner," Mrs Thompson said with great enthusiasm. "You will see the things she does."

They entered a classroom with several paintings posted on the wall. Kimathi's eyes were instantly assaulted by the different colours and his nostrils inhaled the acrid smell of paint. As he scanned the room, he could feel his pupils expanding.

Mrs Thompson walked straight to a picture next to the chalkboard. She stopped and examined the mainly green drawing of a man blowing out six candles on a cake. Another man, standing behind the first, was looking away, his hands curled into claws. A woman was looking at the cake and her face was not happy.

"I think you've got yourself a young Frida Kahlo at home, Mr Tito," Mrs Thompson said as she pointed to Zanu's name on the drawing.

"You mean Zanu did this?" Kimathi asked as he examined the drawing.

"She is brilliant, isn't she?"

"It's fantastic."

"Especially considering that she is only in Grade One."

Mrs Thompson looked at her watch and then at Kimathi. "It's time now. She will be waiting at reception for you."

"Thanks for showing me her work," said Kimathi as they walked out of the room.

"The pleasure is mine."

They found Zanu at reception. She was wearing her school uniform – a yellow check dress and brown shoes. A brown schoolbag hung on her back. The hug that Kimathi gave her lasted for about a minute.

As Mrs Thompson bade goodbye to both of them with a wave of a hand, Kimathi gave Zanu's little hand a gentle squeeze. "I've missed you, sweetheart," he said, leading her out of the reception. "I promise to come and fetch you from school every Friday from now on."

"I've missed you too, Daddy. My friend Nicole's dad comes to fetch her every day at school," Zanu said, an innocent expression on her face.

"I can only come on Fridays. Daddy works every day except Fridays."

"Will you fetch me in the morning as well?"

"I will try, sweetheart."

"Uncle Thami bought me some paint on my birthday," Zanu said as they reached the car. "I have painted something for you."

As they drove away in the direction of Rosebank, Zanu unzipped her schoolbag and pulled out a picture that she showed to Kimathi. He could not make out what it was, but it was bright blue.

"Oh, that is so lovely," Kimathi said as he glanced at the picture. "You must teach me how to paint like you."

"You must frame it and put it on your wall like the one you have inside the house," Zanu said excitedly.

"You mean *Mary*? I definitely will. Thank you very much, sweetheart," Kimathi said, putting the picture carefully on the back seat.

They turned into the McDonald's drive-through on Oxford Road, where they bought two ice creams. Kimathi watched Zanu as she spooned the ice cream into her mouth. He smiled as he saw her little fingers holding the spoon tightly as if it might float away.

"Uncle Thami takes me to school with Tumelo every week."

"Who is Tumelo?" Kimathi asked, glancing at her as they rejoined Oxford Road in the direction of Killarney.

"He is his son. He is eight years old."

"Is he at the same school as you?"

"Yes, but he is in Grade Three."

"I must see you often, my girl. But Daddy is going to Angola for two weeks. When I come back, we will have another ice cream together," he reassured her.

"I will paint another picture for you."

They had come to a stop in front of a block of flats opposite the Killarney shopping mall. It was about half past four in the afternoon. Kimathi pulled out his phone and dialled Anele to let her know that he had arrived with Zanu. As he looked at Zanu again, the gruesome image of the murdered little girl in the Emmarentia Dam intruded into his consciousness once more.

"I love you, baby girl, and please forgive me for not being there on your birthday," Kimathi said, taking her hand. "When I come back I will get a huge jumping castle for you to play on with your friends. I'll also get you some paint to do more pictures with."

"I love you too, Daddy."

"You're my princess."

As he said that, Kimathi saw a man standing at the entrance to the block of flats with a young boy. Zanu slowly pulled her hand away from his and opened the door.

"Daddy, that's Uncle Thami and Tumelo," she said, smiling. "Do you wanna say hi to them?"

"Not today, sweetheart," Kimathi replied, his smile fading. "Daddy has to run. I'll see you when I come back from Angola, okay?"

As Kimathi slowly pulled away he looked in the rear-view mirror and saw Zanu's hand waving goodbye. He kissed his fingers and placed them on the mirror.

"I love you, my little princess," he said to himself.

Chapter 41

Amilcar Cabral camp, Kwanza Norte province,
Angola

The afternoon following Comrade Makana's death, Comrade Idi and Comrade Pilate were sitting in their office at Amilcar Cabral. On the chair opposite them was Lady Comrade Mkabayi.

"We have called you here because we have an exciting proposal for you," started Pilate, a smile on his face. "We are considering sending you to the Soviet Union for two years to do advanced specialist training."

"Thank you," Lady Comrade Mkabayi said doubtfully, confused by the sudden change in attitude. "What does that entail?"

"Well," Pilate said, folding his arms over his chest, "we've actually selected you for a pilot training course."

"Thanks again," she said, hiding her emotions. "And when do I start?"

"That's a good question," answered Idi indirectly and with a satisfied smile. "Several other comrades have also been selected." He paused and shared a second of eye contact with Lady Comrade Mkabayi. "But it's really up to you as to when you want to go. The offer is there, waiting, you just have to show your appreciation."

"What do you mean?" Lady Comrade Mkabayi asked.

"You're an adult, comrade," said Pilate. "Some things don't have to be explained. It's clear, you know."

"If you want me to sleep with you, just forget it," Lady Comrade Mkabayi said, a sickle of rage cutting through her. "The answer is still no."

"With that attitude, Delilah, you'll rot in here," said Idi, looking at Lady Comrade Mkabayi as if he was ready to spit in her face. "I'll make sure of it."

* * *

Later that evening, Comrade Pilate and Comrade Idi drank a lot of mahango beer. In the pre-dawn dimness, just as a storm started to rumble, they decided to visit

Lady Comrade Mkabayi in her cell. The crickets were singing outside and the rest of the prisoners were asleep, waiting for another day of torture. Guided by their drunkenness and the relentless burning of what they called the "friendly assault weapons" between their thighs, they entered her cell.

Idi immediately undid his trousers, stripped them off and tossed them on the floor. Drunkenly, Pilate slammed the door of the cell shut as Idi knelt in front of Lady Comrade Mkabayi. Despite the noise they were making, they were both convinced that she was fast asleep, but when Idi groped her thighs she pressed them firmly together, giving away the fact that she was wide awake.

As Idi's mighty hands tried to pry her thighs apart, Pilate covered her mouth so that her screams wouldn't wake the other prisoners. He could feel her resistance weakening, but when Idi pulled her underwear aside and entered her, she began to wrestle with him again. Summoning the last of her strength, she bit down on Pilate's hand. Screaming, he jerked his hand away and hit her across her face before sucking his bleeding fingers. At the same time, Idi was withdrawing gloatingly from her, but in that moment of disengagement she squeezed his balls so hard that he also screamed in pain.

In order to save his friend from misery, Pilate hit Lady Comrade Mkabayi in the face for a second time. Retrieving a knife from his trousers, Idi used it to stab her in the stomach. She collapsed, and the two hurried out of her cell.

The following morning, during the camp's routine check, Lady Comrade Mkabayi was found dead in her cell by Comrade Bambata and Comrade Muzi. Her face was a mess – she had a black eye and a big wound that ran across her left cheek. Her legs had been left wide apart and dried semen was visible around her thighs. Without any show of remorse, Pilate and Idi instructed four prisoners from the Native Spies block to bury her. They dug a shallow pit under a thorn mimosa tree behind the Doomed Spies block, and that is where Lady Comrade Mkabayi was laid to rest.

Chapter 42

At eight o'clock the following morning, Napo, Lola and Makhanda made their way through passport control at OR Tambo International Airport. Their SAA flight to Luanda was scheduled to depart at nine forty-five, from boarding gate eleven.

"Where's Kimathi?" asked Makhanda as the three of them walked towards the gate. "Is he not supposed to be on the same flight as us?"

"I have no idea," answered Napo, "but I know he is supposed to be here."

At fifteen minutes past nine the gate was opened and the fligh began to board, but Kimathi was still nowhere to be seen. As they boarded the plane, Napo tried to call Kimathi, but his phone was off. Makhanda suggested that they try his friend Sechaba to find out his whereabouts. Panicking, Makhanda called Sechaba.

"Is Kimathi with you?" asked Makhanda with the cellphone pressed to his ear. "We have not seen him here at the airport."

"No. I last saw him at the office the day before yesterday. He told me that he was going to fetch his passport from his house."

"What do we do now? We are already boarding the plane!"

"I suggest you proceed with the trip. Everything has been arranged and paid for. I think Napo also has Mongezi's details, your host in Angola. He will be waiting for you at the airport there."

"But how will he know it's us?"

"I really have no idea."

The call was interrupted by a female voice: "This is the final boarding call for South African Airways flight A340 to Luanda. Will all passengers for this flight please proceed immediately to gate eleven. The gate will close in five minutes."

Kimathi arrived after all the other passengers had taken their seats. He had a newspaper tucked under his left arm; his hand luggage was clutched in his right hand. He was sweating, showing that he had been running. As he made his way to his business class seat, he caught sight of Makhanda, who was sitting next to a young man wearing headphones. Lola and Napo were in the row behind and Kimathi waved at them before the flight attendant found a space for his bag in the luggage compartment.

Kimathi's seat was by the window. Next to him sat a slim brunette, with K Sello Duiker's *The Quiet Violence of Dreams* lying open on her lap. Kimathi made a mental note of the title, promising himself that he would buy a copy as soon as he returned home. When the woman glanced at him, he pretended to be reading the emergency evacuation card.

Once the plane was cruising, Kimathi ordered two small bottles of Johnnie Walker Black and two bottles of mineral water from the overly made-up flight attendant. As she handed him the drinks, he reclined his seat and opened the service tray. After pouring both bottles of whisky into a plastic cup and taking a sip, he opened his newspapers in an attempt to read. For a few seconds, he froze as Ganyani's mug shot and a picture of a car that was nearly submerged in a dam jumped off the page at him. His eyes bulged with fear. His hands began to shake as he held the newspaper, and he could hear his heart pounding hard against his ribs. Without reading the accompanying story, Kimathi immediately closed the newspaper, folded it and put it in the seat pocket in front of him. Clenching his fists as if he was squeezing the panic out of his body, he reached for his drink and downed it in one gulp before closing the service tray.

Within ten minutes he had fallen into a deep sleep.

Chapter 43

Hiding quietly behind a blue gum tree, Kimathi saw their silhouettes outlined in the half light just a few metres away from him. His stubby fingers, splayed out on the tree trunk, twitched as he watched the two policemen lead Lakeisha towards the pine trees in the park between St. Andrews and Empire in Parktown. They had left their van on the side of the road and Kimathi had parked his car a little further down after following them from the police station.

It was about half past one in the morning and the smell of blue gum was constantly in Kimathi's nostrils as he waited for the right time to strike. As the three figures stopped between two pine trees, Kimathi knelt by the tree trunk and picked up the golf club he had brought with him from the car. He listened, then hunched low and crept forward slowly.

One of the officers lit a cigar under the tree. Kimathi was sure it was one of his Cohiba Behike cigars that they had taken from him and the thought made him angry. He kept watching as the other officer began to pull off his trousers, then his shorts. Lakeisha knelt between them as the one smoking the cigar also started to undo his trousers.

Crickets were chirping as both Lakeisha's hands started to work on the two policemen separately. Kimathi waited. He wanted to be sure that the two men were no longer interested in what was going on around them.

A faint breeze blew, causing the pine trees to shudder. The policeman that was smoking threw the cigar on the ground and began to moan.

As the other policeman bent his head down towards Lakeisha, Kimathi leapt up from behind and, without a word, swung his golf club hard. He hit the policeman who had been smoking on the side of his head. The man fell down with a heavy thud without making sound.

Lakeisha screamed.

"Don't run or I'll shoot," Kimathi ordered, although he didn't have a gun. "Stay where you are and remain quiet. This is not about you."

Timidly, Lakeisha obeyed, remaining on her knees as if she was praying.

Kimathi turned to the other policeman. The poor man seemed undecided whether to pull up his pants up or reach for the gun at his ankles. He just stood there facing Kimathi as he swung his club again and hit him in the ribs.

"Fuck! What do you think you're doing?" the policeman demanded, doubling over in pain.

"I'm teaching you guys how to master your appetites," Kimathi said with a wicked smile, swinging his club again and hitting the policeman in the same spot.

The policeman turned to run, but tripped over his trousers and fell. He covered his head with both his hands, anticipating the next blow, but when Kimathi swung his club again, he hit him in the ribs for a third time.

When Kimathi was sure that the policeman was unconscious, he went for the two guns on the ground. Lakeisha watched him, shivering.

"Search him," Kimathi ordered Lakeisha, pointing at the other policeman.

Turning the policeman over, so he lay on his stomach, Kimathi took a fishing line from his pocket and tightened it around the policeman's neck so cruelly that there was no way the man could survive. Lakeisha watched him, holding the first policeman's cellphone and wallet.

"Is there money in that wallet?" Kimathi asked as he removed the bloody fishing line from the second policeman's neck.

"Yes."

"Search this one too. And when you're done, count the money," he ordered Lakeisha.

Kimathi went over to the first policeman, put the fishing line around his neck and pulled as hard as he could. He was now sure that they were both dead.

"How much did you get?" Kimitha asked Lakeisha.

"One thousand seven hundred and thirty."

"That's all yours," he said, squatting next to the dead men. "Come here and help."

"But..."

Kimathi pointed one of the policemen's guns at her an gave her a killer's grin. "You will do as I say," he said, motioning to her to take the feet of the first policeman.

Lakeisha nodded.

"You talk about this and you die," Kimathi said as they carried the policeman to the car. "You hear me?"

Lakeisha nodded again as they came back for the second man. Within ten minutes, they were done putting both dead men in the boot.

"Now, you must walk towards the garage." Kimathi pointed at the BP garage ahead of them. "I know where you live, and I will kill you if you tell anybody about this. If I have to come to Tanzania to kill you, I will."

Kimathi's heart swelled with satisfaction as Lakeish started to cry. Climbing into his car, he started the engine and drove away down Empire Road. After passing the robot by the BP garage, he opened all the windows to let the sharp chill gnaw at his face. He felt his sense of accomplishment grow as, instinctively, he found himself joining the M1 South in the direction of Soweto.

Chapter 44

Kimathi woke up at about twelve fifteen. The plane was making its final descent into Luanda. He rubbed his face with his hand and stared at the mesmerising ocean rolling towards the beach. The dream about the policemen had scared him. Panic was rising so hard within him that he felt he was choking on it. He sat there in silence, but the sound of the plane as it decelerated made him feel like he was bleeding through his ears. Looking down, he caught sight of the newspaper in the seat pocket in front of him. Immediately he felt the burning wrench of his own stomach as nausea attacked him. Cold sweat broke out on his temples. The lady next to him closed the book that she had been reading and looked at him. He tried hard to smile at her, but he was sure she could see the fear in his eyes.

As the plane turned towards the airport, Kimathi caught sight of Kinaxixi Square, where the Portuguese had beheaded slaves centuries before. It was only then that his mind temporarily surrendered to reminiscence, as he remembered The Movement's cultural band that used to perform for the citizens of Luanda in the square. He also remembered the times when he and Comrade Ludwe would leave the camp on the pretext that they were going on a mission, but would end up at the beach, checking out the women in bikinis. The thought was momentarily therapeutic.

As soon as the plane touched down on the long, wide runway of Quatro de Fevereiro International Airport, the flight attendant's voice welcomed them to Luanda in English and Portuguese. Kimathi drank one of his bottles of mineral water to try and calm himself. It felt strange to be back in Angola after such a long time. He had come here for the first time in 1986. Kimathi remembered the day well. He had arrived on a military plane from Tanzania. Immediately after landing, he and the eleven other freedom fighters on the flight were put into a military truck and taken to Mafukuzela Camp near Malange, where he had stayed until the fateful day of the raid by the SADF paratroopers.

As soon as the pilot had shut down the engines, there was the sound of seat belts being unbuckled. Many of the passengers switched on their cellphones.

After disembarking from the plane, Kimathi, Napo, Makhanda and Lola waited to have their documents stamped at passport control before making their way to the baggage carousel area in the terminal building.

"We were worried about you this morning," said Makhanda. "I never thought you'd catch the flight."

"I had a busy day yesterday," answered Kimathi curtly. He was still sweating visibly and his bloodshot eyes flicked this way and that.

After collecting their bags from the carousel, they followed Kimathi to the customs area, where a uniformed police officer raised his hand to stop Makhanda. He was wearing a grey shirt with his ID photo pinned to one of the pockets.

"Stop," the policeman said to Makhanda.

Makhanda looked at the man as if he had just had a brain fart. The man took Makhanda by the arm and began to speak in Portuguese, pointing at his medicine bag.

"Uthini lo? What is he saying?" asked Makhanda in both isiZulu and English.

"Where from are you, sir?" asked the man in broken English, leading him to one side.

"Angimuzwa uthini? I can't hear him," said Makhanda as he glanced over his shoulder at Kimathi.

"Just go with him," said Kimathi. "He probably thinks there are drugs in your bag and he wants to search it."

Makhanda uttered an obscenity in isiZulu as he was escorted to an interview room. Kimathi followed them, but the policeman told him to back off in Portuguese.

Within ten minutes Makhanda was out of the room, the plastic wrap removed from his bag.

Clearing customs and immigration took about an hour. Finally, leaving the air-conditioned confines of the international arrivals hall, they emerged into the Luandan humidity. There were a number of people outside the sliding glass doors of the customs area. Some carried signs with the word *Taxi* written on them while others had boards and papers with people's names on them.

Mongezi was standing next to a white Land Cruiser wearing a short-sleeved white shirt and a black tie. He had light stubble over his chin and a short thick neck that was complemented by thin red lips. He also had a drinker's bloodshot eyes, hidden behind black-rimmed spectacles. As soon as he saw Kimathi, Mongezi stretched out his arms to embrace him. The hug lasted for about a minute. Kimathi felt his clothes sticking to him because of the heat and humidity.

"*Bemvindo*, comrade. Welcome to Angola," Mongezi said as he released Kimathi.

"Thank you."

"*O que se passa*, comrade?"

"I'm good. And you?"

While Kimathi was putting his bags in the Land Cruiser, Mongezi extended his right hand to greet the others. Napo took it tentatively as if assessing the greeting. With a forced smile on his face, Mongezi squeezed Napo's hand a bit too tightly as if he was trying to establish an instant camaraderie with him. He shook Lola and Makhanda's hands with equal enthusiasm.

"Welcome to Luanda," said Mongezi as he ushered them all into the Land Cruiser. "I'm sure you'll enjoy our city."

"Thank you," said Napo, "but I don't think we will be able to enjoy that much as we have a long journey tomorrow."

"I know, but Quibaxe is not that far from here," said Mongezi as he started the car and pulled away. "It's less than two hundred kilometres, and will only take us two hours if we're lucky with the traffic."

"I think we have to rest for tonight," said Napo, looking at his noticeably tired wife. "Maybe when we come back from there we can go around the city a bit."

"But I'm sure you wouldn't want to miss out on the excellent calulu de peixe at Pimm's. How about I come and fetch you around nine tonight at your place?"

"What's that?" asked Makhanda.

"Oh, it's a delicious dish of fresh and dry fish. It's cooked with okra and spinach with a dip of palm oil." Mongezi looked briefly at Makhanda, his eyes glittering with promise. "You have to taste."

Lola didn't show any interest, but when Napo looked at her for her consent she nodded.

The afternoon rush-hour traffic made them stop every now and then. Street vendors were everywhere, selling everything from suits to salt fish; the streets in places looked like a makeshift market. At Primeiro de Maio Square, they stopped at a red light. In the middle of the square was a statue of the late president Agostinho Neto with his right hand outstretched towards the adjacent Independence Plaza.

It took about an hour and a half to reach the B&B. Mongezi left Napo, Makhanda and Lola there, and took Kimathi on to the Hotel Presidente Meridien. He promised to come and fetch them all at nine that evening for the calulu dinner.

Chapter 45

It was about half past two in the morning when Mongezi dropped Kimathi at his hotel. Kimathi was visibly drunk and he walked as if his legs were heavy. It was understandable; they had had a great time. After taking Napo, Lola and Makhanda back to their B&B at about half ten, Kimathi and Mongezi had visited various Luanda nightclubs. They had danced to live music at After Eight, where Kimathi had met a lady from Cabo Verde. She had worked him with her dance moves before disappearing with some young man. Kimathi had been disappointed that she had vanished, but, nonetheless, he'd had a great time. They had also gone to Jango Valiero, where they'd boogied to Kizomba music before moving on to Zanzibar, where Kimathi had flirted with some young Angolan beauties. He hadn't wanted to leave the club, convinced that he had won over a young Angolan girl, who kept calling him "darling", but at two in the morning Mongezi had insisted.

The first thing Mongezi did upon arriving at Kimathi's hotel with him was to ask a guy with a sharply pointed chin at reception to give Kimathi a courtesy wake-up call at five o'clock that morning.

"Thank you for the great night, comrade. I had too much fun with that Cabo Verde chick," said Kimathi as if he was reliving the pleasure of the lady's company in his head.

"Go get some rest," said Mongezi, looking at his watch. "You have less than three hours."

"Don't worry about me." said Kimathi, rubbing his face. "Half past five, I'll be waiting for you on these sofas."

"Have a good rest comrade," said Mongezi. "I promise we'll do it all again when we come back from Cabral."

"And next time I won't come back empty handed," Kimathi promised himself as he pressed the button on the wall by the lift.

"I'm sure of that," replied Mongezi as he walked out of the hotel through the rotating glass door.

In his hotel room, Kimathi opened the minibar and looked inside. After taking out two miniature bottles of Johnnie Walker Black, he sat heavily on the chair next to his bed and tried to remove his shoes. While removing his socks, he once again caught sight of the two miniature bottles of Johnnie Walker Black on top of the table next to the phone and wiggled his big toes in excitement.

After managing to take his clothes off, Kimathi unscrewed the top of one of the bottles and downed the whisky in one gulp. Five minutes later, he was snoring.

Chapter 46

Kimathi put his phone down on his bedside table. *Something is not right*, he thought. Although his cellphone conversation with Ludwe had been brief, he had detected irritation in his friend's voice. He could only guess what was troubling him. They had agreed to meet in Ludwe's hotel room at the Hyatt at ten. Only the two of them, Ludwe had said, which was quite unusual as well.

At about ten to nine, Kimathi parked his BMW X5 at the Oxford Road Engen garage. Pulling a cap down low over his eyes, he climbed out of his car and began to walk slowly towards the hotel, carrying only his red Virgin Active gym bag.

His timing was perfect as there was a swarm of drunken guests by the lifts, singing and chattering. No one noticed him as he entered the hotel through the sliding door behind the reception area; everyone's eyes were on the group of young white males and their partners as they celebrated Manchester United winning some important match.

Kimathi decided to use the stairs instead of waiting with the crowd. Walking along the third-floor corridor, he stopped at room 3113 and pressed his ear to the door. There was the sound of a television inside, so he decided to knock. Seconds later the door swung open to reveal Ludwe.

As Kimathi stepped into the room, the two of them embraced briefly. But Ludwe's was an awkward, one-armed hug. Kimathi spotted a bottle of eighteen-year-old Glenfiddich on the table. Next to it was a small bucket of ice.

"You look different, comrade," Ludwe said as he withdrew from the embrace.

"Oh, yes. When you called me I was busy at the gym," said Kimathi as he pulled off his cap and put his gym bag down on the carpeted floor. "We just finished now, so I decided to come straight here."

"Next time you must invite me," Ludwe said, rubbing his protruding belly that hung over his black trousers. "I need to trade this for a nice six pack."

There was a trace of humour lurking in Ludwe's eyes as he said this, and both men laughed.

Going towards the table, Ludwe opened the bottle of Glenfiddich and poured the whisky into two glasses. "By the way, I have a visitor coming at about twenty past eleven," he said as he dropped some ice cubes into the whisky. "We should be done by then, I think."

"Is it anyone that I know?" Kimathi asked as Ludwe passed him a drink.

"I don't think so," Ludwe said. He passed a glance at Kimathi to see his reaction, but the latter only raised his eyebrows without saying a word.

Ludwe sat down in a chair. "I suppose by now you have guessed why I've called you here," he started, taking a sip from his glass.

"I know," said Kimathi, also taking seat, "I should have come to the meeting earlier, comrade, but . . ."

"No. It's about my niece, Sindi. She was crying hysterically when she told me what you did. Comrade, I think you must reconsider your decision."

"Comrade, you know very well that I meant to empower her," said Kimathi, taking a sip of his whisky before putting the glass on the table. "But I got advice that what we had done did not in fact constitute proper empowerment as defined in the BEE Act. I had to take some action. Otherwise the Act has certain penalties." He picked up his glass again and ran his finger around the rim. "There is a ten per cent penalty on the annual turnover of convicted perpetrators, including individuals and entities. I was only trying to avoid any unnecessary risks to our bid."

Ludwe didn't say anything for several moments. Instead he blinked, rubbed his eyes and then drained his glass until only the ice remained. Standing up, he poured himself another drink and topped up Kimathi's glass. After this, he walked towards the window and stared at the unfinished Rosebank Gautrain station below him.

"I see what you mean, comrade," said Ludwe. "But Sindi told me that you called her yesterday to tell her that you had found another BEE partner. And then you immediately transferred seventy thousand rand into her account to pay her for her shares. And after that you simply took back the shares! That's not what we agreed, comrade. Remember, I'm taking a huge risk here."

"Unfortunately there is nothing we can do about it, comrade. Like I said, I've been advised by my lawyers that committing a fraud relating to BEE is regarded in a very serious light." Kimathi drank the whisky in his glass in one go. "Removing Sindi was the best decision. We don't need to be sentimental about it."

"But you know we are family, comrade. And I promised you that I'd make sure we win this tender. Now it seems we are betraying one of our own family members."

"Comrade, I know I'm making the right choice here. Sindi is still young and inexperienced, and this looks suspicious on our part."

"She's suspicious to whom, comrade?"

"To all the politicians and business people who also have their eyes fixed on this lucrative deal like hawks. We have to play smart, comrade."

"Don't tell me about politicians and business people, comrade," Ludwe scoffed. "They are all criminals sent by the devil to do mischief in this world, and you know that. They are the very root of our current dilemma in this country. The Kimathi that I know from exile cared a lot about family. If that person still exists in you, comrade, you'll find a way of helping that girl."

"Comrade, I guess some choices are easy to make, but some stay with you forever. This is one of those choices."

"Well, in that case, I think relationships are overrated," said Ludwe, draining his glass. "But I'm asking you to think again, comrade, and to do so immediately. Otherwise you're putting *me* in a dilemma here," he continued as he moved to pour another drink for them. "As we speak, Sindi is thinking of approaching the South Gauteng High Court to challenge her removal."

Kimathi rubbed his face hard and fast. "On what basis is she doing that, comrade?"

"I have seen her draft letter, and things might turn nasty for our bid," continued Ludwe. "I'm afraid the court might rule that you did not enter into a genuine transaction when you sold twenty-six per cent of Mandulo's shares to her." He raised his fingers above his head to demonstrate inverted commas after mentioning the word "sold".

"But you know she didn't buy those shares. We were just fronting her."

"I know," said Ludwe, rubbing the tip of his nose. "But that is what she is saying in the letter to her lawyers."

"Are you helping her to do this?"

"What would you do if you were in my position?" asked Ludwe, looking uncomfortable. "I mean, she claims that she bought twenty-six per cent of the shares for only one rand. She wants the Department of Trade and Industry to investigate your actions."

"But this is my company and I'm the chairman and director," Kimathi said as Ludwe handed him a glass of whisky.

"Well, I am just warning you, comrade. Sindi feels cheated by you, and a cheated woman is very dangerous, my friend."

As Kimathi sipped his whisky, Ludwe looked at his watch. It was ten forty. He stared reflectively out at the unfinished Gautrain station building. A sudden, frightening grin spread across his face.

"By the way," Ludwe said, "I've also been approached by another company about this tender. I must say that they put a very generous offer on the table."

"Which company is this?" Kimathi asked.

"I can't say for now. But the offer is more than double what you gave me," said Ludwe.

"But, comrade, we have a deal," said Kimathi. "So far we have given you more than three hundred and fifty thousand rand."

"I know, comrade, but life has taught me that sometimes it is necessary to do the wrong things for the right reasons. At the moment I'm still not decided."

A hundred questions flashed into Kimathi's mind.

"So, what do we do now?" he asked.

"Think carefully about your offer and also about Sindi's future in your company."

"I'm sure we can work out something. Give me two days."

"Two days, you've got," said Ludwe, looking at his watch again. "We need to wrap it up. My guest will be here soon."

Ludwe stood up and staggered towards the toilet. It was the moment Kimathi had been waiting for. He knew that his friend had a small bladder and would go to the toilet every half an hour. Unzipping his gym bag he took out a small bottle filled with a clear liquid. After pouring some whisky into both their glasses, Kimathi emptied a generous dosage of the poison into Ludwe's glass. By the time he heard the toilet flush, he was back in his chair with his glass in his hand. Ludwe looked at his watch again as he came out of the bathroom and Kimathi took it as his cue to leave.

"I'll see you in two days with a counter offer that you cannot refuse, comrade," he said, standing up.

"I'll drink to that," said Ludwe, picking up his glass.

Their glasses clinked before they emptied the contents. Kimathi picked up his bag and walked towards the door. Before he touched the handle, he turned back and looked at his friend.

"The best way of understanding a man is to talk to both his friends and enemies, comrade," said Kimathi. "I guess my enemies are all over the world, but my friends are hard to find."

Ludwe tried to talk but he sounded like he was choking. He staggered backwards and fell against one of the chairs.

Kimathi moved away from the door and walked towards the table, where he picked up his empty whisky glass. As he put it in his bag, Ludwe began to shake violently, saliva running freely from his mouth and mucus from his nostrils.

"I grew up in an organisation where backstabbing is the norm," Kimathi said maliciously. "I know that my father was betrayed by the men he trusted in The Movement. That's why he killed himself."

Kimathi stood for a while and watched his friend convulse on the floor.

When Ludwe started to vomit, with his eyes sinking deeper, Kimathi knew that it was over. He turned and walked away.

It was about twenty minutes past eleven when Kimathi made his way down the stairs, his cap low over his eyes. At the reception, a couple was talking to the lady he had given a generous tip recently. Others were waiting for the lift on the ground floor. Marching out of the building, he quickly walked towards Oxford Road.

Chapter 47

The following morning at sunrise they left Luanda for Quibaxe in two white Land Cruisers. Mongezi led the way, with Kimathi beside him in the front seat, and Napo, Lola and Makhanda in the back. In the second vehicle were Fito, the pathologist, Josina, the forensic archaeologist, and Pena, their helper. A strange anticipation bubbled inside Kimathi as they travelled along the main road. It was a slow drive as they had to follow trucks carrying agricultural products from Luanda and heavy equipment to the diamond mines of Lunda province. The road snaked through the dense vegetation, running parallel to the railway line from Luanda to Malange. Ahead of them was the quiet provincial capital of N'dalatando, at the foot of Pinda Mountain.

"Remember this place, comrade?" Mongezi asked Kimathi, pointing at the gardens that lay neglected and overgrown beside the road. "This used to be the garden city of Angola, but look at it now. It's in ruins."

"I still remember," said Kimathi, his eyes alive with excitement. Despite his nightmare about Ludwe's death, he was feeling more alive than he had in years. "This trip feels like I'm on my way back home," he concluded.

Mongezi glanced at the passengers in the back and cleared his throat to attract their attention.

"The first president of Angola, Agostinho Neto, used to have a modest house here, but it is also in ruins."

"Is that so?" asked Napo with keen interest.

They stopped for a few minutes at Nosso Super Supermarket in N'dalatando to buy water. Turning southwestward, there were now very few trucks on the road, which made the driving relatively easy. They passed Robusta coffee and cotton fields on either side of the road and by eight o'clock they reached a dusty town called Dondo, where they stopped to refuel. At a small liquor store on the banks of the Kwanza River, Kimathi and Mongezi bought a dozen Cuca beers before continuing on. Mongezi steered the Land Cruiser past the hydroelectric plant at Kambambe and the guarded complex of Pousada. Lola, Napo and Makhanda looked impressed by the majestic Kwanza Valley and the hundred-and-two-metre-high curved dam wall near the ruins of the Kambambe Fort. They kept pointing at it as Mongezi drove by.

"It was built by the Portuguese in the sixteen hundreds," said Mongezi, pointing at the fort. "It is the place where about three hundred years ago our unfortunate ancestors suffered their gruesome fate. They were kept here after being captured and before they were transferred to Luanda and America. The church you see over there is a place where our great-grandparents were baptised before they were sent across the Atlantic as slaves."

Kimathi did not say a word. Instead he opened up a beer can. A spray of foam shot out and wet his trousers. Mongezi opened his eyes wide, looked at Kimathi and smiled as they drove onwards.

Crossing the Kwanza River, they drove for about fifteen kilometres to the town of Massangano, at the confluence of the Lucala and Kwanza rivers. The Nossa Senhora da Victoria church was in front of them now, and the road led them to Lucala town. From there they left the Negage-Uige road, turning off before the Samba Caju and Camabatela signposts. Kimathi drank from his beer, let out a little burp and felt good. The alcohol, the swaying of the car and the humidity were already making him tipsy. He fell asleep as soon as they joined the gravel road.

Chapter 48

At about seven o'clock in the evening, Kimathi parked his hired Toyota Corolla in the forecourt of the 1st Avenue Shell service station in Parkhurst. He was in the company of a white prostitute with red hair. After inserting a new SIM card into his cellphone, he gave her Ganyani's number to dial. He put the phone on "speaker" and listened silently as the prostitute spoke to Ganyani.

"Good evening, Mr Novela," she said in a fake French accent. "My name is Laure Fredette from French Channel Activities, and I got your number from Mr Luc Lacasse, the chairman of the FMB company, which you have merged with for the Soutpans tender bid." She paused to make sure Ganyani was listening. "I know this is rather an awkward call, but I was wondering if there was any chance of us meeting to discuss the possibility of investing in your company. We are extremely interested in corporate social responsibility and would like to talk to you about starting upliftment programmes in the Elim area."

The prospect of investment in his company obviously interested Ganyani, just as Kimathi had known it would.

"Well, that can be arranged," Ganyani said.

"Well, I'm in South Africa until tomorrow morning, when I leave for Namibia. I really wanted to meet you before I leave, if possible. I know it's short notice, but I was hoping that I would be able to persuade you to meet with me."

"Well . . ." Ganyani hesitated. "I'm staying here at the Hilton in Sandton. Where are you?"

"I'm based at The Grace hotel in Rosebank, but a friend of mine is picking me up at half past seven for dinner at a restaurant called George's on 4th, in Parkhurst."

"Luckily, I have nothing to do tonight, so I will be there. I might be a bit late, though."

"Fantastic." The red-haired prostitute paused as Kimathi gave her a thumbs-up. "Do you need directions to the restaurant?"

"Don't worry, I know where it is. I'll be there in about an hour."

"It seems parking is a problem in that area. I was there yesterday and it took me forever to find a parking space. So today I have prearranged parking with the owner of the restaurant. One of the car guards who works for the restaurant will reserve a space for us outside the Solly Kramer." She paused. "Do you want me to ask them to reserve a space for you as well?"

"That will be great, thanks."

"What car are you driving, so that they recognise you when you come?" the prostitute asked.

"Oh, it's a black Porsche Cayenne with Limpopo plates."

"Okay, and just so you know, we have reserved a table. Just ask the waitresses at the door as you come in and they will show you where we are. See you soon."

"Bye," Ganyani said, dropping the call.

A smile formed on Kimathi's lips as he took his phone from the prostitute. He thought she had done a great job in tossing Ganyani the deadly bait – the chance to make more money.

"Is this only for calling someone?" the prostitute said, sounding pleasantly surprised as Kimathi handed her fifteen hundred rand "He must be a very important person."

"Yeah, you did a great job," Kimathi answered indirectly.

"Please call me again if you need any help. I don't mind spending ten minutes on a call for one point five."

"Will do," Kimathi said, sounding impatient. "Now, call a metre taxi. I'll pay for that as well."

The woman removed a business card from her handbag and punched the number on it into her cell.

"How much do you think the taxi will cost?" Kimathi asked as she waited for someone to answer her call.

"One fifty will be okay," she said.

Kimathi gave her the money.

The taxi arrived ten minutes later and the prostitute kissed Kimathi on the cheek, opened the door and got out. "Let's do it again, honey," she said, running her fingers through her red hair. "Next time we'll have more fun."

"Yeah," Kimathi replied, nodding.

Kimathi looked at his watch. It was about ten minutes to eight. He got out of his car and put on a neon jacket and a cap. *A country without prostitutes and criminals is not a real country*, he thought as he walked down 7th Avenue towards 4th Avenue. He wanted to avenge the stress that Ganyani had caused him. Earlier, at his Bassonia home, Kimathi had tried to read some of the pile of urgent mail that needed his attention. However, the first three letters had angered him so much that he hadn't been able to read any further. One announced that Ganyani had sued his company, Mandulo, for listing him as one of the directors. He had lodged a complaint with the civil engineering authorities about the improper use of his name by the company. The second letter was a protection order, informing Kimathi that he was not allowed to contact Ganyani and that he must stay at least five hundred metres from him at all times – the letter cited the incident in the parking lot following the tender presentation in Pretoria as justification for these restrictions. The third letter was a reminder from the bank that he was four months in arrears on his bond, and that they would repossess the house if he did not pay up.

Before Kimathi reached Solly Kramer's, it started to rain hard. He ran past the building and stood under the roof of a darkened boutique next to it. At about twenty minutes past eight he saw a Porsche Cayenne approaching. As it slowed down in front of him, he walked towards the car with his hood up as if to protect himself from the rain. As Ganyani tried to reverse into the empty parking space, Kimathi posed as a car guard and directed him. Once he was satisfied with the way the car was parked, Ganyani opened the door and felt the rain with his right hand. Then, removing his seatbelt, he put both his feet on the pavement to avoid the flowing rainwater next to the drain. Before he could even close the door, he felt a gun in his back.

"If you move or look back you're dead," said Kimathi, pressing the gun harder into Ganyani's back. "Get into the car now and drive."

"Please take whatever you want and leave me alone," pleaded Ganyani, squeezing his eyes shut. "I have a special meeting."

"Get into the car now or I'll blow your brains out!" ordered Kimathi, his heart brimming with hate.

Without any further resistance, Ganyani climbed back into the car. He started the engine and swung into the road again, tyres squealing. Kimathi sat in the back seat with his gun pressed against Ganyani's neck.

Ganyani glanced in the rear-view mirror. A crease appeared in his brow when he saw Kimathi.

"Comrade Kimathi!" he said, his voice shaking and his eyes wide with bafflement and terror.

"So, I'm 'comrade' today?" Kimathi said with a forced smile. "You should have thought of that when you sued me. You bloody monkey!"

Ganyani's tongue peeked out to wet his dry lips. He closed his eyes for a second and then shook his head without saying a word.

The rain drove harder against the windscreen as they passed the Parkhurst Bowling Club, where 4th Avenue changes into Braeside Road. They continued until Muirfield Road, where Kimathi ordered Ganyani to turn right.

"Where are you taking me?" asked Ganyani as he slowed down to allow another car to pass them. "Why are you doing this to me?"

"You can never tell what people have inside them until you start taking their hope away," answered Kimathi as they crossed Clovelly Road.

They passed the Greenside Animal Hospital on the corner of Barry Hertzog Avenue. As they crossed Komatie Road, the headlights picked out Emmarentia Dam ahead of them. The sight of the shining water sent a chill down Ganyani's spine.

"But what have I done to you?" Ganyani asked, his voice sounding as if fear had frozen his vocal cords.

"Enemies like you deserve to be hung by their balls for selling our country to the highest capitalist bidder," said Kimathi. "Suing my company for using your name after you ditched us at the last minute! You don't deserve to live."

"Please, don't do this!" pleaded Ganyani, jerking his head back nervously.

"Shut up and keep driving," ordered Kimathi, his face twisting with rage.

"My strong advice to you is to let me go right now and minimise the damage. I will pretend this never happened, I promise."

They came to a T-junction; the orange street lights on Louw Geldenhuys Drive reflected off the water in the dam in front of them. The gun was almost touching Ganyani's neck. His eyes stayed wide with fear as Kimathi instructed him to drive into an area between some tall pine trees and down towards the edge of the dam. He stopped the car and switched off the lights.

"Please, comrade, I'll give you anything you want," begged Ganyani, looking at the water in front of him. "Don't kill me, please."

"Open the front windows," ordered Kimathi, changing the position of the gun and pressing it against Ganyani's head. "I don't want anything from you except your life."

"I can transfer five million to you now, comrade," sobbed Ganyani. "Please don't kill me."

"It's already too late," said Kimathi, looking at him with cold, malicious eyes.

"Please, I beg you."

"Shut up, you fucking dung-eating baboon!"

Ganyani felt his mouth and legs quivering at the same time. He blinked several times before closing his eyes completely as he felt Kimathi slowly pulling the trigger. His face tensed like a child anticipating a doctor's injection. The single shot splattered blood over the windscreen and onto Kimathi's jacket.

It was still raining hard as Kimathi opened the car door. He searched Ganyani's body and found a wallet and two cellphones. He pulled the automatic gear lever to drive, released the handbrake and pushed the car into the dam. As the car plunged into the water, Kimathi turned and began to walk away.

As he made his way towards the set of robots at the junction of Olifants Road and Louw Geldenhuys Drive, Kimathi tossed both the gun and Ganyani's cellphones into the dam. After passing the robots, he opened Ganyani's wallet. It contained about three thousand rand in notes, which he removed and put in his pocket. He chucked the wallet into some bushes. Satisfied with his work, Kimathi walked back towards Barry Hertzog Avenue along Ingalele Road and called a metered taxi. He breathed in deeply, and the sweet smell of the rain settled in his nostrils.

The taxi found him less than ten minutes later at the Greenside Animal Hospital, and took him back to the Shell station where he had left his car.

Chapter 49

Kimathi woke up bemused by the violence of his dream. He was completely disoriented and for a few minutes he didn't know where he was. He glanced at Mongezi who was driving silently, then at the passengers in the back seat. Napo and Makhanda smiled at him reassuringly while Lola stared out through the window. Kimathi blinked several times and shook his head but it was only when he rolled the window down completely and stuck his head out that his mind came back to the present.

They arrived at Quibaxe at about half past nine in the morning. The place only had one street and was not large enough to be called a town. There were a few typical Portuguese colonial buildings with white walls, wide verandas that were supported by pillars, low windows with shutters and wooden doors. The air was humid outside and the temperature hovered around thirty degrees.

Leaving Quibaxe, they passed a shallow stream. The name Quibia came into Kimathi's mind, but he was no longer sure if it was correct. It had been a very long time since he had been in this place. The sight of the villages ahead awakened bittersweet memories and his mouth felt dry. He and Comrade Ludwe used to sneak out of the camp at night to visit the surrounding villages of Quipanzo, Bondo, Camatambo, Vuanga, Quindulo, Quissaco and Peso, where they would get drunk on homemade mahango beer. Sometimes they would visit the villages for business with the locals, bartering a bag of sugar for a goat, a box of tinned fish for a pig, a pile of clothes for a cow or a bag of rice for some marijuana.

Kimathi popped open another can of beer and took a long swig.

They passed a low rocky hillock, where the ground sloped down towards a stream. About twenty metres to their right was a shell rock, projecting into the air towards some nearby bush. They passed a village that lay on the brow of the hill. The sight of the thatched, red mud-brick houses brought the name

Quipanpungo to Kimathi as they passed three huge ovens that the locals had built to produce bricks.

The dusty road led them to a huge anthill next to an almost dry river. From there, they drove for about twenty minutes through the bush until they saw five dilapidated white buildings. It was Amilcar Cabral. *Nothing has changed*, Kimathi thought as he saw some cows ahead, with herd boys running after them. At the side of the road, he saw another boy herding a flock of goats and sheep through the open fields, the animals stepping nimbly through the weeds and rocks. As soon as he saw the Land Cruiser, the boy waved at them. Kimathi thought about the unprotected sexual encounters he had enjoyed with some of the local women, and wondered if the boy could be his son.

Chapter 50

The heat thickened as Fito, the pathologist, carefully dug out the shallow grave. As Kimathi watched, he noticed the crescents of sweat under his arms, staining his yellow T-shirt. He was hit by an attack of the dry heaves that left him weak and short of breath. Closing his eyes, he exhaled in an exaggerated expression of impatience.

Finally, Fito put the spade aside and pulled on a pair of cream latex gloves. His face was dripping with sweat after his hard work. He used the back of his hand to wipe it off.

Ants were busy making their daily rounds as Fito entered the grave. He removed the skeleton cautiously, bone by bone, for the autopsy. Lola sobbed tearlessly and hid her face in her hands. After he had removed all the bones, Fito studied the remains closely before putting them into a thick plastic bag. As he watched the pathologist work, Makhanda wiped a layer of sweat away from his forehead with a cloth. The humidity was unbearable, and the harsh reflective sand irritated their eyes as none of them were wearing sunglasses. The ever-present sand flies and other insects crawled on their legs. Suddenly Lola collapsed.

Kimathi's heart pounded in fear as the others moved in to help Lola. His eyes were fixed on a spiny lizard as it ran up a nearby mimosa tree towards a spider's web. The lizard stopped and looked at him for a few seconds, then it bobbed its head and climbed out of sight. Out of the blue, an owl landed on a branch in the tree. Kimathi's heart jumped in his chest with shock. Recovering himself, he looked up and saw the owl flying directly above him. *But owls only fly at night*, he thought. The bird defecated and the droppings landed on the bridge of his nose as the owl flew away in the direction of one of the old camp buildings.

Wiping off the droppings with the back of his hand, Kimathi looked around, but no one seemed to have noticed anything, the were too busy attending to

Lola. His lips began to tremble when he discovered blood on his hand instead of bird droppings. He blinked rapidly, his face a mask of courage and confusion.

Instinctively, Kimathi left the rest of the group and waded through the thick grass between the five blocks of the camp. He ran his finger over the bridge of his nose, but the blood had already begun to congeal. As he walked, Kimathi scanned the trees that had grown up a few metres from the buildings, forming a deep green wall that could conceal anyone and anything. Fearful of what might be hiding in the trees, he walked towards the open doorway of one of the buildings.

Inside what used to be the Doomed Spies block, there were mounds of dried animal dung. As he stood in the middle of the room, a wave of nostalgia passed over Kimathi as his eyes darted around. Suddenly, he noticed a mist drifting through the broken windows. As it reached the corner of the room, it took on a human form. Filled with fear, he collapsed to the ground. It was at that moment that the ghost of Lady Comrade Mkabayi appeared in front of him.

"Comrade Pilate," she said, "where do you want me to live now? You and your sangoma have chased me out of my parents' house in Soweto."

"But you are dead," Kimathi said, fear creeping into his voice. "That is why we are here, to fetch your spirit."

"Comrade Pilate, I thought you knew that a person does not simply disappear when they die," Lady Comrade Mkabayi said to him. "They go to another world, just like Ganyani did when you killed him two days ago."

"Why?" Kimathi asked, his eyes glowing with fear. "Why can't you leave me alone?"

"Because you did not tell the truth about what you did to me."

"What do you want me to do now?"

"I want you to tell them everything. Tell them that your career as a freedom fighter was motivated by your dark and hidden desires. Inform them that I was imprisoned here in Amilcar Cabral for two years for nothing."

"But I was merely following the orders of The Movement," responded Kimathi.

"That is a beautiful, generous lie. But your sins will follow you everywhere, Comrade Pilate. Whether you were merely following the orders of the others or not."

"I'm really sorry," Kimathi pleaded, tears flowing freely down his cheeks.

"That's not enough. You and I know that human beings lie to each other more often than they tell the truth, Comrade Pilate. But fate doesn't lie – not today."

"But my commanders felt that you had attempted to overthrow The Movement's leadership. I had no choice."

"There is always a choice. Sometimes the cost of telling the truth is greater than any heart is willing to pay."

"There is no burden as heavy as the regret that I'm feeling right now. I want us to reconcile, Lady Comrade Mkabayi," Kimathi said, with fear clinging to his throat.

"It's too late for that, Comrade Pilate," the ghost said, "Don't you think?"

"Tell me what I must do now?" Kimathi asked seriously. "I'm willing to do anything. That is why I came here with your parents, to help put your spirit to rest."

"My time and your time are not the same time, Comrade Pilate," Lady Comrade Mkabayi responded. "We live in a world that is out of our control, and sometimes death is preferable to the harsh life of imprisonment that we are living now."

Lady Comrade Mkabayi gave Kimathi a searching look and then a mocking sympathetic laugh. She watched as he removed his belt from his trousers.

"Why do you keep on manipulating my mind?" Kimathi asked, blinking several times. "My life doesn't belong to you."

"If we live in the hearts of those we killed, we will never die," the ghost of Lady Comrade Mkabayi answered. "And that is why I am stuck with you. The best way of dealing with your pain is to acknowledge your part in causing it, Comrade Pilate."

"I'm very sorry for what I did in the past," said Kimathi, his eyes full of tears. "I was very selfish, cruel and stupid."

"But the man inside you knew the difference between right and wrong," the ghost said. "Remember the saying: 'do unto others as you would have them do unto you'?"

"Yes. It was the monster in me. I beg for your forgiveness. I'm a changed man."

"You have just passed the point of no return, Comrade Pilate."

"Oh, my God, please let me live," begged Kimathi, dropping to his knees.

"Let me remind you that this is Amilcar Cabral Camp, Comrade Pilate. God is far away in the sky, leaving men here on earth alone," Lady Comrade Mkabayi replied. "It is a long way home from here."

Chapter 51

Outside, Fito and his team had finished their work. Lola was sitting silently under the tree, recovering from her collapse. Napo held her hand as if trying to absorb her grief. As they prepared to fill the empty grave with soil, a large amount fell into the grave on its own. Makhanda was about to go and look for Kimathi to complete the ritual before they took the bones away for the autopsy, when, suddenly, Mongezi burst into tears.

"I have been looking for this opportunity to meet you and tell you what happened to her. I just didn't have the guts," he said as tears ran down his face.

Makhanda and Napo looked at Mongezi as if they were preparing themselves for an explosion. Lola had to bite her lip to avoid crying; she blinked rapidly as if her eyelids were crammed with sand.

"There is a monster behind that man," said Mongezi, pointing in the direction of the dilapidated camp buildings. "He is a freak of nature."

"What are you talking about, son?" asked Napo, sounding confused. "I thought he was your friend."

"It's Kimathi that killed her," Mongezi said finally.

"That dog!" cursed Lola loudly. "He has a nerve to lie to us. He must pay for what he did to my daughter."

"Why did you wait so long before you told us?" questioned Napo impatiently. "Why now?"

"I had to observe The Movement's protocol. No one is supposed to say anything. They say what happened in the bush stays in the bush." Mongezi paused. "And also, I was ashamed. It was me . . . I was the one who betrayed her. They tortured me and I betrayed her."

"So why tell us now, then?" asked Napo, pain and anger fighting inside him.

"I could not take it any more, pretending as if nothing had happened as the man who killed my friends walks around happy." Mongezi paused and wiped his face. "That is why I have made it a point that he pays for everything, including this autopsy."

"So, you knew our daughter?" asked Napo.

"Senami was my best friend. I left home with her in 1987 because the police were looking for us." Mongezi loosened his tie. "We were the leaders at Pace Commercial High School. She was the head prefect and I was her deputy. Me and other comrades like Lwazi Sibisi used to come to your house in Protea North to discuss politics. I don't think you remember me, but I used to live in Pimville Zone 2. That's where I come from. The five of us, comrades Lwazi, Senami, Thulani, Luvo and myself went into exile via Botswana. We crossed the border at Lobatse, from Zeerust."

"What happened to the others?" asked Makhanda.

"Kimathi killed them. First, he buried Comrade Luvo and Comrade Thulani alive, then he kicked Comrade Makana – that was Lwazi Sibisi's nickname – to death. I'm the only survivor from that group. Kimathi killed Senami in the middle of the night. I kept quiet because I was the one who'd told him that she was a spy, but I knew that one day I'd avenge her death." Mongezi paused as the image of Senami's dead body intruded on his conciousness. "In Zeerust we met a Ndau healer who gave us muti for strength. His name was Emilio. Senami was so special and very brave. That's why she was given the name Lady Comrade Mkabayi here in exile. I was known as Comrade Bambata then..."

"So that explains it," Makhanda said, looking at Mongezi. "The Ndau spirit."

"But why did he kill her?" asked Lola.

"He was in love with her. And jealous that she didn't love him back. He called her a spy before putting her into prison. This camp was nothing but The Movement's prison." Mongezi pointed randomly at one of the buildings. "He and Ludwe also robbed me of my life during the torture. I can't have children of my own."

As Pena and Fito refilled the grave, Makhanda removed his sandals and knelt down. Opening his medicine bag, he took out his bones and some ground umnono bark, which he mixed with pink-flowered umsokosoko. He put a spoonful of the mixture into his mouth and started gargling. After looking into the sky for about three minutes, he spat the muti on the bones.

"Senami, my child!" he called, addressing the bones. "We have come here from far away back home in South Africa, in Soweto. We have long been travelling, looking for you. You have been lost for many years." He spat again on the bones. "But we have found you on foreign soil here in Angola. Your father Napo and your mother Lola are here with me and want you to come back home. Please, allow us to take you back with us. We plead to you also, our ancestors, to guide us well on our way back home with Senami."

A strong wind started to blow as Makhanda spat again on the bones. Dust rose from the gravesite and coiled upwards like a snake. They watched as the column of dust moved slowly in the direction of the buildings.

"Where is Kimathi?" Makhanda asked, standing up and looking around for signs of his presence. "We have to find him now."

They all went looking for Kimathi. Makhanda moved before them as if he was familiar with the territory. He followed the direction of the coiling dust. Upon entering what used to be the Doomed Spies block, they found Kimathi hanging by his belt. He was dead.

"Blood doesn't wash off easily, does it?" said Makhanda, staring at Kimathi's lifeless body.

"You're right," said Napo, his eyes wide with fright. "The filth of crime and corruption can never be erased. At least we have found closure and we'll be able to carry our daughter's spirit home with us."

Acknowledgements

Thanks to:

The IWP – International Writing Program in Iowa, USA – and the Bureau of Education and Cultural Affairs at the US Department of State for the residency opportunity in 2008. That's where I conceptualised and wrote the first few chapters of this book.

The Brussels literary organisation Het Beschrijf in association with the Flemish Community's Cultural Department for the residency in Passa Porta, Belgium. That's where this book took shape.

The 2009 MA Creative Writing class and the supervisors at Wits University for all the feedback.

All my friends who read the book in its manuscript form.

NIQ MHLONGO was born in Soweto in 1973. His first novel, *Dog Eat Dog*, was published by Kwela Books in 2004 and awarded the Mar de Lettras Prze in 2006. *After Tears,* his second novel, was published to critical acclaim in 2007. *Way Back Home* is his third novel.